THE KILLER SEEMED
TO BE SNIFFING THE AIR....

I stared in cold-sweat panic as the figure looked cautiously around, then turned and strode purposefully toward the utility room. Never have I experienced such undiluted terror. I backed away from the door, struggling at the same time to pull the gun out of my handbag. But it had gotten tangled up in the hairnet I carried in the bag! I could hear the doorknob twisting slowly, quietly. Very carefully, the door was being coaxed open. A heartbeat later, the killer stood in front of me, framed in the half-open doorway. I was looking into a face contorted with menace.

"What is this all about?" the deceptively soft voice demanded.

"P.I. Desiree Shapiro has a wonderful New York way with words and an original knack for solving homicides. She's one sharp gal in voice and in detection. Intriguing and fun."
    —Elizabeth Daniels Squire,
        author of *Who Killed What's-Her-Name?*

MURDER CAN KILL
YOUR SOCIAL LIFE

MURDER
CAN KILL
YOUR
SOCIAL LIFE

by

Selma Eichler

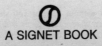

A SIGNET BOOK

SIGNET
Published by New American Library, a division of
Penguin Putnam Inc., 375 Hudson Street,
New York, New York 10014, U.S.A.
Penguin Books Ltd, 27 Wrights Lane,
London W8 5TZ, England
Penguin Books Australia Ltd, Ringwood,
Victoria, Australia
Penguin Books Canada Ltd, 10 Alcorn Avenue,
Toronto, Ontario, Canada M4V 3B2
Penguin Books (N.Z.) Ltd, 182–190 Wairau Road,
Auckland 10, New Zealand

Penguin Books Ltd, Registered Offices:
Harmondsworth, Middlesex, England

First published by Signet,
an imprint of New American Library,
a division of Penguin Putnam Inc.

First Printing, November 1994
15 14 13 12 11

For Mollie

Introduction

I'm no Sam Spade.

Mostly I handle divorce and insurance cases, with some child custody and missing persons thrown in. Once, there was even a missing cat. *That* was a funny story. But I'll tell you about it later.

Right now, I want to tell you about THE CASE. The one that changed my life.

My name is Desiree Shapiro. Go ahead, laugh. Everyone else does. It *was* Desiree Soulé, but then I got married.

Anyway, I've been a private investigator for about twenty years. (Of course, I started when I was prenatal.) A long time ago, that seemed like a pretty exciting thing to be, especially for a woman. I'd go to parties and when people asked what I did for a living, it was a real kick to say I was a P.I. To appreciate just what kind of an impact that made, picture this. I'm five-foot-two with auburn hair (abetted somewhat by Egyptian henna) and blue eyes. *Plus* I've got dimples. Not—unfortunately—on my face. But on my elbows and hands and knees and a lot of places the world will never see.

Now, that may lead you to believe I'm a little overweight. Wrong. I'm a lot more than a little overweight. I won't tell you what I weigh, but I once lost over twenty pounds and hardly anyone noticed. I didn't get discouraged, though. I went and lost fifteen pounds more. This time, *everyone* noticed. My friends thought I looked "fabulous," "sensational," and all those other nice things. But it didn't get me Robert Redford. Or even a reasonable facsimile. And *that* discouraged me. So I put back the thirty-five pounds. And then some.

Eventually, I met and married Ed Shapiro, who was also a P.I. It only lasted five years, because Ed choked on a chicken bone and died. I know that sounds bizarre, but, believe me, it's no joke. We were very, very happy.

Anyway, I started to tell you about this case of mine. . . .

It was a double homicide that had the police and everyone else completely stymied. And I figured out the whole thing. For the first time, I realized that I was a highly competent investigator and that I could do a lot better than the schlock stuff I'd been working on. In fact, right away I started getting some very interesting referrals.

But the case didn't only affect my career. It turned my whole world upside down. Which is the reason I'm writing this. You see, if I don't, I think I may just explode. . . .

Chapter 1

I'd never have gotten involved with the investigation at all if, on a particular Monday late in October, my apartment was not being painted. And if, on that particular Monday, I did not have a truly disastrous dinner date. *And* if, on that very same Monday, I did not have to walk up a zillion flights of stairs.

The morning started off all wrong—and wound up being the high point of my day. The painters were due at 8:00 a.m. and showed up at 9:45. Then I had to give them about twenty-five minutes worth of last-minute instructions (most of which, I discovered later, they chose to ignore). It was almost 11:00 when I got to the office.

I rent space from a couple of lawyers named—are you ready for this?—Gilbert and Sullivan. It's a terrific deal for me. Not only do I have a much nicer office than I could otherwise have managed, but Elliot Gilbert and Pat Sullivan are two unbelievably sweet guys who throw business my way whenever they can. Also, it means I have the services of a secretary. And that's something I'd never have been able to swing on my own. Even if I could, I wouldn't have found anyone like Jackie. She's smart, efficient, pleasant, kind, helpful, *and* she knows how to say I'm out when I'm in and have people believe her.

I spent what was left of the morning trying to catch up on my paperwork and hardly making a dent in it. I had plans for dinner that evening with Stuart Mason, so at lunchtime I ran over to Woman of Substance to pick up the dress they were hemming for me.

My idea of a colorful outfit used to be anything that

wasn't black. I'd buy something navy or gray or brown and try to convince myself that it was a really spiffy number. Which it wasn't. And that it made me look a lot slimmer. Which it didn't. Of course, fashion had long since decreed that it was okay for us well-rounded ladies to wear bright colors. But I still hadn't dredged up the courage to break out of my shell. *Until that dress.*

It was cream silk with coral and pale pink flowers. I know that sounds pretty putrid, but it was nothing if not gorgeous. It took a lot of nerve for me just to try on something like that. But once I did, the sales-woman practically had to pry it off my back.

Anyway, that day the shop was unusually crowded, and I had to wait forever for a fitting room. Then the hem wasn't even, and I had to sit around for another eternity while they fixed it.

When I got back to the office, it was past 2:00, and an irate client—my 1:30 appointment—was lying in wait for me in the reception area. I spent a half hour placating him. Naturally, that made me late for my next appointment and *that,* in turn, made me late for the dentist. I left the dentist's at 5:00, the absolute worst time to try and get a cab. After twenty frustrating minutes, I put my conscience on hold and pushed a polite business-type out of the way, just as he was reaching for the door handle of what I'm positive was the last available taxi in Manhattan.

It was 5:40 when the cab dropped me off in front of my office. And Stuart was due to pick me up at 6:00! Never has anyone so slow moved so fast. I could hardly believe my own mirror image, but by 5:55, there I was in the ladies' room, all dressed, made up, and spritzing my hair. After the third healthy spritz—which guaranteed that not a strand would come free even in a hurricane—I was finally satisfied. I have this thing about neatness. I decided years ago that while people could call me fat, I'd never give them a reason to call me fat and sloppy. I always make extra sure there are no runs in my panty hose or lipstick smudges on my teeth or spaghetti stains down the front of my dress. And, most important, I never go out without hurricane-safe hair.

I checked the results of my efforts in the full-length mirror. As I stood there simpering at my reflection, I remember thinking that, fashion-wise, I had finally caught up with the rest of womankind. I looked at my watch, simpered one more time, and hurried back to my office to wait for Stuart. I can't tell you how much I was looking forward to a good dinner and a chance to unwind.

Ha!

I suppose I should fill you in on my relationship with Stuart Mason....

We've known each other for fifteen years. At first he was just my accountant. Later, he became my friend. And when Ed and I married, Stuart and his wife, Lynne, became *our* friends. The four of us used to have dinner together at least once a month—until Stuart and Lynne split up. To this day, I have no idea what happened between them; Stuart never really talked about it. I have the feeling—based on nothing, I admit—that the divorce was Lynne's idea and that Stuart was actually quite devastated. But, like I said, it's just a feeling.

After the divorce, Ed and I continued to see Stuart on a regular basis. Sometimes he'd bring a date, but mostly, it was the three of us.

Then Ed died. Stuart was absolutely wonderful to me. Talk about a shoulder to cry on! I cried on that man's shoulder, wailed in his ear, and sniffed my way through at least a dozen of his classy monogrammed handkerchiefs.

I have to tell you the rest, much as I think it's the tackiest thing in the world for people to talk about their sex lives. But this story would make no sense at all if you didn't know that I had planned to stay over at Stuart's apartment that night. (I'm sure you don't consider it any big deal. But I guess I'm sexually retarded or repressed or something, because it took a lot for me to admit that to you.)

The turning point in my friendship with Stuart oc-

curred more than a year after Ed died. We had gone
out to dinner, and Stuart came up for some coffee
afterward. All of a sudden I started feeling weepy,
which still happened pretty regularly in those days. He
put his arms around me to comfort me, and, well,
things progressed from there. It's funny, though. Until
that evening, I'd never been attracted to Stuart. Not
in that way, I mean. It isn't that he's homely or anything; he's a good-looking man: tall and blond with
nice, regular features and a very decent build. It's just
that I'd never thought of him for me. I've always been
a pushover (so to speak) for little skinny guys. Robert
Redford being the understandable exception.

I'm sure Stuart was as surprised as I was when our
dates took on this added dimension. I'm not exactly
the kind of svelte, sophisticated woman he's used to.
(You should have seen Lynne!) Maybe he was lonely
or something. Probably we both were.

At first I thought I was in the throes of this grand
passion, and I started to feel really guilty because of
Ed and all. But it didn't take long before the initial
excitement died down and things got back to normal—
with one small, pleasant exception. Stuart was still my
accountant. We were still good buddies. And we still
had dinner together fairly often. Only now I spent the
night at his place afterward. Which, that Monday, I
considered a lucky thing, since the smell of wet paint
makes me vomit.

But back to our disastrous date. . . .

When I opened the door to my office, Stuart was
already there, sitting in the visitor's chair next to my
desk. He turned around. "Wow!" he said, his mouth
at half mast. It wasn't the sort of "wow" I'd been
hoping for.

"What's that supposed to mean?" I demanded,
bristling.

Stuart, a reasonably intelligent man, immediately realized he had stepped onto a minefield and was now
proceeding very, very carefully. "You just look different, Dez, that's all ... but nice, really nice. It's just
that you don't usually wear anything that ... uh ...

bright. But you *do* look nice. *Really* nice." I translated that slop with no problem: You're too fat to wear a dress like that.

I was positively crushed by Stuart's reaction, but almost immediately my mood switched to hostile. Good and hostile. By the time we got to the restaurant—which has the best French food in the universe—I was barely speaking to him. Soon things got worse. I started talking again. Stuart, meanwhile, was being exceptionally patient. Which only made me bitchier.

I had ordered all my favorite things: a lovely pâté, Caesar salad, and roast duckling a l'orange with wild rice and mushrooms. Plus a little broccoli with hollandaise sauce on the side. Normally I would have attacked a dinner like that with unrestrained ecstasy. But that night, when my appetizer came, I mostly just jabbed at it, pretending it was Stuart's heart. When the busboy finally removed my victim, I excused myself to go to the ladies' room. There was a phone just outside the door, and I dialed my niece Ellen.

She answered on the first ring. "Can you put me up for the night?" I asked, skipping the niceties.

"Aunt Dez?"

"Uh-huh."

"Are you okay? You sound funny."

"I'm fine. But I need someplace to stay tonight."

"You *sure* you're okay?"

"Sure I'm sure." I *almost* smiled. Ellen is so earnest. "The apartment's being painted and the smell of paint kills me."

"Oh, I know what you mean. Of course you can stay here. I brought the sofa bed with me. It's very comfortable. You remember."

I did. And it wasn't. But at that point, who cared? "That's great," I said. "I appreciate it."

"Don't be silly. Do you have the address?"

"You gave it to me last week," I reminded her. Ellen had moved five or six days before, and the very second the phone was installed, she called with her new number and the rest of the particulars. "I'm at a restaurant now with Stuart." I said his name between clenched teeth. "So I might be a little late. Is that all right?"

"Don't be silly," she said again. "Come whenever."

"Look, don't wait up. I can let myself in. Just leave the key for me."

"Okay. I'll put it under the mat. It's apartment fourteen-A. Right next to the elevator."

When I got back to the table, the salad was there. So was a bottle of red wine. When I'm out with Stuart, we hardly ever order anything to drink. Even wine is a real rarity for us. It did the trick, though. After I'd drunk just half a glass, I was almost mellow. And by the time I'd finished my duckling—and another half a glass—I was a bona fide human being again. I was also a little ashamed of myself.

"I'm sorry I've been acting like such a bitch tonight," I began. "It's just that I was so hurt about the dress—"

"I know. And it's my fault. But—what I said—well, I didn't mean it to come out like that. The truth is, you look very nice. Exceptionally nice, in fact. I was just surprised at seeing you in something ..." He paused, working his way cautiously through the minefield again and finally deciding on "with flowers." There was another pause before he continued. "I wanted to tell you that all through dinner, but I was afraid of putting my foot back in my big mouth."

I assured him I understood. Then I apologized again. Then he apologized again. Then we had more wine. And some chocolate mousse (which was divine). And some coffee. And some more wine. . . . Soon we were back to being best of friends. The only problem was that when we were leaving I had to explain about going to Ellen's. Stuart suggested I call her back, but I checked my watch and saw that it was past 11:30. "Ellen's usually asleep by now," I told him, shaking my head. He looked so disappointed that I added, with what I hoped was a voice full of promise, "Next time."

Being a sex symbol isn't always easy.

*   *   *

It was just starting to drizzle when we stepped outside. But, fortunately, there was a taxi at the door. About ten minutes later, we pulled up in front of Ellen's building. She lives on one of those blocks in Chelsea that has new luxury high-rises alongside old run-down brownstones alongside just as old and even more run-down apartment buildings. The most run-down of which was Ellen's. In other words, it was a pretty typical New York neighborhood. Still, I was surprised that Ellen would move into such a dilapidated building. Of course, rents in Manhattan being what they are, I don't suppose she had a bunch of places to choose from. And, as she'd gushed to me at least a hundred times since taking the apartment, it *did* have a fireplace.

Stuart wanted to see me upstairs, but, since the rain was coming down really hard now, I insisted it wasn't necessary.

By the time I made it the short distance to the entrance, I was soaked. I ran into an even bigger problem when I tried opening the inner door to the lobby. The damned thing was locked! I couldn't believe that neither Ellen nor I had considered that. I decided stupidity ran in our family—until I remembered that Ellen was actually Ed's niece.

There was nothing to do but call upon one of my finely honed private investigator skills. So I fished around in my seriously lacquered hair, retrieved a hairpin, and picked the lock.

As soon as I entered the lobby, the elevator—that's "elevator," singular—was in plain sight. So was the sign that said OUT OF ORDER.

I thought, with something like horror, about walking up fourteen flights. Then I thought about the alternative. I could go home and gag on paint fumes all night long. And while, right then, I might even have settled for that, I didn't relish going outside in that downpour to try and find a cab. Also, rain or no rain, the very idea of venturing out alone in this neighborhood so late at night turned me to jelly. Without my .32-caliber security blanket—which I'd never had occasion to so much as point at anyone—I'm not a fearless P.I. I'm just another pigeon. And one that can't run worth spit, besides.

So I took a deep breath and headed for the stairs.

Chapter 2

Climbing up all those flights was the most physically exhausting—and dumbest—thing I've ever done in my life. Looking back, I realize it would have been less hazardous to sleep in the street than to tackle so many stairs carrying so much weight. But my I.Q. has never been up there with my poundage.

So I climbed.

I had only gone as far as the second floor when I was forced to sit on the landing to catch my breath. After making it to the third floor, I sat on the landing a little longer and breathing was a little harder. En route to the fourth floor, I plunked myself down in the middle of the flight and could barely breathe at all. I won't bore you with a blow-by-blow account of my perilous ascent. It's enough to say that it took so much time and energy for me to go up each succeeding flight that I had serious doubts about seeing fourteen before dawn. If I saw it all.

To make everything even peachier, the floor numbers on the landings were faded to the point where they were illegible, so I had to count to myself as I went up. "Twelve," I silently huffed. "Thirteen," I gasped. And, at last, with what was unquestionably my one remaining breath, "Fourteen."

I opened the stairwell door and spotted the elevator at the end of the hall. Somehow I was able to drag myself to the apartment alongside it. There was no mat on the floor! I tried to read the name over the door buzzer, but the hall was so poorly lit I couldn't make it out. If only I had some matches. This had to be the right apartment, though. It was the only one

next to the elevator. Obviously there'd been a mis-
communication. Maybe Ellen had put the key on top
of the doorframe. I stood on tiptoe to check, but I
couldn't reach it! I was so tired and waterlogged and
frustrated that I was *that close* to what could turn out
to be a most intense and prolonged bout of hysteria.
(I told you I'm no Sam Spade.) Just then I heard a
noise down the hall. I looked around to see a tall,
thin, and very wet man in his late twenties coming out
of the stairwell. He was carrying an even wetter large,
fluffy dog and, I noted with malicious satisfaction,
breathing with almost as much difficulty as I was.

"Can I help you?" he croaked as he set down his
burden of fluff.

"I'm looking for Ellen Kravitz," I managed to croak
back, propping myself against the wall to keep from
falling on my face. I let the almost-brand-new and
probably unsalvageable Italian leather pumps that I'd
removed somewhere between the second and third
floors drop from my hands. Immediately the fluff
began to chomp on them.

"There's no Ellen—what did you say her last name
was?—living there," the man informed me, indicating
the apartment to which I had been so desperately trying to gain access. "That's the Blinder apartment."

"She said fourteen-A." I could feel the tears threatening again.

"This is fifteen-A."

"Oh, God!"

"Walking down's not nearly as bad as walking up,"
he offered encouragingly. He was so winded it was a
problem getting the words out. Nevertheless, he was
now manfully attempting to disengage the fluff, who
was—since I didn't have the strength to do anything
about it—still gnawing on my pumps. "Philip here
wouldn't budge after the ninth floor," he wheezed,
handing me a pair of now definitely unsalvageable
Italian leather pumps. "I had to carry him the rest of
the way."

I murmured something sympathetic.

"I'm getting used to it. This crummy elevator's always on the blink, and Philip's a very lazy guy." He glanced at the dog with a combination of love and despair. "At this rate, I'll develop a great set of muscles." He chuckled. "If I don't die of a heart attack first."

I eked out two faint clucks to commiserate. Then I just *had* to ask. "What time did the elevator break down?" I swear if he'd mentioned any time after 11:00, I'd have thrown myself down fifteen flights of stairs.

"Well, naturally *we* didn't have to go out this evening while it was still working, God forbid." He glared down with mock reproach at an unrepentent Philip. "But my neighbor told me it conked out around ten."

I could live with that.

I left whatsisname and Philip and backtracked, practically on my hands and knees, to the fourteenth floor. The mat was, as Ellen had promised, in front of her door. With a superhuman effort, I bent down and retrieved the key.

I was asleep five minutes later. New dress and all.

Chapter 3

It was early afternoon before I woke up. But I'm absolutely a hundred percent certain I'd still be stretched out on that lumpy sofa if the aroma of fresh coffee— one of my many weaknesses—hadn't penetrated my unconscious.

I was one big ache. I know you won't believe it, but even my eyebrows throbbed. Just getting myself into a sitting position was a major accomplishment. But, somehow, I found the strength to haul my protesting body off the sofa and inch it into the kitchen.

Ellen looked up as I got to the doorway. "Morning, Aunt— Oh, my God! What happened?"

"Your elevator's broken. I had to walk up fourteen flights of stairs," I replied accusingly.

"Oh, my God!"

"Stop saying that," I demanded. I deposited myself in a chair as Ellen poured some coffee for me.

"You look awful."

"Thanks. Just what I needed to hear."

"You know what I mean. Are you all right?"

"I guess so, or I will be after all my muscles stop complaining," I told her, a little more kindly.

"I'll fix you some breakfast, and after that I'll run you a nice hot bath." No wonder she's my favorite niece. (And I'd feel that way even if I *did* have more than one.)

"Sounds wonderful." I took a few more sips of coffee. "But I think I'd better call the office first."

Jackie was very relieved to hear from me, but in spite of that, there was an unmistakable edge to her voice. "You had me worried sick. I kept trying your apartment all morning and getting no answer. You always call if you're detained or anything."

"I'm sorry, Jackie. Honestly. But I couldn't help it."

My contriteness pacified her a little. She went on a bit less irritably. "Good thing Stuart phoned you. I was all set to run over to your apartment when he called. He said you'd spent the night at your niece's—only he didn't know her name. When I told him you weren't in yet, he got pretty upset." She paused and her tone suddenly softened. "Is anything wrong, Dez?"

"Not really. I just had a very exhausting night. I'll see you tomorrow morning, and I'll explain everything. I'm really sorry I worried you. Oh, and Jackie, do me a favor and call Stuart, will you? Tell him I'm okay and that I'll speak to him later."

After a leisurely breakfast and a lot more coffee, Ellen, bless her, ran a bath for me and helped me into the tub. I soaked for so long I started to pucker.

As I was drying off, the doorbell rang. I heard a man's voice, although I wasn't able to make out a single word. I slipped on my once-gorgeous dress, which Ellen had pressed as best she could. Unfortunately, it still looked as though I'd slept in it. Which, of course, I had.

I don't know who was more shocked when I limped into the living room, Ellen's visitors or me. Sitting there were two men from homicide, Sergeant Tim Fielding and Detective Walter Corcoran. And Fielding and I went a long way back. . . .

I first met Tim when I got involved with a case he was handling—that was years before he transferred to homicide. And then I happened to mention his name to my husband Ed, who at that time wasn't even my husband yet. Now, before turning P.I., Ed had been a member of the force, and it turned out he and Fielding had worked out of the same precinct. They'd been pretty tight in those days, too. But once Ed left the department, they gradually drifted, the way people do.

Anyway, you should have seen the smile on Ed's

face when I brought up Fielding's name. He spent hours that night reminiscing about their days on the force together, and the next morning he picked up the phone and called his old friend. After that, they started meeting for a drink every so often, and sometimes I'd join them. Then, when Fielding transferred to homicide, his new partner started tagging along. Right away, I thought his partner was an impossible young snot. The same impossible young snot that was shooting his mouth off now.

"Hey, Dez, looks like you had a big night." Walter Corcoran smirked, checking me out. Corcoran's a big man with a thin, high-pitched voice that sounds like it doesn't belong to him. It makes me want to laugh every time. But, being a nice person, I always restrain myself.

"Never mind that, Walt," Fielding admonished as I sank into the first available chair. "We have to ask you some questions, Dez. I hear you came over around midnight last night."

"Around. Why? What's going on?"

Fielding—for my money, one of the nicest guys on the force—ignored the question. That really wasn't like him. I figured he must be pretty stressed out. Anyway, it was obvious he wasn't here collecting for the Police Athletic League. "You see anyone besides Mr. Lambeth when you came in?" he wanted to know.

"Mr. Lambeth?"

"Tall, skinny guy on fifteen. He's got this big white dog."

"Oh, Philip's friend."

"Who?" Corcoran demanded.

"Philip's the dog," I explained. I looked at Tim and tried again. "Now, are you going to tell me what's going on?"

"There was a homicide upstairs. We're talking to everyone in the building."

"Oh, my God!" That was Ellen, of course.

"Who was killed?" I asked.

"Old lady in fifteen-D. Sort of eccentric, they say. A recluse. I don't suppose you saw anything."

"Don't be a boob, Tim. Wouldn't I tell you if I did? When did it happen?"

"Coroner figures around one a.m. But he hasn't completed the autopsy, so that's just an educated guess. What about you, Ms. Kravitz?" He turned to Ellen, who was now a very ghostly white.

"I didn't see anything," Ellen replied, her voice barely above a whisper.

"You go out at all last night?"

"No."

"You're sure?"

"She *told* you she didn't," I interjected.

"Your niece can speak for herself, Dez," Fielding said, with only a trace of impatience.

Walter Corcoran took up the questioning. "You know the old lady in fifteen-D?" he asked Ellen. "A Mrs. Agnes Garrity?"

"No." She looked so frightened it almost broke my heart.

"Ellen's lived here less than a week. Besides, you fellows said the woman was a recluse," I pointed out.

Corcoran grunted something—no doubt a four-letter word—and frowned at me.

"How was she killed?" I wasn't going to let his rotten temperament intimidate me.

"Shot. Looks like her door was jimmied open," he informed me grudgingly.

"Burglary?"

"We can't tell yet," Fielding answered, "but nothing was disturbed. So if that's what it was, someone knew exactly where to look."

"I gather you've been talking to the neighbors."

"Been doing that all day."

"No leads?"

"Not a one. From everything we've been able to find out so far, the woman was pretty much alone in the world. No friends and no relatives."

"Enemies, maybe?"

"I doubt that. She was a recluse, as you so kindly reminded us a few minutes ago."

"Think that would rule out a crime of passion, Dez?" Corcoran asked snidely.

Fielding stopped me from having to come up with an equally snide answer. "Come on, Walt," he said, getting up. "I think Dez and Ms. Kravitz here have told us all they can."

"But have *we* told Dez all *we* can?" Corcoran retorted, rising. "Listen, Dez, if there's anything else you want to know, you call us—day or night—hear?"

None of us realized then that before long, that's just what I'd be doing.

Chapter 4

Ellen had taken some time off from work for her move, and she wanted me to stay at her place for a few days so she could "look after" me. Now, while I was pretty charley-horsed from my sudden, unwanted involvement with physical activity, I wasn't exactly what you'd call incapacitated. Besides, much as I love her, I knew I'd go bonkers if I spent very long under Ellen's ministrations. On the other hand, having someone cater to me for a *little* while didn't sound half bad just then. I finally agreed to stay until morning. Ellen looked so relieved at finding out I'd be there even one more night that I'm not sure her motives were entirely altruistic. The muder had left her pretty shaken.

At about five that afternoon, Ellen went down to the grocer's to pick up a couple of frozen dinners. My niece's culinary talents end with breakfast. As for me, I love to cook almost as much as I love to eat. But Ellen insisted I just sit and relax. And I wasn't up to arguing.

Ellen came back about twenty minutes later. It seems everybody in the grocery store was talking about the murder. Mrs. Garrity, I was informed, used to order from there by phone all the time, and the delivery boy went to her apartment a few times a week. "The police asked *them* questions, too—Mr. Martinez, I mean; he's the owner of the store. And Jerry Costello, who's the delivery boy. I told them you were a private investigator and knew the detectives real well," she said smugly. "Everyone was very impressed."

I smiled. Ellen is twenty-seven but, as you may have already gathered, she's a very, very young twenty-seven. Inside that slim five-foot-six frame is the soul of a ten-year-old, with all the ingenuousness and wonder that goes with it. "I bet you told them I'm a regular Sam Spade," I commented dryly.

Ellen turned crimson.

On Wednesday morning, I got up very early and went home to change my clothes. The paint smell was overpowering. I opened the windows wide before leaving for the office. And I kept them open wide when I came home—even though it was unusually cold for October. I was really exhausted, so I went to bed at a little after 9:00. My teeth chattered all night long.

Not surprisingly, I woke up on Thursday with a beaut of a cold. I felt so rotten I didn't even attempt to go to work. After fixing myself some tea and toast, I just crawled back into bed and stayed there. I was beginning to doze off when the phone rang.

"Hi." It was Stuart. "I just spoke to Jackie, and she said you were home sick."

"Dat's true," I snuffled. "I've dot a told."

"I can tell." He sounded a little amused, but either compassion or cowardice kept him from coming out with anything that sounded remotely like a laugh. "Look, I called to find out if we're still friends."

"Don't be silly. Of dourse we are."

"Good. Say, suppose I pick up some Chinese and come over tonight. I'll get some nice hot therapeutic egg drop soup and—"

"Dat's sweet," I interrupted. "But I don't want to infect you. Besides, I have do appetite. All I feel like doing is sleeping."

"Okay ... if you really feel that way ..."

"I do, honest. But danks."

"Do you need anything?"

I assured him I didn't, and we hung up. I was a mere second or two away from sleep when the phone rang again. This time it was Ellen.

"I just called your office, and I know you're not

feeling well, Aunt Dez, but could I possibly stop in later? It's terribly important."

I explained about being contagious.

"This is *terribly* important. Anyhow, I have very good resistance." I didn't answer right away, so she added, "I swear I won't stay long."

The last thing I wanted was company, but I couldn't say no. Disappointing Ellen is like stealing candy from a baby or kicking a puppy. It could leave you with a terrible case of the guilts. Very reluctantly, I agreed to let her come over.

"Uhh . . . is it all right if I bring someone with me?"

"Ohhh, Ellen . . ." I wailed.

"I wouldn't ask, but I told you, this is really, *really* important."

"Who else is tumming?" I figured I was entitled to know.

She said it would take too long to explain and that she'd be here at 7:00.

By evening, with the help of three Actifeds and a handful of vitamin C, my stuffed nose was gone. Unfortunately, however, the cold had traveled from my nose to my chest. And the snuffles had been replaced by a hacking cough. Mildly cursing my favorite niece, I put on a decent robe and some lipstick.

At 7:00 on the button, the doorbell chimed. Ellen was standing there with a dark, chunky man in his forties, who was looking at me with an astonished expression on his moon-shaped face. I led the way into the living room, and when we were seated, Ellen made the introductions. The gentleman in shock was Ellen's grocery store owner, Mr. Martinez.

"*She's* the private eye?" he asked her incredulously.

I responded with a bristly "Yes," but the man was deaf where I was concerned.

"You din tell me she was a *woman*." He glared at Ellen accusingly.

"I *said* my *aunt* was a private investigator."

"I din hear the aunt part," he retorted sulkily. Clearly, he felt he'd been tricked.

"Well, that's not my fault! Anyhow, what difference does it make?" Ellen was getting shrill. "She's as good—better—than any man!"

"She don' even *look* like a real private eye!" Martinez countered, his voice rising, too.

"Well, it so happens—"

I cut off Ellen's defense of me. "I think Mr. Martinez would feel more comfortable consulting another investigator," I said. "I can recommend a couple of very competent—" I began to cough then, loud and long. Ellen ran to get me a glass of water.

By the time my coughing fit was over, Martinez had evidently had a change of heart. Maybe he thought that with a cough like that—and any luck—I'd be dead by morning, so why not go along with this thing? Or maybe he figured my recommendations wouldn't be any better than I was. At any rate, he addressed me directly for the first time. "Listen, lady, you gonna do fine. I 'pologize for how I been actin'. I jus' not been myself the las' few days. An' I wasn' expectin' no lady, is all. No offense?"

"No offense," I agreed, without really meaning it.

"Mr. Martinez needs your help." Ellen was now all sympathy. "He's sure they're going to arrest Jerry for murder. You know, the murder in my building."

"Jerry?"

"Jerry Costello, my delivery boy, Meez Shapiro," Martinez clarified.

"Call me Desiree. Or Dez, if you'd rather." He looked so miserable that I was suddenly sorry for him, too.

"Okay, thanks. Anyway, Deseeray, I'm real scare' for Jerry. He's the only one Meez Garrity ever let into the apar'ment. Excep' maybe the super. But he, the super, he say he wasn' never inside the place. She wouldn' let heem in to paint or fix things or nuthin'. He jus' come to collect the rent, he say. Besides, the night of the killin' was hees birt'day, an' he hab comp'ny that come sleep over. He say they gonna swear he couldn'a gone out that night." Martinez sighed deeply. "So who's tha' leave? Jerry!"

"Wait a minute. You mean the police suspect Jerry just because he's the only one Mrs. Garrity used to let into the apartment?" I was floored.

"Yeah, right. They sayin' he know where she kep' her money an' everythin', see. So he could go in and rob her without messin' up the place. But Jerry wouldn' never steal nuthin'. An' forget murder! Why, Jerry's the best kid ever work for me. Supports hees mother; she's a widow, see. Even goes to church reg'lar counta she wants that he should go with her. There's two other boys in the fam'ly, but they're no damn good—excuse me, Meez ... uh ... Deseeray. Always in trouble, them two are. But Jerry's differen'. Boy's like my own son. He wants to go to college for to be a lawyer. I was goin' to help heem with his school money an' ..." Martinez choked up. Taking a handkerchief from his pants pocket, he dabbed vigorously at his eyes, which were filling up at an alarming rate.

"It doesn't seem to me they've got much of a case," I said, trying to reassure him but meaning it, too. "You want me to look into this for you?"

"Yeah. I sure do. Ever since Ellen here mention the other day that her ... her aunt, I guess she say ... was a private eye, I been thinkin' about it. An' I made up my min' tha's wha' Jerry needs."

"Okay, then, that's what he's got." We shook hands on it.

They stayed a few more minutes, during which time Martinez and I discussed some minor points like my fee (which I kept almost ridiculously low). As they got up to leave, I told Martinez—or Sal, as he asked me to call him—that I'd find out exactly what the police had on Jerry. "I'll want to talk to the boy as soon as possible, too. And don't worry. We'll get this thing straightened out."

I've got to admit I wasn't nearly as confident as I sounded. I mean, stray cats and philandering husbands are one thing. But murder's another story. . . .

Chapter 5

Well, you see what I meant before. If I hadn't had to contend with all those stairs Monday night, I wouldn't have still been at Ellen's on Tuesday afternoon when Fielding and Corcoran showed up. Which, of course, means she couldn't have bragged about her aunt being a P.I. on intimate terms with the police, and Martinez would never have thought of hiring me.

But to continue ...

The next day, although I was practically at death's door, I forced myself to get out of bed and pay a visit to the Twelfth Precinct.

Fortunately, Tim Fielding was in. Just as fortunately, Walter Corcoran was not.

Fielding's back was to me when I walked in, his short, muscular torso bent over his desk, his fingers wound tight in the close-cropped salt and pepper hair. I cleared my throat and he looked up from the folder he'd been studying. I got the impression he wasn't terribly pleased to see me, especially when I informed him that I was on the Garrity case. But I knew he was too nice to refuse to help an old friend. So I invited myself to have a seat alongside his desk and asked him to fill me in on the evidence they had against Jerry Costello.

"Listen, Dez," he told me, closing the folder and shoving it aside, "no one's trying to frame your client. We've pieced together a pretty decent case against him."

"Why don't you arrest him, then?" I challenged.

"We will. Soon."

"Don't make things tough for me, Tim. Tell me what you've got."

He took a deep breath. "Okay. Let's start with what we don't have. We don't have a victim here who was killed for gain. I'm talking gain like in inheritance. Not only haven't we been able to come up with a single relative, but even if there are any, they won't be getting her money. I've seen a copy of the old lady's will, and whatever money she had—and it wasn't a hell of a lot—goes to some bird society. I checked it out, and it's a legitimate organization, by the way.

"I'll tell you what else we don't have—a murder for revenge. If Agnes Garrity wasn't a total recluse, she was close to it. The only person she had any real contact with was your client when he delivered her groceries. And we're certainly not claiming the kid wasted her because he was mad at her.

"Okay. We eliminate those motives, plus—in case you're interested—a crime of passion." He grinned mischievously at his reprise of Corcoran's tasteless joke. "So what does that leave?"

"You tell me."

"We figure it had to be a burglary. Nothing else it could be. Except maybe some sort of psychopath, and there's no indication of anything like that."

"Hey, back up. You said you *figure* it had to be a burglary. Don't you *know* if anything was stolen?" I guess that must have come out with more force than I intended it to, because Fielding glanced quickly around the room, obviously embarrassed.

"Calm down, Dez. We don't have any actual proof, but we found out the victim *did* leave the apartment occasionally—once a month, as a matter of fact—to go to the bank. The one on the next corner. She cashed a check for over three hundred dollars around . . ." He searched through a pile of folders on his desk, finally coming across the one he wanted near the bottom. He flipped through it. "Here it is. The check was cashed only eight days before the murder. But there was very little money found in the house. What happened to the rest of it?"

"Maybe she had bills to pay," I said in a tone that reflected my disdain for the question. "Hey, wait a minute. You said 'very little money' was found; then there was *some*. Why didn't Jer—the killer—take it all?"

"We think something woke the victim up. She called out, and the kid got scared. So he ran over to the bedroom door and blasted her. Then he grabbed a handful of cash and took off. Or maybe he already pocketed some of the cash *before* she woke up, so he split with whatever he had."

"Why didn't he just take off? Why shoot her?"

Fielding shrugged. "I'm not in his head. Could be he was afraid she'd scream and wake the neighbors. Most likely, though, it's what I said before. He just panicked."

"Was there only one shot?"

"Uh-uh. The kid's no marksman. There was a bullet in the headboard eight or nine inches above the bed and another one in the wall about a foot to the left of the bed and a foot and a half above it."

"Did anyone hear anything?"

"They all say not. That's a pretty old building, you know—prewar. Good solids walls. Also, there's a utility room on one side of the apartment, and the tenant who lives on the other side's been in Europe for three weeks."

"Where'd she keep the money, anyway?"

"In the freezer," he answered, grinning.

I couldn't help it. I grinned, too.

"The kid admits knowing the money was there. He used to come in and put the grocery bags on the table for her. After he gave her the bill, she'd make him wait outside in the hall while she got the cash. But he says the money always felt ice-cold. And once or twice, when she thought he was already out in the hall, he heard the refrigerator door open and close."

"Your client's an idiot," I announced to myself.

Aloud I said, with all the incredulity I actually felt, "And that's it? That's what you've got?"

"Hold on. Before you get on that high horse of yours, just think about it. Nothing in that apartment was even a little out of place. And the kid was the only one who knew where the victim kept her money."

"Who says? You can't be sure of that. Besides, you admit you don't know for a fact any money *was* stolen. Excuse me, Tim, but the case you have against my client sucks."

Fielding's voice turned quiet. "That's not quite all."

"What else?"

"We've got the kid's fingerprints on the refrigerator door."

That one threw me. But I tried hard not to let it show. "I suppose you asked him how they got there?"

"Sure we did. He tells us he doesn't remember."

"Maybe that's because it happened so casually he never gave it a second thought."

Fielding's "Yeah" was dripping with irony. "Look, Dez, I don't want to chase you, but I gotta get back to work. So I *am* chasing you."

"I'm on my way. Just one more question, though. Who discovered the body?"

"The super and some neighbor." He shuffled through his papers and picked up one of the typewritten sheets. "Name's Robert Levy. Lives across the hall from Garrity." He returned the sheet to the folder, but I continued to look at him expectantly. He sighed and went on. "This guy Levy was going to work Tuesday morning when he noticed that Garrity's door was ajar. He called to the old lady a few times, and when she didn't answer, he got nervous. So he went down for the super, and they found the body together. She was lying in bed, a bullet through her head. Here." He slid a photograph toward me.

I shuddered as I examined it. (I'm not used to murder, remember?) The victim was lying on her left side, a bullet hole in the right side of her head, about an inch below the temple. I noticed that the blanket was pulled up to her chin. "It doesn't look like she was reacting to a noise or anything," I commented, more to myself than to Fielding.

His response was only the slightest bit testy. "I can see that, too. Poor woman was probably too petrified to move."

"Get a definite fix on the time yet?"

"The coroner says between twelve and two. He can't pin it down any closer than that. Although, personally, I'd be inclined to say the shooting took place sometime after twelve forty-five."

"How do you figure?"

"It was teeming that night, if you remember, and that's when it stopped—around quarter of one."

"So?"

"So Garrity's kitchen floor was clean—no streaks, no mud, nothing."

"Maybe the perp took off his—or her—rubbers and shook himself off before he broke in," I suggested, mostly in jest.

"Sure," he countered sarcastically, "or maybe he mopped up after himself."

"*Or,*" I said meaningfully, "maybe the killer never went *into* the kitchen."

"Christ, Dez," Fielding said abruptly, "I really *do* have work to do."

"I know. But just one more thing. What about the gun?"

"We haven't found it yet, if that's what you mean?"

"Any reason to believe Jerry owned a gun?"

"No, but he wouldn't have a problem getting one. Not in this city. Besides, we picked up his oldest brother for possession twice this year. Your client's got two big bad brothers, you know."

"What caliber was it? The gun that killed Mrs. Garrity."

Fielding made a big production out of checking the folder. Then he very deliberately shut it and pushed it away from him. "Thirty-eight."

"I'm going," I said hastily, not wanting him to think I was too insensitive to take the hint. I picked up my

attaché case, which was propped against the chair, and
started to leave. But I thought of something else. "Just
one more question—"

"What now?" Fielding bellowed. I was afraid I'd
really worn out my welcome. But I looked at his face.
He was smiling. It was sort of a forced smile, but
you've got to admit the man had to have some kind
of great disposition to even manage that.

"Was the freezer door open or closed?"

"Closed." He seemed uncomfortable with the answer. "The kid must have slammed it shut—you know,
like a reflex—when the victim called out." I looked at
him skeptically. "Or it's possible he closed it *after* he
killed her, so as not to draw attention to the theft."

I didn't for one second believe that *he* believed his
explanations, but I didn't say a word. I mean, how far
can you press your luck?

"If that's all . . . ." Fielding said sarcastically, getting
to his feet.

I decided to *find out* how far you can press your
luck. "I'd like to check the apartment."

"Dez, Dez," he said, shaking his head from side to
side. "You know better than that. Court's got it
sealed."

Actually, I didn't know better than that. They don't
seal apartments with my usual cases. "Till when?"

"Until we're all through with it. Anyway, there's
nothing there to help you. Trust me. Why don't you
just talk to the super and that other guy . . . Levy?"

"I will. And listen, Tim, I really *do* appreciate your
time and everything."

"It's okay. And if you run into any problems, call
me. I mean that."

I had started to walk to the door by then. I turned
back. "Thanks. You're a doll. I almost feel guilty
about having to make you look like a jackass on this
thing."

I was beaming at him over my shoulder as the paper
clip whizzed past my ear.

Chapter 6

In less than half an hour, I was in Martinez's grocery store. Jerry was out on a delivery, so Sal treated me to a Coke while I waited. Ten minutes later the kid returned, and we went into the back room to talk.

It was a small, narrow room filled with cartons and crates of all sizes. Jerry found a couple of empty crates, turned them over, and set them opposite each other. He straddled the smaller one. Apparently I was expected to sit on the other one. I complied, but with only half a cheek and much trepidation.

Jerry Costello was small and skinny, with light hair and a pale complexion decorated here and there with bright red zits. He was wearing a pair of faded jeans about two sizes too big for him and a faded plaid shirt about a year too small for him. He looked thirteen years old, but I gave him the benefit of the doubt and put him at fifteen. I found out later he was close to eighteen.

At first the kid was quiet, almost wary. But he seemed to be pretty straightforward about answering my questions.

Yes, he'd been delivering groceries to Mrs. Garrity for a long time—since he started working here after school two years ago. And no, he didn't have anything to do with her murder. Honest he didn't. And no again, there wasn't anyone who could vouch for his whereabouts at the time she was killed. He'd been to a movie with friends on Monday night. It was past 11:00 when he came home. His mother was already asleep, and both his brothers were still out. In fact, they didn't get in until 3:00 or 4:00 in the morning.

Well, that took care of that. Actually, it was what I expected. If he'd had a decent alibi, Fielding and friends would have been forced to find themselves another killer.

"Did you like Mrs. Garrity?" I wanted to know.

"I guess I shouldn't say it, because she's dead, but not very much," he admitted, blushing. "She was real unfriendly. And rude. Boy, was she rude! And she never gave me a tip, either. Not even once. Not even at Christmas."

"When was the last time you delivered an order to her?"

"On Monday, the day before ... you know."

"Now I want you to think really carefully," I ordered. "The police found your fingerprints on the refrigerator door. Do you have any idea how they could have gotten there? It's important."

"I don't know. Honest. I thought the cops were making the whole thing up. Like to trap me."

"I'm afraid not." I took a stab at a possible scenario, trying to refresh his memory. "Could she have been putting something away in the fridge and maybe you held the door open for her?"

"Uh-uh. She never used to put stuff away while I was there. I always set the bags on the table for her, and then I'd wait in the hall while she got the money out of the freezer."

Oh, how I wished he hadn't admitted knowing about that! "Did you mention to anyone else that Mrs. Garrity kept her money in the freezer? I'm talking about before she was killed."

"Uh-uh ... at least I don't think I did. . . ." He considered the question some more. "No. I'm pretty sure I didn't," he concluded more definitely.

Which let me know he didn't have the slightest idea if he'd told anyone or not. "How about your brothers?" I asked.

That touched a raw nerve. "Hey! They wouldn't murder an old lady!" he shouted. He was calmer in an instant. "I'm sorry. But they wouldn't. Anyway, I'd never tell them about a thing like that."

I believed him. In spite of the boy's protestation, he was obviously smart enough not to put temptation in his brothers' path. I went back to our biggest problem. "I want you to keep thinking about how your prints could have gotten on that refrigerator door. Maybe it wasn't even the last time you were there. It could have happened the time before. Just concentrate on it." I took my business card out of my handbag and scribbled my home phone number on it. "Please call me right away if . . . when you remember. Okay?"

"Okay." That's when Jerry smiled for the first time. It was one of the warmest, sweetest smiles I'd ever seen, completely transforming his face.

I'm not sure whether it was my maternal instinct or just because I'm a little soft in the head, but from that smile on, I was wholeheartedly in Jerry Costello's corner. He probably could have been standing in a locked room with a dead body at his feet and a smoking gun in his hand, and I'd still have been convinced of his innocence.

After getting the kid to promise again that he'd keep thinking about the fingerprints, I left for Ellen's building.

Within ten minutes, I was pressing the buzzer that read s. CLORY, SUPT.

"Yeah?" The voice that came over the intercom was somewhere between a bark and a growl.

I had to stand on tiptoe to respond. "Mr. Clory? I'm investigating the Garrity murder."

He buzzed me in, but not before letting loose with some really colorful expletives.

The super's apartment was on the first floor. I walked toward the back through a dirty hallway until I came to an open door blocked by an even dirtier man. He was about forty-five and huge—easily six-three, with a barrel chest and an enormous stomach that dropped way below his very ample waistline. He had sparse yellow hair and teeth to match.

And we detested each other on sight.

I introduced myself politely, even extending my

hand. Which, predictably, S. Clory ignored. "My name is Desiree Shapiro. I'm a private inves—"

"Private!" he snarled, starting to close the door in my face. "I don't have to say nuthin' to you!"

I shoved my foot in the door, bravely disregarding the fact that this slime would have no compunction about crippling me for life. "I'm working very closely with the police on this case. I wouldn't like to report that you refused to cooperate. They might decide you have something to hide." This sounded reasonably threatening to me.

"Your ass!" he replied.

Plan B went into operation. I opened my left palm to reveal the twenty-dollar bill I'd taken from my wallet as soon as I heard that melodious voice on the intercom. "I just want to ask you a few questions. It won't take long," I cajoled.

Clory licked his lips. I could almost read his mind. As much as he wanted the twenty, he also wanted to give me a hard time. In the end, spite triumphed over greed. "Shove it!" he said.

It was time for Plan C. "You've heard, I suppose, that Jerry Costello, Martinez's delivery boy, is a suspect in the killing."

He glared at me expressionlessly. From his lack of reaction, it was apparent I wasn't giving him any big news.

"I would hate to tell the Costello boys—who I understand are as mean as they come—that you're helping to send their little brother to jail."

Actually, I'd had very little hope for Plan C. But, amazingly, it did the trick. The door opened wide.

"Look, I don't have nuthin' against the Costello kid, so don't go spreadin' vicious lies." He lowered his voice and practically bent himself in two, so that we were at eye level with one another. I now had the pleasure of smelling S. Clory's breath, which was heavy with liquor and tobacco and as nauseating as I might have imagined. "You don't mess with them Costellos. They got Mafia connections, them boys," he whispered. He then offered proof positive: "Fam'ly's Eyetalian."

"I *heard* they were involved with the mob," I lied.

"Yeah, well, I got a wife and kid," he said hoarsely, his eyes darting up and down the hall. The man was really scared, I was delighted to see.

"You have nothing to worry about if you cooperate," I informed him in what was intended to be a very official tone. "Can we go inside?" Since it wasn't really a question, I didn't wait for an answer.

Pushing past my gracious host, I entered a dreary, but surprisingly clean living room. I quickly appropriated what I was certain was Clory's chair, so he reluctantly settled his substantial bulk in the less comfortable chair alongside it. "Now, how well did you know Mrs. Garrity?"

"I din hardly know her at all. I just useta go up and collect the rent once a month. That ole bitch wouldn't even let me come in and fix stuff. Once, we got a leak in fourteen-D we was pretty sure was comin' from her place. Wouldn't even let me in to check. Anyways, it turned out to be from somewheres else."

"One of the tenants claims to have seen you on the fifteenth floor the morning of the murder," I threw out. "I'm talking about the *very early* morning—hours before you went up there with Levy." It's not for nothing that I watch old grade-B detective movies on television.

Clory's face turned a brilliant and extremely unflattering purple. "That's a fuckin' lie!"

Well, it was worth a try.

"But you *did* know she kept her money in the freezer, didn't you?"

"How the fuck would I know *that*?" He half rose out of his chair. I was afraid for a second that he wanted to get within striking distance of me, but he settled back again immediately. "I told you I never went into that fuckin' apartment. I just seen her once a month for maybe a coupla seconds, like I said."

"I thought you were going to be cooperative," I reminded him.

"Look, lady, I *am* being cooperative." Beads of perspiration appeared on his forehead, and he took what
had to be the world's filthiest, most disgusting handkerchief from his pocket. "I'm tellin' you the fuckin'
truth," he declared, mopping his face. "I din know
about no freezer, and I wasn't up there that morning.
Anyways, not till Levy come and got me."

"Okay, okay, forget it," I said magnanimously. "It
was probably a mistake." I glanced behind me toward
the rear of the apartment. "You say there's a *Mrs.*
Clory?"

"What about it?"

"I'd like to talk to her later. Is she in?"

"She's workin'. She don't get home till five-thirty."

I checked my watch. It was almost 5:00. "Fine. In
the meantime, why don't you tell me exactly what
happened the morning of the murder. Start with when
Levy came to get you."

"Yeah, okay. Levy rings my bell and—"

"What time was that?"

"Around quarter to eight. The wife had just left
for work."

"Go on."

"He says how he seen the ole lady's door open, so
he calls out to her, but she don't answer. Natcherly, I
went upstairs to check things out. Had to walk up all
them stairs, too, account of the damn elevator broke
down, for a change. Anyways, me and Levy go inside.
There's no one in the livin' room or the kitchen, so
we look in the bedroom. First I see this little gray
head with the covers pulled up and all. I din' even
realize she was dead. Then I call 'Miz Garrity! Miz
Garrity!' you know? I'm still standin' at the door, but
when she don't answer, I walk in. Jesus, whatta shock!
She's layin' there, light shinin' right down on her head
so's you could see all the blood and—"

"Light?"

"Yeah, one of them real tiny things."

"You mean a night-light?"

"Yeah. A night-light."

"All right. Now, as you're facing Mrs. Garrity, which side was the night-light on?"

"Left side. On a little table."

I nodded absently. That would mean it was on the old woman's right. "Mrs. Garrity was lying on her left side?" I asked for no reason at all, since the police photo was still clear in my mind.

"Yeah."

"How was she facing?"

"I don't know what you mean."

"I want to know if she was facing the door—or what?"

"She was facin' the other way, towards the window."

I chewed that over for a minute. Let's say—just to consider all the possibilities—that Fielding was right and that the woman was too frightened to sit up in bed when she heard the intruder. Okay, maybe I could buy *that*. But if she called out, it would have been positively unnatural for her not to turn in the direction of the sounds. By the laws of common sense, Agnes Garrity should have been found on her *right* side, facing the doorway—that is, if Fielding's premise was correct.

But Fielding's premise, I was convinced, was for the birds.

"Continue," I told Clory.

"Where was I?" he demanded petulantly. "Oh, yeah. I warned Levy, 'Don't touch nuthin'.' Then we went to his apartment, and I called the cops. And that's it. There ain't nuthin' else to tell."

"All right. Thanks. What time does Levy get home?"

"How the hell should I know?" he snapped. Then, apparently remembering the Costellos, he amended grudgingly, "Around six, most times."

My watch said 5:15, so I figured it might be a good time to go out and replenish myself with some coffee and just the tiniest piece of cake. "I'll be back in a little while," I informed Clory, "to talk to your wife."

I couldn't quite make out the muttered response, but it was probably better that way.

Just then I heard a key in the door. The lady of the house—poor thing—had come home a little early.

Erna Clory entered the room tentatively. She was tall. Almost emaciatingly thin. And completely colorless. She was neatly and unbecomingly dressed in a long-sleeved tan turtleneck sweater—which revealed the absence of breasts—and baggy khaki slacks—which emphasized a too-flat bottom. She wore no makeup, except for the merest trace of pale pink lipstick. And I noted, a little sadly, that her dull brown hair was cropped short, elongating an already unattractively long face.

"My name's Desiree Shapiro. I'm a private investigator, and I'd just like to ask you one or two questions, Mrs. Clory," I told her gently.

She looked quickly at her husband, who shrugged. "All right," she agreed in a small voice.

It was apparent Erna Clory was frightened. And not of me. I was willing to bet Clory abused her physically. I couldn't actually *tell,* since her clothes covered her from the neck all the way down. But it was hard to miss the way she reacted to him.

"On October twenty-second—that was the Monday—" I started to say.

"I know. It was Sean's birthday that night, so I couldn't forget the date."

"What the fuck you babblin' about? Just answer what she asks ya!" Clory exploded.

"I'm sorry," Erna murmured timidly.

That slob uses her for a punching bag, all right, I told myself with conviction. "It's okay," I assured her. "You can say whatever you want to." I presented Clory with a withering glare before turning to his wife again. "You had a party that night, I believe."

"Yes."

"What time did it start?"

"Around eight."

"And it lasted until ... ?"

"I'm not real sure. Maybe two."

"Who was there?"

"Just Sean's brother and his girlfriend. And my sister and brother-in-law—they came in from Philly. And, of course, Sean and me. Our daughter Colleen—she's ten—stayed over at her girlfriend's."

"I'd like all their addresses, if you don't mind."

"Now?"

"No, next year!" Clory spat out.

I ignored him, but Erna cringed. She went into the kitchen and came out with a piece of paper on which she'd hastily written the information I asked for.

"Just one more question. Did anyone leave the apartment at any time that night?"

"No."

There was just the least bit of hesitation before she answered, but I caught it and pressed her. "Someone *did* leave for a little while, didn't they? Was it your husband?"

She glanced at Clory, but he turned away. "Sean did go out for some ice," she admitted in that wispy voice of hers. "But he was only gone a few minutes."

"What time was that?"

"Nine or so, wasn't it, Sean?"

"Yeah, that's right. Nine or so," he repeated, gloating.

I realized then that, because of my dislike of Clory, I'd been particularly intent on getting something incriminating on the man. And it bothered me a little. But it bothered me a lot more that I hadn't succeeded.

I bid the Clorys good night and went up to the fifteenth floor. A large sign on the door of 15D announced that the premises had been sealed by the court. But I wasn't there about the apartment. I wanted to have a look at the utility room next to it.

The space was very small, only about three feet square, and packed with assorted junk: soiled rags, a broken mop, a whiskerless broom, a couple of buckets, some collapsed cartons, and piles and piles of old newspapers. The room didn't tell me anything at all—

except that it might be a convenient place for someone to hide.

I decided to see if Robert Levy was home from work yet. He was. He was also a pleasant change from Sean Clory. But he didn't add a thing to what the super had told me.

I went home feeling pretty discouraged. But that was nothing compared to how I felt when I played back the messages on my answering machine. The first one was from Martinez. He thought I should know that Jerry Costello had just been arrested for murder.

Chapter 7

At 7:30 the next morning, I was on the New Jersey Turnpike, on my way to an appointment with Erna Clory's sister and brother-in-law.

Bill and Evelyn Anderson lived on a quiet street of one-family homes in a nice middle-class section of Philadelphia. When Evelyn Anderson opened the door, I was struck by two things. First, how much different she looked from her sister. And second, how much alike.

Evelyn was as tall as Erna. And as thin. But on her, that bony frame wasn't pathetic; it was chic. She had the same angular facial structure and the same shade of medium brown hair her sister had. But this woman's hair shone with warm auburn highlights. And it was smartly styled to add fullness to her face. She was carefully made up, too. And the long-sleeved sweater Evelyn had on was a soft shade of coral. It was also cashmere.

I wondered if Evelyn was younger than the unfortunate Erna; she certainly looked it. But then, *she* wasn't living with Clory.

We entered a large, comfortably furnished living room. Bill Anderson was seated in one of those big leather recliners and was just putting down his newspaper when we walked in. He was a rangy, good-looking man in his fifties with an easy smile. He stood up and introduced himself, holding out his hand. I liked him on sight.

The Andersons insisted I have some refreshment, and who wanted to be contentious? So over a cup of steaming coffee and warm, buttery—and absolutely delicious—miniature Danish, we discussed Sean Clory's birthday party.

"Erna tries so hard to please that man," her sister sighed. "His birthday was last Monday, so naturally the party had to be that day, too. Erna didn't want to have it on for the weekend, because she felt dear Sean should be able to celebrate his birthday *on* his birthday. Imagine? It didn't make any difference to us. Bill's his own boss—he has a pharmacy not far from here—and he's got people working for him, so he can take off without any problem. And I don't work—at least, not outside this place." She made a sweeping gesture of the room. "But Erna waits tables during the week. And, of course, you know Clory'd never give her a hand with a thing, don't you?" She definitely did not expect an answer.

"Somehow, though, Erna managed to prepare a lovely dinner—Lord knows where she found the time—and it turned out to be a pretty good party, because Clory got crocked and passed out." Evelyn stopped suddenly. "I hope this is the sort of thing you want to know. I suppose I should let you ask some questions."

"You're doing great. Where did Clory pass out?"

"On the living room sofa. Which was just fine. We all sat around the kitchen table and told stories and everything. Sean's brother Patrick has a marvelous sense of humor."

"His girlfriend's kind of a pill, though," Bill Anderson interjected.

"True, but it was better than having the birthday boy around."

"Amen," said her husband.

"What time did he pass out?" I asked.

"Must've been around ten."

"No, it was later," Bill corrected. "The phone rang when it was almost ten-thirty. I remember wondering who it could be at that hour." He turned to me. "It was Colleen, their little girl. She was sleeping at her girlfriend's, and she wanted to ask her mother about something. But Clory was the one who answered the phone."

"He's right," Evelyn agreed.

"How soon after the phone call did he lie down?"

"Oh, it was very soon after." Evelyn looked at her husband.

"Yes, it was," he concurred.

"Could you see him from where you were sitting in the kitchen?"

"No. The kitchen's down the hall and off to the left. You can't see into the living room at all from there," Bill explained.

"Was he passed out all evening?"

"Yup," Evelyn replied. "When Patrick and Hedy— that's Patrick's significant other, or whatever they call them these days—well, when they went home, we walked to the door with them; it's right in the living room. Sean was stretched out on the sofa and snoring to beat the band."

"What time was that?"

"Around two, wasn't it, Bill?"

"It was closer to two-thirty," he contradicted, with an apologetic little smile for his wife. "I know, because I wound my watch a couple of minutes later."

"That's when you went to bed?"

They both nodded.

"And Erna?"

"She went to bed just a little while after we did. She wanted to rinse out the coffee cups first," Evelyn said.

"What about Sean?"

"He was still on the sofa, snoring away, at seven the next morning when we left for home."

"Let me ask you this. Did any of you go into the living room between ten-thirty and two-thirty?"

"I don't think so. I know *I* didn't," Evelyn told me.

"I didn't, either. But I think Erna did once," Bill put in. "I guess it was to check on him." Then, anticipating my next question, "But I have no idea what time that was."

"Was it around eleven? Twelve? One?"

"Maybe twelve-thirty, one. But that's just a guess."

I don't know why I was so anxious for the answer. If Clory *wasn't* asleep on the sofa when Erna went into the living room, there was no way she'd admit it to me or anyone else. Not if she wanted to stay in one piece, that is. But right then, feeling as I did about Sean Clory, it was enough to know he *could* have left the apartment, and he *could* have murdered Agnes Garrity.

Sometimes it doesn't take a whole lot to please me.

Chapter 8

The first thing I did when I got home late that afternoon was call Sal Martinez. Jerry was still in jail, and Martinez was in a terrible state of depression. "The most important thing right now," I said, "is to get Jerry a lawyer."

He was way ahead of me. "I got this guy suppose to be the best." He mentioned the name, and I was impressed. Also surprised. The man was a crack criminal lawyer and a very expensive one. Apparently Martinez was in much better financial shape than I figured. "He—thees lawyer, Pheelpott—he tell me the cops mess up the paperwork or somethin', so Jerry he habbin been able to see the judge yet. But he—the lawyer I got—say not to worry. By Monday, they be gettin' Jerry watchacallit—I don' know the word . . ."

"Arraigned?"

"Yeah, that's it."

"I'm sure this Philpott will be able to arrange bail, too. Jerry doesn't have a criminal record. And he supports his mother."

"Tha's what Pheelpott tell me, too. Jesus, I hope so!"

"In the meantime, I want you to know that I'm following a couple of very promising leads." Sure it was an exaggeration, but the truth wouldn't have been nearly as kind.

"Tha's good. Tha's real good."

"So take it easy, huh? You've got Jerry one of the best lawyers around, and things are coming along at my end. Everything'll be just fine."

By the time our conversation was over, Martinez

sounded a little less discouraged than when it had begun.

The next day, Sunday, I phoned Patrick Clory. Would he be home that afternoon and could he see me for a few minutes? He would and could. What about his friend Hedy? She'd be there, too.

It was about 3:00 when I got to the Tribeca loft the couple shared. I don't know what I *thought* Clory's brother would be like, but it certainly wasn't anything even remotely resembling what greeted me.

Patrick was thirty, tops. He was also extremely attractive: tall, tan, and muscular, with eyelashes any woman would die for. Hedy Van Dam might have been his twin. They were both dressed in white shorts. Hers were very *short* white shorts, which showed off her absolutely sensational legs. Now, some women might have hated Hedy just for those legs. Not me, I'm proud to say. It didn't matter, though. She soon gave me plenty of other reasons to despise her.

"We've just been bike riding," Patrick told me, obviously in explanation of the shorts. He indicated a pair of stationary twin bikes in a corner of the huge room, then motioned for me to sit down on the large modern sofa. "Now, you had some questions for us?"

I asked them pretty much the same stuff I'd asked the Andersons. And got pretty much the same answers. Except that getting an answer from Hedy took some extra work. Also, this couple was a lot less certain about times. They couldn't remember what time Colleen had called her mother or what time Clory had passed out. And they had no idea what time they'd gone home.

"Did either of you look in on Clory after he fell asleep on the sofa?"

"No, we didn't," Patrick said.

I turned to Hedy for confirmation. Nothing. I locked eyes with her. Still nothing. I finally realized she was playing games with me. What's worse, I had to let her win.

"Is that your recollection, too, Ms. Van Dam?"

"Is *what* my recollection?"

"I'd like to know whether either of you looked in on Clory after he passed out," I said, controlling my temper only with a great deal of difficulty.

"Why in heaven's name *would* we?" Even if she'd been loaded with cellulite, I couldn't have liked her.

"What about Erna?" I asked them. "Did she check on him?"

"I honestly can't say," Patrick replied. "I don't think so, but she may have."

I had to repeat the question for Hedy, who, lifting one perfectly shaped eyebrow, replied coldly, "I didn't notice." It was obvious this bimbo couldn't be bothered with anything as trivial as a murder investigation.

I was about to go into something else when Patrick blurted out, "I know what you're getting at, but Sean didn't budge from that couch all night! Believe me, he was in no condition to move, much less walk up a dozen flights of stairs."

"Look, Patrick, I'm not accusing your brother of anything. I just want to find out what happened that night." This was delivered in my most reasonable voice.

"Sorry. It's just that everyone thinks the worst where Sean's concerned. I admit he isn't always easy to take, but you'd find out that he's actually a pretty decent person—if you ever got to know him." The thought sent chills through me. "And he's no murderer," Patrick stated firmly, "that much I'll swear to."

I couldn't think of an appropriate response, so I said, "I only have one or two more questions."

"Okay, shoot." Patrick sighed, with zero enthusiasm.

"Did either of you know Mrs. Garrity?"

I got two no's on that one.

"Just one more thing. Did Clor—uh, Sean—ever mention Mrs. Garrity to you?"

"Before the murder?" Patrick asked.

I nodded.

"Only once. But that was a long time ago."

"I'd appreciate your telling me what was said."

At that moment, Patrick realized he'd made a mistake. But it was too late for him to back down. "It was over a year ago—well over. In fact, it was probably closer to two years ago," he added defensively. "We were talking about money, and Sean said people hide it in nutty places. We had a good laugh about it—her keeping her money in the freezer. But listen, that doesn't mean a damn thing. I'll bet everyone in the building heard about the old woman's freezer. Just ask around."

When I left Patrick and the charming Hedy, I was feeling a whole lot lighter. It was like I weighed ninety pounds! I decided to walk awhile before catching a cab back to my apartment, and, I swear, my feet hardly touched the ground. I had finally learned something that could make a real difference: Jerry wasn't the only one who knew about that freezer. Sean Clory knew about it, too!

I had only covered a block and a half when it started to pour. (Thanks once again, WNBC, for your impeccable forecast.) But even the rain didn't faze me. I was one smug little P.I.

Needless to say, I couldn't get a taxi, so I had to settle for the subway—complete with a flasher, a pot smoker, and a kid with a boom box. I got back to the apartment dripping wet. But smiling.

There was a message on the answering machine from Stuart. He said to call him if I felt like having dinner that night.

Now, you *know* how paranoid I am about my hair. And plastered down like that it looked like a skin rash and felt like flypaper. But not to worry; I'm like the Boy Scouts—or is it the marines?—always prepared. I keep a spare head of hair in the closet, which is exactly like my real hair—only it's removable.

I checked it over. Not bad. A few spritzes here and there, and I could live with it.

I called Stuart back and left a message on *his* machine. I'd be ready at 7:00.

We went to an excellent Spanish restaurant, where

I stuffed myself silly with positively no shame. (I was still confusing myself with a featherweight.)

All in all, it was a wonderful evening. Stuart was very good company. And I was inordinately pleased with myself and the investigation.

My euphoria ended less than twenty-four hours later, when all hell broke loose.

Chapter 9

The next morning, I called Tim Fielding to ask if he knew where Erna Clory worked. (Oh, I realize I said I'd never be able to get a thing out of her. But I had to try, didn't I?)

"Don't tell me you want to pin this on Sean Clory," Fielding said, with what sounded like a snort. "You're wasting your time, you know. Your own client's the perp."

I countered with, "You wouldn't want to bet." Or something equally effective.

We sparred for a few more rounds, but Fielding came through as usual. "It's called the Bus Stop," he informed me, supplying me with the address.

I left as soon as I put down the phone.

The Bus Stop was a small coffee shop in Chelsea, not far from Ellen's apartment building—which is how I think of the place. There were five counter seats and six or seven tables, just one of which was occupied at the moment. Erna was the only one waiting tables, so I didn't have to worry about taking a seat at her station.

She actually looked terrified at seeing me.

"I just want to ask you a couple of questions," I told her extra kindly.

She didn't look any less terrified. Maybe because she'd heard something like that from me before. "I'm not allowed to visit when I'm working," she replied in her little voice.

I ordered coffee and a Danish and tried to persuade her. "It won't take long," I assured her. "And you're not real busy now." I glanced around the room to make my point. The man who'd been seated at the other table was heading for the door.

"Okay," she reluctantly agreed, "I'll be right back." A few minutes later, she returned with my order. As she set the cup down in front of me, I noticed ugly purple bruises high on both arms peeking out from under the short sleeves of her uniform.

I had been positive Sean Clory was a wife beater. And now, with this brutal evidence to attest to my perception, I felt just the tiniest bit self-satisfied. And mad at myself for feeling that way.

I got to the reason I was there. "The night of the party, Mrs. Clory, I understand your husband passed out on the sofa. Did you go in and check on him at all?"

"Two or three times," she said, almost defiantly.

"Can you tell me when?"

She furrowed her brow as if trying to recall. But I knew she was attempting to come up with the times that would do Clory the most good. "Around twelve," she responded finally, "then just before one and again at two o'clock or so."

"And he was asleep?"

"Yes, fast asleep."

"If you're saying that just to give him an alibi, Mrs. Clory, he doesn't deserve it. Anyhow, that's not what your sister and brother-in-law told me. According to them, you only looked in on him once."

"If they said that, then they made a mistake. Besides, I don't know why you're asking me these things. The police already have the murderer locked up."

"The police may have arrested Jerry Costello, but he didn't murder anybody. And the truth is bound to come out sooner or later."

"Sean didn't murder anyone, either. He couldn't have. He was asleep the whole time."

I gave up. There was no way in the world I would get any straight answers from Erna Clory, and, looking at those arms of hers, I couldn't altogether blame her.

In the cab heading for the office, I went over everything again and again. The elation I'd felt the night before was fading fast. I was still absolutely convinced of my client's innocence. And I was just as convinced of Sean Clory's guilt. But how was I going to prove it?

I vowed to put the whole thing out of my mind for a while. It was time I paid some attention to the rest of my workload.

When I got to the office, I immediately pulled out the file on another case to make sure I kept my promise to myself. I quickly reviewed it to refresh my memory. To be honest, it was about a hundred times more challenging than what I usually handled, and under normal conditions I'd have been thrilled to work on anything like that. There was your standard attractive young wife with your standard rich elderly husband. There was also, of couse, a young hunk in the picture that you could bet the farm was the lady's lover. Well, it seems—and this is the interesting part—that the woman's very pricey jewels had disappeared under circumstances none of the three principals could agree on.

Anyway, the insurance company had hired me to investigate the theft, and when I read the woman's original statement to them, I picked up on a really dumb lie. I knew I should have made an appointment to see her days ago, but practically from the minute Martinez hired me, I'd let everything else go to pot.

I reached for the phone and dialed the lady in question. She agreed to let me come over at 4:30. It turned out to be a very profitable meeting. For me, at least. When I brought up her obvious lie, she got rattled enough to—as we say in the trade—come clean. She admitted having had an affair with the hunk and confided that the night the jewels were stolen she'd been engaged in a ménage à trois with her lover and his former girlfriend. Which, she subsequently found out, her lover had arranged when *he* found out that the husband had found out about them. It's all pretty involved—and very juicy. And I guess it's too complicated to go into now. I'll tell you about it later. . . .

The main thing about *that* case, though, isn't that it

allowed me a badly needed degree of success; it's that it kept me from thinking about *that other* case. Of course, the second I got home that night, I was at it again.

Believe it or not, until then, it had completely slipped my mind that Jerry should have been out on bail by now. (I guess I was more disciplined than I gave myself credit for.) The least Martinez could have done, I thought, was to let me know what was going on.

I was not about to call *him,* I decided childishly. Unless, of course, I didn't hear from him by morning.

Chapter 10

The phone rang at 7:00 a.m. *Martinez!* Instantly awake, I grabbed it on the second ring.

But the call was from Elliot Gilbert, one of the lawyers I rent space from. There was a man he was supposed to meet with in Greenwich, Connecticut, in connection with an embezzlement case he was handling. But something else had just come up, and he asked if I could fill in for him. I said "No problem," then jumped out of bed and tore around the apartment like a crazy person. I only had a half hour to get ready if I wanted to be on time for the appointment Elliot had set up. And it usually takes me that long just to brush my teeth.

It turned out to be a wasted day. The Greenwich guy wasn't available when he was supposed to be, and I had to wait around for hours to get in to see him. Then, to top it off, what he had to tell me wasn't worth a walk around the corner, much less a drive to Connecticut.

When I got home, it was close to 9:00, and I was so exhausted my palms itched. (Don't ask me why, but they always do when I'm *really* tired.)

I walked into my living room/dining room/guest room/office to find the answering machine winking at me. I pressed playback.

"Hello, Dez, Tim Fielding. If you get home before eleven, give me a call at the station."

I called back without stopping to take off my coat.

"We had another homicide in your niece's building today," he told me. "Her floor—fourteen-D."

The first thing that popped into my head was,

"Thank God nothing's happened to Ellen!" The next was a very fervent hope that Jerry had been denied bail.

No such luck. "Seems strange it should happen the morning after your client gets out, don't you think?" I couldn't tell from the voice whether Fielding was serious or just riding me. But either way, I didn't like it.

"C'mon, Tim! That is so stu—" I began angrily. Then I remembered that it *was* nice of him to keep me posted like this, so I forced myself to cool off. "Do you happen to know what time Jerry was released?" I asked in a nice, calm voice.

"Don't *you* know?" He sounded surprised. "It was yesterday afternoon—a little after four."

"Who was hit?"

"Man named Constantine. Neil Constantine. He was an artist of some kind."

"How'd it happen?"

"Pretty much the same as with the Garrity woman. Same M.O. The lock was jimmied, and the victim was shot to death. Constantine bought it in the hallway between the living room and bedroom. The bed looked slept in and the victim was in his shorts, so we think he must've gotten out of bed when he heard someone in the apartment. Happened around the same time, too—somewhere between twelve and two, the cornoner estimates."

"Same gun that killed Garrity?"

"Could be. The ballistics report hasn't come in yet."

"Was Constantine shot in the head, too?"

"Uh-uh. He got hit once in the lung and once in the heart."

"No one heard anything, I guess."

"Good guess."

"Anything taken?"

"I don't know that yet, either. The place wasn't messed up. But maybe the killer knew just where to find whatever he was looking for. Constantine's girl-friend—she lives with him—may be able to tell us something about that when we talk to her. She's the one who discovered the body. Found him when she came home at eleven this morning."

"Came home?"

"She's been out of town more than a week. Seems she's taking this thing real hard, too. Guy across the hall's a doctor, and he had her sedated all day. We'll be going over to get her statement tomorrow morning; she's staying with a girlfriend for a few days. I'll drop by and pick you up on the way over if you're interested."

I told him I was interested.

I had barely put the phone back in the cradle when it rang again. It was Ellen, and she'd been trying to reach me for hours.

"Why didn't you leave a message on the machine?"

"I didn't want to talk to any machine; I wanted to talk to you!" She was in a state somewhere between agitation and hysteria, but a lot closer to hysteria. "There's been another m-m-murder." It was the first time I'd ever heard Ellen stutter.

"I know. Tim Fielding just told me. I was about to call *you*."

"He and his partner were here a couple of hours ago, asking me questions. I'm scared, Aunt Dez. There must be a maniac running around loose!"

I did my best to calm her. "You have nothing to worry about, Ellen. There's a definite connection between those two murders, and whatever it is, it has nothing to do with you. You didn't know this fellow Constantine, did you?"

"No. I don't think I ever even saw him."

I had been positive of her answer. Still, I was relieved to hear her say that. "Look, Ellen, you're in no danger. But I think you should hop in a cab and come over anyway."

"Oh, no. I'm okay. I feel better now that I talked to you."

I could tell that all she needed was a little coaxing. "I want you to throw a few things in a bag and get over here. You'll stay with me for a while. The truth is, I could use a little company." Which wasn't the truth at all. But knowing how nervous Ellen was, I didn't want her to have to cope by herself.

"You mean it?" she asked hopefully.

"Why would I lie?"

"I'll be over in about an hour."

While I was waiting for Ellen, it suddenly came to me that I hadn't had anything to eat since 1:00 in the afternoon. Now, that is not like me. Ordinarily, I'd have to be unconscious to miss a meal. This damned case was affecting every aspect of my life!

I dragged myself out of my nice cushy chair and went into the kitchen to heat up a Kraft macaroni and cheese dinner. (The hell with the calories; can a normal person not eat pasta?) I intended to follow it up with a respectable portion of Häagen-Dazs macademia brittle, a quart of which was lurking seductively in my freezer at that very moment. The phone rang just as I was about to put away my first mouthful of macaroni.

"You hear?" Sal Martinez asked.

"A little while ago. I also heard Jerry was out on bail. I was surprised I didn't hear it from you." I tried not to sound as petulant as I felt.

"I was gonna call you thees morning. Hones'. I jus' get so beesy. An' then I figger Jerry already call you heeself."

"He didn't."

"Oh. . . . You know, Deseeray, I don' know if I done heem no favor for to get heem out on bail."

"What do you mean?"

"Now he's out, the cops are on hees ass again— excuse me, please. But now they wan' know where he was when Con . . . that other fella . . . was murdered."

"Constantine," I offered automatically.

"Right. Well, Jerry din even know tha' man. He wasn' even a customer, I swear. He come in once, maybe twice, three times in all the time I got the store. Jus' when he run out of somethin'. Prob'ly done his shoppin' at the supermarket over by Seventeenth."

I told Sal the Constantine shooting was actually a break for Jerry. "Now they'll have to start looking for someone with a motive for *both* killings, don't you see?"

"I guess so. But I dunno. What if they say thees new murder habbin got nuthin' to do with the other? They'll still be on Jerry's ... on Jerry ... for the firs' one, even if they fin' out who done thees one."

I insisted that the two homicides had to be too much of a coincidence even for the police. But I had my fingers crossed when I said it.

Then Sal asked what I was afraid he'd ask. "You got somethin' new on the ol' lady's murder?"

I didn't tell him about Sean Clory and the freezer. While Clory retained the honor of being my prime— make that my *only*—suspect, I'd finally come around to admitting to myself that what I'd found out wasn't exactly hard evidence. Except to me. "I've made some headway," I said, "but there's still a long way to go. This second murder should help a lot, though. You wait and see. Jerry's going to be just fine, so stop worrying. Tell him I'll be dropping by the store tomorrow to see him."

I sat down to my cold macaroni and cheese a little after 10:00. Before I was halfway through the meal, the buzzer sounded. It was time to reassure Ellen some more.

Chapter 11

On Wednesday morning, a much calmer Ellen fixed breakfast for us both. I left her dressing for work and went downstairs to wait for Tim. Promptly at 8:00, he and Corcoran pulled up in front of the building.

As soon as I got in the car, someone brought up Jerry's name. It was probably me. "You can't really still consider him a suspect," I challenged. "You think this Constantine kept money in the freezer, too?"

"Don't be such a smart-ass," Corcoran retorted. "He coulda wasted this guy for lotsa reasons. Maybe he found out Constantine saw something the night he offed the old lady—like maybe him sneaking around the place. Or maybe the kid figured it would throw us off the track. Or maybe—"

I didn't let him finish. "You've got to be out of your mind! He's in all this trouble over one murder, so the minute he gets out on bail—and knowing you're sure to suspect him—he commits another murder!" I was so incensed it's a wonder smoke wasn't pouring out of my ears.

"Hold on, Dez," Fielding, the voice of sweet reason, intervened. "No one ever said a word about the kid committing *this* murder. All I pointed out to you last night, if you recall, was the coincidence of the timing. If it *was* a coincidence." I didn't get a chance to interrupt. "Look. Before you say anything, the fact is, since Costello wasn't locked up anymore, he *could* have done it. It's a possibility, that's all."

"It's also a possibility a lot of other people could have done it. Why don't you find out where Sean Clory was last night?"

"We know where he was," Corcoran shot back. "He was down at the station."

"Are you serious?"

"He got in a fight in a neighborhood bar Monday night. The two of 'em—this other jerk and him— started breaking up the furniture. So the bartender called the station, and they both got picked up. That was around ten-thirty. They weren't released until nine o'clock Tuesday morning."

None of us said anything more until we pulled up in front of a posh high-rise on East 63rd. "Not bad," Corcoran muttered, giving the building a quick and appreciative once-over.

The door to 5G was opened by a smartly dressed young woman in a pink wool suit, a brown suede top-coat tossed casually around her shoulders. She was carrying an attaché case that informed us she was just about to leave.

She stepped aside, and we entered a small, mirrored foyer. Right away, I knew this was *some* place. "I'm Frannie Eppinger, Selena's friend," we were told. "Selana's waiting for you in the living room. You don't need me, do you?" she asked, her hand on the knob of the still-open door. She didn't wait for an answer. "Selena insists she'll be better off by herself today; she just wants to sleep, poor baby. And I'm already late for work."

Fielding said he didn't think it was necessary for her to stay but that he might want to talk to her another time. "Sure. Whenever," she replied. And with that, Ms. Eppinger was gone, the door closed firmly behind her.

The living room was enormous—by my humble standards, at least—and magnificently decorated in gray and peach (one of my favorite color combinations), mostly in art dèco (my *very* favorite style). There was a deep, curved-arm sofa in dark gray wool accented with pale peach throw cushions. On either side of the sofa was a graceful black lacquer chair with a shell-shaped back, which was upholstered in a tiny peach and beige check. The cocktail table in front of the sofa was modern—a large glass square on lucite block legs. And there was this gorgeous gray geometric rug, bordered in peach, that almost completely covered the beautiful parquet floors. Speaking of gorgeous, I wish you could see the breakfront in that room. It was black lacquer embellished with gold chinoiserie (I have an interior designer friend who educates me about things like that)—and so huge it took up an entire long wall. Which now brings me to the best part. Hanging above the sofa and on the remaining two pale gray walls were no fewer than half a dozen absolutely drop-dead impressionistic paintings!

I'm telling you about this living room not because it has anything whatever to do with the case, but because I was so damned impressed. I mean, that room was *me*. Not mine, unfortunately, but me.

Now, where did I leave off? Oh, yes . . .

A young woman of about twenty-eight was sitting on the sofa, her legs drawn under her. She was wearing a yellow bathrobe, and her thick dark hair was all disheveled, as if she'd just awakened from a very restless night's sleep. Her red-rimmed eyes were glazed over, and she looked at us vacantly. I got the impression we didn't seem quite real to her. The girl—I consider every female person under thirty a girl—appeared to be in the throes of a triple whammy: shock, grief, and a strong sedative that hadn't entirely worn off yet.

"I'm terribly sorry to bother you at a time like this," Fielding told her solicitously, "but we have some questions we have to ask you."

She nodded in acknowledgment. "Please sit down," she invited listlessly, as if by rote. "Can I get you some coffee?"

Both men declined politely. But I decided she was in dire need of a little jolt of caffeine herself. "That sounds good." She started to get up. "No, sit there," I instructed. "You just tell me where it is, and I'll make some for all of us." She stared at me blankly. "Never mind," I said. "I'll find it."

From the kitchen, I could hear the girl responding

tersely to the questions Fielding put to her, her voice flat and unemotional.

"You and Neil Constantine were living together?"

"Yes."

"For how long?"

"Seven months."

"It's *Mrs.* Warren, isn't it?"

"Yes."

"You're divorced?"

"Separated."

"I understand you were in Chicago this past week, visiting your mother."

"That's right."

"She's been ill?"

"Yes."

"I hope it's nothing serious."

"Gallbladder surgery."

I put up the coffee and rejoined the others in the living room.

"You went out to your mother's on Sunday the twenty-first?" Fielding was asking.

"Yes."

"And you came home around eleven yesterday morning?"

Selena nodded.

I had to feel for Tim. It was really like pulling teeth. "Please tell me what happened. You got to your front door ..." he prompted.

"Yes. And it was open. I don't mean *standing* open, but it wasn't locked. I was surprised. Neil and I always keep the door locked."

"Go on, please."

"Well, I went in, and I called out, 'Neil! I'm home!' But there was no answer. I put my bags down in the living room and started to walk to the bedroom. When I got to the little hallway, he was there. On the floor. And there was blood all over...." She covered her face with her hands.

Corcoran, to my amazement, told her it was all right and that she should take as much time as she needed. In a minute or two, Selena had composed herself.

As soon as she saw Neil lying there, she continued, she ran across the hall to her neighbor, Dr. Ellison. She didn't know if he'd be home or not, but she prayed he'd be there. "He's semi-retired," she explained, "so he doesn't have office hours every day and I have no idea of his schedule, but I had to see if he was in. His office is on East . . ." The too-brief answers had given way to frenetic rambling.

Tim tried to get her back on track. "And the doctor was home?"

"What?" She had that vacant look again. It was obvious she was no longer with us.

"When you went to get the doctor—Dr. Ellison— was he at home?"

She returned from wherever it was she'd gone and, for the first time, focused on Tim as she answered his question. "Yes. He came back to the apartment with me. He could tell Neil was dead right away. And he didn't want to touch anything. So then we both went to his apartment, and he called the police from there."

"And then?"

"Dr. Ellison gave me some kind of shot to calm me and told me to go and lie down in the bedroom— his bedroom. He said not to worry; he'd wait in my apartment for the police to come."

"You didn't go back to your apartment after that?" Corcoran asked.

"No."

I was becoming more and more annoyed with the direction of their questions. They had, I was sure, gotten the same information from Dr. Ellison yesterday. So why put the poor girl through all this—particularly since there was so much new ground to cover? I clamped my mouth shut hard and kept reminding myself that I was a guest at this inquisition.

"What time did you sleep till?" Corcoran wanted to know. Although I'm positive he already knew.

"Around six. When I woke up, Dr. Ellison said the police were probably still going over the apartment, and anyway, he didn't think I should stay there. So he called Frannie—you met Frannie, didn't you?—and then he fixed me some scrambled eggs and then Frannie came for me and brought me to her place—here. I didn't even take any clothes with me. Just my handbag. Dr. Ellison got it from the apartment for me. This is Frannie's robe. . . ." She ran out of steam suddenly, and her voice trailed off.

"Is there anything in your apartment you think someone might want bad enough to kill for, Mrs. Warren?" Hallelujah! They were finally asking the right questions. The only surprise was that Corcoran was the one doing the asking. And in an unusually (especially for him) deferential tone.

"Oh, no. We don't have anything valuable. Except for my clothes—I have a fox jacket—and Neil's paintings, of course."

"Jewelry?" Corcoran persisted.

"Well, I do have a diamond watch and a few other good pieces. . . ."

"When you get back to the apartment, we'd like you to look around—as soon as you feel up to it—and see if anything's missing."

"All right," Selena agreed.

There was a pause before Corcoran asked, "Did you and Mr. Constantine plan to be married?"

"He wanted to, and I guess that eventually we would have. But we didn't have definite plans."

"*He* wanted to?"

"Marriage wasn't important to me. But if that's what Neil wanted . . ." She began to cry.

Corcoran, believe it or not, said something soothing. (Was this the same snide Walter Corcoran I'd come in here with? Or had aliens invaded his body?) Then, incredible lame-brain that I am, it dawned on me that our Walter was smitten! Now I knew why he'd been keeping one hand in his pocket—the hand that had the finger with the plain gold band on it. Well, Selena Warren, even with red eyes and rag mop hair, was a very good-looking girl. But as to that jerk's timing . . .

That's when I remembered the coffee. I jumped up and hurried into the kitchen. After turning off the coffeepot and putting up some toast, I checked out the cabinets. I found a little tray which I loaded down with four cups of extremely overperked coffee, a sugar bowl, a container of milk (sorry, Mom, I couldn't find a creamer) and a plate with a couple of slices of buttered toast.

I walked back to the living room very, very gingerly.

Selena looked at me gratefully when I handed her the toast. I think it made her realize how hungry she was. But she took a few tiny bites and gave up, as though eating were too much of an effort.

Watching her brought back my own not-too-distant loss with a sharp pang. "I hope you'll be staying here for a few days," I told her. "It isn't good for you to be alone right now."

"I'm going home tomorrow," Selena said firmly, taking a sip of coffee. (Without, I might mention, making a face of any kind.) Then, noticing my expression, she added, "I'll be fine."

"Why don't you wait and see how you feel tomorrow morning?" I urged. "Is there someone to take care of the funeral arrangements?" Turning to Fielding, I asked, "They *will* be releasing the body soon, won't they?"

"Probably tomorrow."

"Louise—that's Neil's ex-wife—is handling everything," the girl told me. A second later, she said "You're very nice," put down the coffee cup, and began to sob.

Corcoran cleared his throat to get my attention. That accomplished, he favored me with the dirtiest look he could dredge up. I ignored him. "Where did you and Mr. Constantine meet?" I asked, as soon as Selena had pulled herself together. I knew I'd pay for taking over like this, but I couldn't seem to keep a lid on myself any longer.

"We met at the Lavery Art Gallery, where I work."

"How long ago was that?"

"Seven months ago."

"And you started living together right away?"

"After our third date."

"You were separated at the time?"

"Of course." She was hurt that I'd even ask. "Jack and I had been separated for almost a year by then."

"If you don't mind, *Missus* Shapiro!" Corcoran put in. He had lowered his squeaky voice at least an octave in an attempt to sound menacing. "Sergeant Fielding and myself will be taking over from here." Very deliberately, he turned his back to me. "Mrs. Warren, can you think of anyone who'd want to harm Mr. Constantine—anyone with a grudge against him?"

"No." It was a very tentative no.

Corcoran pressed her. "Look, don't you want us to find out who killed him? We can't do it if no one will cooperate with us."

"I want to cooperate. Only I *know* he wouldn't kill Neil."

"Who?"

Selena hesitated, then hunched her shoulders as if to say, *What's the use?* Aloud, she replied, "Bill Murphy. He used to be Neil's partner."

"There was trouble between them?" Corcoran persisted.

"Maybe a little. Neil owed Bill money."

"How much?"

"Ten thousand dollars."

"That's a pretty good chunk of money."

Reluctantly, she went on. "Neil used to gamble once in a while. He needed the money to cover his losses."

"When was that?"

"Last year sometime. Before Neil and I met."

"Mr. Constantine wasn't able to pay him back?" I swear that just slipped out. Both men glowered at me.

"Well, no ... not really. Neil inherited quite a bit of money about a year and a half ago, when his father's sister died. But the will's still being probated. There was some kind of mix-up, I think."

"And Mr. Murphy didn't want to wait any longer?" Fielding asked.

"I think it was more that he just didn't believe the money was still tied up."

"When was the last time Mr. Constantine saw this man Murphy?" Fielding wanted to know.

"It's been a couple of months." Then, grudgingly, "But they talked on the phone Monday night."

"*This* Monday—the night before the murder?"

"Yes."

"Mr. Constantine tell you about the phone call?"

"Yes, he did. I called him Monday night at nine o'clock—I called him every night at nine when I was in Chicago—and he said he'd just had a big argument with Bill about the money."

"That's nine Chicago time?" Fielding asked.

"Uh-huh; ten o'clock here." She looked around helplessly at the three of us and spread her hands. "But Bill's a very decent man. He *couldn't* have done this thing."

Then Tim Fielding asked the question that had been sitting perilously on the tip of my tongue. "You say Mr. Constantine was coming into money. I suppose he had a will?"

"He made a new will a couple of months ago."

"Who were the beneficiaries?"

"Alma, that's his daughter—she's eighteen—and I. We're the cobeneficiaries."

"You said a *new* will," Fielding pointed out. "Who were the beneficiaries under the old one?"

"Alma and Louise, his ex-wife."

Corcoran took up the questioning. He asked how long ago Constantine and his wife had split up. Selena said it had been about ten years. That was when Neil left his business—as co-owner (with Murphy) of a successful advertising agency—and moved out on his wife and daughter to pursue a career as an artist.

"He was good, too. Really good. And he was just beginning to make a name for himself," Selena told us proudly, brushing away a stray tear with her fingertips. "He was such a talented, wonderful man. I don't know what I'll do without him. You know how most handsome men are so self-centered? When I met Neil, I was sure he'd be like that, too. He was so . . . Wait." She got up quickly and left the room. In a moment she was back, carrying a large cowhide shoulder bag. She dug out her wallet and extracted a photograph. It was a color head shot of a man in his middle or late forties, with silver hair and the kind of even white teeth you usually see in toothpaste ads. But the most remarkable thing about him was his piercing blue eyes. I tell you, this Neil Constantine out-Newmaned Paul.

"You see?" Selena demanded.

I knew exactly what she meant. "Yes, I do. He was a very handsome man."

She smiled the smallest smile. "Yes, he was."

I took a deep breath and, carefully avoiding eye contact with Fielding and Corcoran, dared to ask one last question. "How did your ex-husband feel about Mr. Constantine?"

"Jack only met him once; it was outside a movie and I introduced them. But they didn't really talk."

"That isn't what I asked you," I reminded her softly.

"Well, I guess you could say he was jealous of Neil. They were jealous of each other, actually." Things were looking better and better for Jerry.

"The breakup with Jack was your idea?" (Okay, so my last question wasn't my last; but this could be important.)

"Yes, that's right."

"And you say he was jealous of Neil."

"Jack always wanted us to get back together again. He thought we would have, if I hadn't met Neil. But that's not true. I still care about Jack, but I'm not in love with him anymore."

"Why was Neil jealous of Jack?"

"Who knows? He didn't have any reason to be. Maybe it's because Jack just wouldn't give up. He still calls all the time."

"Did he ever get you to see him?"

It took her a long time to answer. "Well ... sort of. He was hanging around outside the building when I came home from work one night. Neil was taking Alma to dinner that night, and he'd gone out to meet her. I guess Jack must have seen him leave, because he asked me if he could come up for a few minutes to talk. I didn't want to, but I didn't know how to get out of it, so I said yes. It was a mistake. We started to argue the minute we walked into the elevator, and by the time we got to my floor, I was so mad at him I wouldn't even let him into the apartment."

"What was the argument about?"

"The usual—giving our marriage another chance. But he was kind of obnoxious that day."

I waited for her to be more explicit, but she'd already divulged more than she cared to. "Just what did he say?" I coaxed.

"I can't exactly remember."

"I think you can. Listen, Selena, do you want the person who killed Neil to get away with it?"

"Of course not. But it wasn't Jack. He never even used to go fishing, because he couldn't stand to hurt the fish." Selena may have been defensive about Bill Murphy, but she was practically defiant when it came to her almost-ex.

"Nobody's saying it *was* Jack. But we have to follow up on everything—even if it's just to eliminate someone." She looked at me doubtfully, so I had to close in for the kill. "You owe it to Neil," I told her.

She didn't say anything for quite a while, just sat there frowning and staring into space. "All right, you win," she replied finally. She was acting like she'd just gone three rounds with Mike Tyson, and, very briefly, I loathed myself for causing her further pain. But humanity was something I just couldn't afford at the moment.

"What did Jack say to you?" I asked again.

"Some things about Neil that I didn't like."

"Such as?"

"He called Neil a user and a no-talent bum. But he didn't *mean* anything by it. He didn't even *know* Neil. He was just talking."

"When did all this take place?"

"Seven or eight weeks ago; it was right at the end of the summer."

"You told Mr. Constantine about it?"

"Some of it. I told him Jack came to the building and wanted to come up and talk and that we had a fight in the elevator about getting back together, so I wouldn't let him in. But I shouldn't have said anything at all. Neil was jealous enough before. He said if he ever caught Jack 'staking out the building' again—that's what he called it—he'd clobber him. But it never happened again."

Fielding cut in then. (Actually, I'd had the floor a whole lot longer than I'd expected to.) "Excuse me, won't you, Dez?" he said sweetly. "I can't tell you how much Walt and I appreciate your doing our job for us, but it isn't fair to leave all the work to you." I admit I *did* get carried away, but the expression on his face was absolutely poisonous. Of course, it softened considerably when he addressed Selena.

"Mrs. Warren, who knew you were going out of town?"

"I'm not sure."

"Your husband know?"

"*I* didn't tell him."

"But he called your office frequently?"

"Yes."

"Would they have told him if he tried reaching you there?"

"I guess so."

"How about Constantine's wife and daughter? Think they could have known?"

"Neil might have mentioned it to Alma, and it's possible she told her mother."

"And Murphy? Never mind," he put in quickly. "Constantine could have said something to him when they talked on the night of the murder. Just one more question, Mrs. Warren—and *I* mean it. Did you or Mr. Constantine know Mrs. Garrity upstairs?"

She shook her head.

"You do know who Mrs. Garrity is?"

"Oh, yes. Neil told me about her on the phone. She's the woman who was . . . who was . . . murdered."

I could tell we were only a minute or two away from a fresh deluge of tears. Tim Fielding knew it, too. He asked Selena for a few names and addresses, and the three of us left.

*   *   *

We walked the short distance to the elevator in uncomfortable silence. I broke it. "I could really use that
list of addresses, Tim."

Fielding mumbled something that sounded like,
"Over my dead body." But he was gritting his teeth
at the time, so I couldn't be sure.

"I wouldn't want to go back and bother Mrs. Warren—"

"Let her have it, Tim," Corcoran said disgustedly.

Fielding reached into his jacket pocket and handed
me the list Selena had written out for him. I copied
it in record time as we waited for the elevator. He
didn't so much as glance at me when I returned it
to him.

I had often wondered what it would take to get Tim
Fielding really angry. I was sorry I'd found out.

In the elevator, I permitted myself an observation.
"She seems genuinely grief-stricken, and I'm *sure* she
was in Chicago. But someone should check out her
alibi anyway, don't you think?"

"We already have," Fielding growled, "and it
checks." I didn't have time to get him any madder at
me, because by then we'd reached the lobby.

I figured they'd be going to see the ex-wife next.
Or maybe the ex-partner. But I never found out.
Would you believe they didn't invite me along?

Chapter 12

I had become a real manic-depressive lately. And right then I was at my most manic. I felt like singing. I felt like dancing. I settled for walking. I needed to get my thoughts in order while everything was still fresh in my mind.

I headed downtown for a few blocks, then turned west and walked over to Lexington Avenue. It was a beautiful, sunny day. The air was crisp and invigorating, without being raw. I mulled over what I had learned from Selena. Neil Constantine's death had presented me with a bona fide group of suspects. Who cared what Tim or anyone else said? Sooner or later, this second murder was going to put Jerry in the clear.

The weather that morning must have been acting like a magnet for the entire neighborhood. Just about everyone who wasn't chained to a desk was out jockeying for sidewalk space. It was a little after 10:00—a time when you have every right to expect the streets to be navigable, even in that area. But I could barely take two steps without getting mauled. After the third elbow to my ribs, I ducked into one of those little French patisseries. In self-defense, of course.

The place was small and clean and inviting, with an aroma that was too exquisite for me to attempt to describe. I walked over to a table in the corner and carefully negotiated my weight onto one of those flimsy little bistro chairs that always groan in protest when I sit down and which, I am certain, will one day crumple under me in total surrender.

A well-dressed middle-aged man was seated at the table behind me, working a crossword and licking some crumbs from his fingers. Across the room, an elderly couple was getting ready to leave. The woman was complaining in a high, strident voice about the check. "Mr. Rockefeller here can't have coffee and a roll home. No, he has to come to a patser—whatever they call it—and get these fancy things that give me heartburn." She picked up the check and glared at it with disgust. "Almost five dollars. And for what?" Mr. Rockefeller didn't answer. "Heartburn, that's what."

My fellow diner's digestive problems did not deter me from ordering a palmier with my coffee. In case you've never had one of these buttery puff pastry confections, let me assure you that heartburn—even if I were prone to it, which, thank God, I am not—would be a very meager price to pay.

As soon as I'd finished off the palmier—and talked myself out of ordering a second—I got a refill on the coffee and went to work.

First, I listed all the suspects. (And at this point, I considered just about everyone a suspect.) Then, alongside each name, I wrote down the motive. Which in some cases, I admit, required a bit of speculation.

1. Selena Warren   Inheritance. (Check alibi.)
2. Alma Constantine   Inheritance. Also, latent hostility over parent's divorce, activated by father's involvement with S.W.
3. Louise Constantine   Woman scorned; younger woman now taking her place
4. Jack Warren   Jealousy over estranged wife.
5. Bill Murphy   Feud over money.
6. Sean Clory   ??? (Double-check alibi.)

I looked over my list. Next to Louise Constantine's name, I added, "Inheritance." It was just possible the woman wasn't aware that her ex had written her out of his will.

I looked over my list again. I had to admit his name really didn't belong there. So, with tears in my eyes, I put a line through number six.

Another cup of coffee—and no pastry—later I grabbed a cab over to Martinez's store.

Martinez was waiting on a customer when I got there. He spotted me and waved. "Jerry's gonna' be back in a—" he began, then gestured toward the door. Jerry was just walking in.

He was terribly pale. And pitifully scrawny. Still, I was relieved at what I saw. He looked exactly as he had before his ordeal. "Can we sit down somewhere and talk?" I asked.

"Sure." He turned and took a couple of steps toward the rear of the store. Remembering the seating accommodations back there, I reached out and grabbed his sleeve. "How about I buy you lunch?"

"I'll just ask Mr. Martinez if it's okay." He turned away, then turned back to explain. "I don't usually go out for lunch. I usually bring a sandwich from home in case there's a rush delivery."

Now, I ask you, is that a good kid or what?

He walked over to his mentor, who nodded vigorously to the request, and a few minutes later Jerry and I were seated at a local McDonald's gorging ourselves on Big Macs, fries, and shakes. (And, since I'd denied myself that second palmier, I did not have the slightest qualm about this little repast, either.)

Jerry was the one who brought up the Constantine killing. "I guess you heard," was how he put it.

"You mean about the second murder?"

"Yeah."

"Yes, I heard. In fact, I was with the police this morning talking to the victim's girlfriend."

"Will this help me, do you think? I didn't even know the guy." His eyes were begging me for reassurance.

"I'm sure it will. There are quite a few people who might have wanted to see Mr. Constantine dead. So now all we have to do is find a connection between one of those people and Mrs. Garrity, and you're off the hook." How ridiculously simple I made that sound! But riding on my crest of optimism, I refused to let anything as deflating as reality set in.

"I hope so. But the cops wanted to know where I was Monday night, so I was afraid they had me pegged for that murder, too."

"Don't worry. I'm sure it's just routine."

He seemed to let out his breath. Then he smiled and took a healthy slurp of his shake.

"Where were you by the way?"

"I went to bed at nine—jeez, did that bed feel good!—and I slept right through till eight o'clock Tuesday morning. I said they should check with my mother. She told me she was so relieved to have me home, she must of looked in on me ten times that night."

His mother. Swell.

"Uh, I don't suppose you've been able to figure out how your prints could have gotten on that refrigerator door," I said without much confidence.

Jerry slapped his hand to his forehead. "I'm so stupid! I can't believe how stupid I am! I should have told you right away. When I was in jail, I had a lot of time to think, and I remembered something." He paused, waiting for my reaction.

If he wanted drama, I didn't disappoint him. I got so excited I choked on my Big Mac. For a couple of seconds, it even looked like someone might have to use the Heimlich maneuver on me, but Jerry got me some water and that did the trick.

"Well?" I asked when I was finally able to emit something from my throat besides "Aargh."

"Well, it came to me that when I made this delivery to Mrs. Garrity—I don't mean the day before she was killed, I mean the time before that or maybe even two times before that. . . ." He broke off and searched my expression for a sign that I was following him.

"Gotcha," I assured him. "Go on." I was so keyed up I could barely get the words out.

"Well, see, the grocery bag split when I went to put it on the table. There were some vegetables in the bag, and they were rolling on the floor and I was picking them all up and some of them ended up over by the refrigerator. I can't be positive, but when I was crawling around on the floor I might have put my hands on the refrigerator door. You know, like to help myself up. That'd be a pretty natural thing to do, wouldn't it?"

"A *very* natural thing to do," I amended.

A big part of the evidence against Jerry had just evaporated. At least as far as I was concerned. I knew the kid's explanation wouldn't mean diddly to the police. But it was still important. It tied up that one little loose end that had been troubling me. And you have no idea how I hate loose ends.

I got to the office around 2:00 and called Louise Constantine. After a bit of cajoling, she agreed to let me come over at 8:00 that evening. She wasn't terribly enthusiastic about it, I might add.

Chapter 13

It was a rainy night, so, anticipating trouble getting a taxi, I'd allowed myself extra time. Naturally, there was an empty cab right outside my building. I arrived at Louise Constantine's East 34th Street apartment at quarter of eight. Now, I happen to think that being early is a lot more inconsiderate than being late. So, to keep things from starting off on the wrong foot, I walked around the block until my shoes squished and my wig had become waterlogged.

"Five-G," I was informed when I finally presented myself to the doorman. "Mrs. Constantine is expecting you."

Louise Constantine was a dainty blond, somewhere in her forties. She smiled politely—and automatically—when she greeted me. Although still quite pretty, the woman was completely bland-looking. In fact, everything about her was bland. Her voice was flat. Her eyes were expressionless. Her manner was remote. Even the environment she'd created for herself lacked any sort of spark, with one exception.

It was a traditional room done entirely in beige and brown. The only real color came from two stunning floral watercolors, one over the sofa, the other above a small credenza on the opposite wall. If I had been playing shrink, I'd have said that the room—aside from the watercolors (which I had a strong feeling were the work of the deceased, so they didn't count)— was a dead giveaway to Louise Constantine's emotional makeup. This was the home of a woman who had a tight rein on her feelings, someone who didn't believe in taking chances. Either that or my hostess had had a lousy decorator.

Mrs. Constantine graciously relieved me of my dripping umbrella and the equally sodden raincoat that I'd been meaning to have rewaterproofed for the last three years. But she wasn't quite able to conceal her distaste. "I'll just hang these in the bathroom," she told me, holding my belongings about three feet in front of her. "Have a seat. I'll be with you in two minutes."

I barely had time to lower myself into a chair when she was back.

After telling the woman how sorry I was about her husband's death and having her promptly correct me with "Ex-husband," I got down to business.

"What kind of terms were you and your ex-husband on?"

"We were very friendly. We have a daughter, you know."

"Yes, I know. How often did you see Mr. Constantine, would you say?"

"Oh, quite often. That is, until Mrs. Warren moved in with him. Before that, Alma used to go up there all the time, and many times I'd accompany her. Particularly when she was younger."

"I see. Would you say you used to see him once a week? Once a month?"

She thought for a moment or two. "I'd say once every few weeks. Maybe a little more often."

"When was the last time you saw him?"

"It must have been a month or two ago."

"Did Alma continue to visit her father once Selena Warren moved in?"

"The first couple of months she wouldn't go near the place. She insisted on meeting Neil at restaurants or at the theater or the movies or whatever. But then she got over it, and she'd sometimes go up there to call for him, although she didn't feel quite comfortable spending any real time in the apartment once he began cohabiting with Mrs. Warren." The unemotional voice stressed the "cohabiting" just the tiniest bit.

"Your daughter didn't care for Mrs. Warren?"

"Oh, I wouldn't say that. I don't think it was anything personal, just circumstances. You can understand that."

I nodded. "I hope you don't mind my asking you this, Mrs. Constantine, but in a murder investigation it's necessary to explore the victim's relationships. . . ."

"Go on," she instructed, but for the first time I saw something in Louise Constantine's eyes. They were wary.

"How did you feel when you and your ex-husband separated?"

"You mean, when he left me?" She was smiling now. It was a smile that sent shivers through me, and it vanished almost at once. "I felt betrayed," she said. "Also abandoned. Angry. Maybe even homicidal. But it didn't last long. We talked things out soon after he left. And Neil explained that his leaving had nothing to do with me; it was our entire lifestyle. He gave up his business at the same time. Did you know that?"

"Yes."

"It was just that he wanted to devote his energies to his art. He's a painter and, from what everyone says—I myself know nothing about art—a good one. These are his," she told me, gesturing to the florals.

"They're beautiful. I admired them as soon as I walked in. But you were saying?"

"Nothing, really. Just that it helped knowing Neil's leaving wasn't because of me. Or at least his *saying* it wasn't because of me." She smiled again. But this time the smile was so sad I had to restrain myself from patting her on the shoulder and clucking, *There, there.* I was beginning to feel very uncomfortable poking away at Louise Constantine's wounds.

I took a deep breath. "Were you still in love with your hus—your ex-husband at the time of his death?"

"I probably shouldn't admit it. I'm sure you'll decide it gives me a motive, but yes, I was still in love with him. I was always hoping that maybe ... He didn't even ask me for a divorce until he met her. Isn't that something?"

This was a real revelation. I assumed the couple had divorced years ago.

"Oh, well," Louise added resignedly, biting on her lower lip. "It didn't work out the first time. It probably wouldn't have worked out this time, either." She drew herself up then, straightening her back and lifting her chin. Suddenly she was in complete command of herself again. Which made it a little easier for me to continue with my questions. But not much. I mean, here was a woman who had seemed so in control, and then she suddenly allows me to see how hurt, how vulnerable she is. I might have taken some small consolation if I could have attributed this to my interrogation skills. Or at least to my sympathetic nature. But the truth was, Louise Constantine had been looking for an excuse to unload, and I'd been the one to give it to her.

She was checking her watch now, apparently having satisfied her need for catharsis. "I have an appointment soon," she told me flatly but firmly.

"I won't take up much more of your time," I said. "I just have one or two more questions. I *do* appreciate this."

"All right," she agreed with a very audible sigh. "But please try to get through with this. I really have to leave in a few minutes."

"How did you feel when your ex-husband changed his will?"

She looked at me blankly.

"You *are* aware that Mr. Constantine made a new will shortly before he died, dividing his estate between your daughter and Mrs. Warren?"

She shook her head slowly from side to side. She appeared to be genuinely stunned. "You think I killed him because I was angry that he changed his will?" she asked finally. "I had no idea he'd made a new will."

"What about your daughter?"

"Alma didn't know anything about it, either. She

would have mentioned it if she did. Besides, the new will wouldn't make any difference to her if she was a beneficiary under both wills."

"But your husband recently inherited some money—quite a lot of money—and that *would* make a difference."

"An inheritance? Neil? I think there's some mistake. Who'd leave Neil that kind of money?" She seemed as surprised by my news as I was to find out it *was* news.

"His aunt died about a year and a half ago," I said by way of explanation.

"Aunt Edna?"

"Was she his father's sister?"

"Yes, but it never occured to me she had money." If Louise Constantine was putting on an act, she was playing to a very gullible audience.

"Do you think he might have told your daughter about it?"

"No. Definitely not. Alma and I don't have secrets from one another. Look, I really have to go," she said, getting to her feet.

"Please, you've been *so* helpful, and I've got just one more question. Maybe if we can wind things up, I won't have to bother Alma." When it comes to obtaining information, I am not opposed to a strategically placed lie here and there.

She promptly sat down again. But on the edge of the seat to let me know this was going to be a very temporary arrangement.

"How did your daughter feel when you and her father separated?"

"She was fine with it. After all, she continued to see Neil on a regular basis. Actually, he devoted more time to her than when he worked twelve to fourteen hours a day at the agency. And don't forget, Neil and I had a friendly relationship. I'm sure that helped, too." She was starting to stand up for the second time.

"I'm sure it did," I put in quickly. "Just one more question. Please."

"I'm sorry, but—"

"Would you mind just telling me where you were on Monday night?"

Louise settled back in her chair. She actually seemed anxious to supply me with the details. "Let's see," she began, "I had supper here around seven."

"You were alone?"

"Yes. Alma got her own place a few months ago. And then after I ate," she went on purposefully, "I showered and dressed. At about twenty to nine, I took a taxi uptown to the Biograph to meet Alma. The movie started at nine-fifteen."

"What was playing?"

"*A Star Is Born.*"

"And after the movie?"

"I went straight home. Alma came with me, because I wasn't feeling well. I had developed a terrible headache about halfway through the picture, and then I started getting stomach cramps—probably a touch of virus or something. In fact, I really didn't think I'd be able to sit through the movie, but with a couple of trips to the ladies' room, I was able to make it through to the end. Anyway, since I was feeling so lousy, Alma insisted on sleeping over."

"What time did you get home?"

"It must have been about midnight. You can check with the doorman. He might remember. Englehardt his name is—he's on from eleven till seven a.m."

"And neither of you went out after that?"

"Oh, no. I took a couple of aspirins and Alma fixed me some hot tea. In a little while I began to feel better, so we both went to bed. That was just past one." She stood up then, and this time there was no doubt the interview was over. "I'll get your things," she said. She returned with my coat and umbrella before I was able to struggle to my feet.

"By the way," I asked her at the door, "did you know a woman named Agnes Garrity?"

Louise made no attempt to hide her impatience. "No, I did not," she replied curtly.

As she was closing the door, I threw out my final

question. "Did you ever hear Mr. Constantine mention her?"

"No," she said as the door clicked shut.

It would be more than two hours before Englehardt came on duty, and the 34th Street Showplace was right down the street, so I sloshed over. Of the four movies playing there, only one was about to start then. It was some Arnold Schwarzenegger thing I'd been planning for weeks to miss, but at least it would be dry inside.

The picture turned out to be a lot less painful than I'd anticipated, and by the time it was over the rain had stopped. I walked back to Louise Constantine's building to find a short, thickset man on the doors. Englehardt. In an impossibly dogmatic manner, he informed me that Mrs. Constantine had come in with her daughter around midnight on Monday and that neither woman had gone out again during his shift.

"Maybe they left without your seeing them," I suggested.

"No way. If they'da gone out, I'da seen 'em." He said it in a voice that dared me to contradict him.

Chapter 14

The following afternoon, I decided to take a chance that Alma Constantine would be home and willing to see me. I figured if I called, she might stall me for a day or two, and I just didn't have that kind of patience. I wouldn't even consider the possibility that any of my suspects might refuse to talk to me.

The girl lived in the east thirties, not far from her mother, in a building that made Ellen's place almost luxurious. And I was willing to bet that Alma didn't even have a fireplace!

I checked the apartment listings in the outer lobby. There was a small black metal plate that read, CONSTANTINE/WILLIAMS. I rang the bell and was buzzed in almost immediately. *Didn't these kids know what intercoms were for?*

As soon as I shut the door behind me, I was attacked by the smell of cabbage. (Ever notice how these run-down old buildings alway smell of cabbage? Not steak. Or ham. Or even hot dogs. Cabbage.)

I got in an elevator no sane person would trust and held my breath until it stopped with a shudder on the second floor.

A young girl was waiting outside an apartment at the end of the hall. She was very blond and Waspy-looking—and pretty enough to make me want to go home and break my mirrors.

"Alma?"

"No, I'm Tess Williams, her roommate."

"I'd appreciate it if I could see Alma. It would only take a few minutes. Is she home?"

The response to my request was pleasant but non-committal. "Uh, could you tell me what this is about?"

"I'm investigating her father's death, and there are some questions I'd like to ask her."

"Do you have any identification?" In the last couple of seconds, Tess had unobtrusively maneuvered herself so that she was now standing between me and the open door.

I fished in my pocketbook and on the third try managed to come up with my P.I. license.

"Wait here, would you?" She left without closing the door.

In a couple of minutes she was back. "Alma says for you to please come in."

I followed Tess into a living room that consisted of a few very old—or shamefully abused—beige and brown uphostered pieces and a badly scratched travertine coffee table. It was apparent that Alma Constantine's apartment was furnished in Early Mother.

Curled up in a worn, dark brown vinyl chair, wire-rimmed glasses down around the tip of her nose, was a girl who had to be Alma. There was an open book balanced on her knees.

"This is Alma," Tess told me unnecessarily as she seated herself cross-legged on the floor next to her roommate's chair.

"I'm Desiree Shapiro," I said, extending my hand. Alma shook it limply and dropped it immediately.

"What did you want to ask me about?" Clearly there were to be no formalities with this kid.

"Mind if I sit down?"

"I guess not."

I walked over to a beige corduroy sofa, every inch of which was covered with soiled throw pillows, and gently thrust a few of them aside. Now I knew why there were so many pillows. The thing was practically in shreds!

I plunked myself down and, under the pretense of getting comfortable, took a little time to study the girl facing me.

She was about as animated as her mother was. But

while the older woman was on a tight emotional leash, Alma went the I-don't-give-a-shit route. It extended from her stringy brown hair—which appeared not to have been washed more recently than last spring—to her spotted T-shirt to her dirty bare feet. What's more, to be certain her message came across, the kid didn't wear a trace of makeup. And I was sure that wasn't just because she was in her own living room.

"Well?" She wasn't exactly rude. Just making it clear that this interview was on the clock.

"I'd like to ask you some questions about your father, if that's okay."

She shrugged. "I guess so."

"How did the two of you get along?"

She shrugged again. "As well as could be expected."

"Your mother says you and your father got along very well."

"It makes her feel better to think so."

"It's not true, then?"

"Yes and no." She shifted a little in her chair and the open book clattered to the floor. She appeared not to notice.

"Look, I'm sorry to have to intrude on your privacy, especially under these circumstances, but I have a client—a young man about your age—who's been falsely accused of another murder, and his life could depend on finding the person responsible for your father's death." As soon as the words left my mouth, I was sorry. Now she'd ask a million questions that I didn't want to take the time to answer. I needn't have worried.

"Okay, you want to know about my father and me? He split when I was eight years old. I hated his guts all the time I was growing up."

I don't know what took me back more: the frankness of her admission or the matter-of-fact manner in which she'd delivered it. "But you went to see him, just the same," I continued after a moment or two.

"Yeah. Because my mother dragged me there."

"But you kept on visiting him even when you were older—when you were old enough to refuse to go."

"Yeah." She gave me another one of those shrugs. "But by then it didn't matter. I was used to it, so what the hell?"

"You didn't hate him anymore?"

"Nah. But I didn't like him, either. I guess I just learned to tolerate him."

"When was the last time you saw him?"

"Sunday."

"This past Sunday?"

"Yeah."

"Would you mind telling me what you did?"

"We went to the museum—Modern Art—and later we had dinner somewhere up around there. Some Italian place. I don't remember the name."

"Just the two of you?"

"That's right."

"How did you feel about Selena Warren?"

"Hey, if that's what he wanted, it was okay with me."

"You didn't dislike her, then?"

"I didn't like her, and I didn't dislike her. The truth is, I didn't give her much thought."

"Your mother said Mrs. Warren's living with your father made you uncomfortable."

"Yeah. Well, I suppose she thought it *should,* so she decided it did."

"I understand you didn't go near the apartment when Mrs. Warren first moved in."

"Because I was busy with school, that's all."

"Tell me, did you know your father had made a new will?"

"I didn't even know he'd made an old one."

"But you *did* know he'd recently come into quite a bit of money?"

"I don't give a flying fuck about money."

"It's true. No one cares less about money than Alma," Tess piped up from her station on the floor. For a moment I was startled. I'd completely forgotten she was there.

"You *are* young," I said jokingly, mostly to Alma.

"Money stinks," Alma retorted. "It's everything

that's wrong with the world. Why do you think Selena Warren wanted my father?"

"So you *did* know about the money."

"Sure. You just told me about it. Say, are we almost finished? I have a lot of studying to do."

"I won't keep you much longer. But I'd appreciate your telling me where you were the night of the murder."

"I went to the movies with my mother—the Biograph. The show started at quarter after nine. Before that, I had dinner with Tess at Mumbles on Thirty-third and Second. We finished around eight-thirty, and then I left to meet my mother in front of the movie."

"And after the movie?"

"Look, I know my mother already told you this, so why are you asking me the same questions? I really *do* have to get back to studying."

"I know, and I promise I won't be much longer. But it's my job to verify things. You've really been *so* cooperative. If you could just give me two minutes more . . ."

"Okay. Two minutes. That's all." To Alma, "two minutes" was not just a figure of speech. I could almost hear the clock ticking away in her head. "What else do you want to know?"

I found myself talking faster. "What did you do after the movie?"

"We went straight to my mother's. She was feeling pretty putrid, so I slept over. I left about ten the next morning and came home to pick up my books. I had a twelve o'clock class. I go to NYU."

"What time did you get to your mother's?"

"It was right around midnight, I guess."

"How did you like the movie?" To this day, I don't know why I asked that. Maybe I just wanted to touch on some humanity in the girl.

The question surprised her. It also put her on guard. "I liked it a lot."

"*A Star Is Born,* wasn't it?"

"Yeah." She was beginning to look more and more uneasy.

"I saw it years ago, and I loved it. I remember that the very next day I ran out and bought the album. I still get chills every time I listen to her sing 'The Man That Got Away.' There's only one Judy, isn't there?" I choked up, as I usually do whenever I think about my all-time-and-forever favorite entertainer.

"Judy?"

"Judy Garland." *What was with this kid, anyway?*

"It so happens Judy Garland wasn't the one who sang it," Alma informed me, casting a sly look at her roommate that I wasn't supposed to catch. "It was Barbra Streisand. We saw the remake."

Now I understood the reason for the look. Alma was feeling very self-satisfied at having avoided my trap. But actually, I hadn't been trying to trap her at all. I'd just been trying to share a little Judy.

"I hope you won't be offended, Alma, but I have to ask Tess about these things for the record." I turned to the other girl. "Can you confirm any of this for me?"

"Yes, I can. We grabbed some dinner at Mumbles, and then Alma went to meet her mother."

"She didn't come home that night?"

"Tess wouldn't know," Alma put in before her friend could answer. "She slept over at her boyfriend's, and she didn't get back here until after classes on Tuesday. About four. Right, Tess?"

"That's right."

"Okay. I guess we're through here. You've both been terrific about this," I told them, attempting to hoist myself up from the battered sofa. "Oh, just one more thing, Alma. Have you ever heard of a woman named Agnes Garrity?"

"Sure," Alma replied. "I read the papers, you know. But I never met the old lady, if that's what you mean." She looked down meaningfully at the obliging Tess, who was instantly on her feet, ready to escort me to the door.

As soon as I was back in the office, I dialed the Biograph. I got a recording. I spent the rest of the day typing up my notes and trying to decide what, if anything, I'd learned. But I didn't make much headway.

At 7:00, I called the Biograph from home. This time, a real live person picked up. She confirmed that on Monday, October 29, the Barbra Streisand remake of *A Star Is Born* was playing at the theater. The last show started at 9:15 and let out at 11:35.

Later on, when I was sitting around watching *Cheers* and trying to avoid fracturing my teeth on a frozen Snickers, it dawned on me: I hadn't seen a single one of her father's paintings hanging in Alma Constantine's apartment.

Chapter 15

The next day, I called Jack Warren at his office—
Goldfinger Real Estate in Manhattan—hoping to set
something up for that evening or, at the latest, the
early part of the following week. I really didn't anticipate too much trouble in getting the man to see me.
Particularly since I was holding a very persuasive little
argument in reserve.

The voice that announced "Jack Warren speaking"
was a warm, rich—almost melodious—baritone. The
warmth vanished as soon as I stated the purpose of
my call.

"Miss Shapiro," I was informed in an exasperated
voice, "the police have already taken up enough of
my time. I told them everything I know, which is a
big fat zero. And I can't see a reason in the world
why I should repeat myself to someone who has no
real authority in the case."

I explained about my representing a fine young man
who had been falsely accused of another murder and
how I was sure the two murders were related and how
the only way I could clear my client was to find out
who killed Neil Constantine. Jack Warren was
unmoved.

"I repeat. I know nothing—nada—zero—zilch—
about Constantine's murder. So good-bye and have a
nice day."

"Wait!" I yelped, trying to forestall the impending
click. It came anyway. Warren either hadn't heard me
or hadn't wanted to.

It was time to drag out that persuasive little argument I mentioned. I dialed the number again. "Look,

before you hang up, there's something I think you should be aware of. Selena is absolutely devastated over this and—"

"I know all about it, lady," Warren retorted, in a voice that was at least thirty degrees colder than the one that had answered my first phone call. "I've spoken to her twice a day since this thing happened."

I sensed that I was a second or two away from another click, so the words tumbled out at record speed. "Mr. Warren, your wife is very anxious to bring Neil Constantine's murderer to justice. I don't think she'd appreciate your not wanting to help. If you would—"

The strategy boomeranged. "You've got one hell of a nerve blackmailing me, lady!" he shouted.

"It isn't blackmail. I was just trying to—"

"I know what you were 'just trying to,'" Warren mimicked snidely, "and it won't work. I will not see you; I will not even talk to you—now or at any other time. Have you got that?"

It was apparently a rhetorical question, because before I could answer, the conversation had been terminated. With a bang.

For a couple of minutes I just sat there, receiver in hand, listening abstractedly to the monotonous drone of the dial tone. I had only myself to blame for this. I'd really screwed up this time, antagonizing Warren to the point where the chances of his seeing me hovered between zero, as he put it, and one in a million, as I, more optimistically, calculated it. I decided to drag out the heavy guns.

I figured that by now Selena Warren must be back at her own apartment again. She was.

"This is Desiree Shapiro. I came to see you on—"

"Oh, sure," she said, "I know who you are. You were at Frannie's with the police Wednesday morning." I was happy to note that she sounded pretty much in control.

"How are you feeling?" I inquired gently.

"I'm better than I was. But I'd almost have to be, wouldn't I?"

There was an awkward pause. I didn't feel too good

about involving Selena in my manipulations. After all, she must still be hurting terribly. (Unless, of course, she'd polished off Constantine herself.) But without her help, I knew there was no way I could convince Jack Warren to meet with me.

I related Warren's reaction to my phone call. Then I went into this whole long explanation about people often having important information they don't know they have. And I pointed out that sometimes even the smallest thing can turn an investigation around. I made it clear that this was the reason it was so vital that I talk to everyone who had even the slightest involvement with Neil Constantine, no matter how indirect. (I mean, remembering Selena's staunch defense of Warren, I was not about to sabotage things by betraying that I considered the man a suspect.)

"Give me your phone number. I'll see that he calls you," Selena promised when I'd finished my song and dance.

I gave her both my office and home numbers and hung up. About two hours later, as I was about to go out for lunch, the phone rang.

"You win, Desiree," said the warm, rich—almost melodious—baritone. "Looks like we'll be having our talk, after all. I've leave the where and when to you." I was absolutely floored by how gracious Jack Warren was in defeat.

"Wherever you say. Any time that's convenient for you."

"You could stop by my apartment tonight, if you like. But I live in Queens, so maybe you'd rather wait until after the weekend. We could get together Monday after work, if that's better for you."

"Queens is fine. I have a car, so it's no problem at all."

"Good. Around eight o'clock?"

"Around eight o'clock," I agreed.

Traffic on the Brooklyn-Queens Expressway was heavy, but I'd allowed myself plenty of extra time. It was 8:05 when I pulled into a parking space about a block from Warren's building.

The man who answered the door of 4C was medium height and slim, with dark, wavy hair and a smile that could curl your toes. (If you happen to be susceptible to classic good looks, that is. Which, as I've already told you, I am not.) He was neatly dressed in a blue and yellow plaid shirt and tight faded jeans that showed off a flat midsection and a nice round tush.

We walked down three steps into a living room that could have hopped straight off the pages of *House Beautiful.* It was all done in chintz and velvet, punctuated with gleaming mahogany tables, striking silk floral arrangements, and an eclectic selection of beautifully framed artwork. But what really knocked me out were the contents of the handsome étagère that stood in a corner next to the windows. Shimmering behind those glass doors was the most extensive collection of Lalique crystal this side of Bloomingdale's.

Now, while I personally prefer more contemporary surroundings, there was no doubt that this place had been put together by someone with taste. Expensive taste.

"Selena did this room," Jack Warren told me with pride, evidently aware that I'd been admiring it.

"She did a fabulous job," I said honestly, sinking into the down-filled sofa. Warren sat—not too comfortably, I thought—in one of the Queen Anne chairs. I began by reassuring him that I would try not to take up too much of his time.

"It's okay," he said pleasantly, "I promised Selena I'd do whatever I could to help, so just fire away." But before I could fire, he jumped up. "I'm sorry. It's been a crazy day, and I must have left my head at the office. Can I get you something to drink? Maybe some wine? A Coke? Coffee?" It was almost impossible to reconcile all this affability with the guy who'd hung up on me twice that morning.

I told him a Coke would be fine, thank you, and stole an appreciative glance at his tush when he went to get it. Warren may not have been my type, but a cute tush is a cute tush.

As soon as he returned with the Coke and what looked like a gin and tonic for himself, I got down to business. "How well did you know the victim?"

"I didn't." After a few seconds he added, with a rueful smile, "I knew *of* him, of course."

"Your wife says she introduced the two of you in front of a movie theater."

"That's right. But we didn't say more than hello. If you consider that *knowing* someone . . ."

"You never spoke to him at any other time?"

"Never."

"I understand your wife found you waiting in front of her building one day." I refrained from using the word *lurking*.

"That's right. It was a stupid thing to do. And I'm not terribly proud of it. Or of the way I behaved."

"How *did* you behave?"

Warren went on to repeat what Selena had told me about his aborted visit to her apartment. "I really *do* know better than to criticize someone to the person who's in love with them—or a least *thinks* they are. Expecially someone as loyal as Selena. But she was making a terrible mistake with that guy, and I just couldn't help myself. She means too much to me to just let it go by the boards like that."

"You were trying to reconcile with her?"

"You bet I was! I know it's not nice to speak ill of the dead, but Neil Constantine was the kind of a guy who used women and tossed them away. Look what he did to his wife. Walked out on her when their kid was hardly more than a baby, so he could devote himself to his 'art.' He didn't deserve a woman like Selena. Hey, maybe I don't, either." He grinned sheepishly when he added, "But I refuse to let myself think about that."

"How long had you—have you—and Mrs. Warren been married?"

"It'll be three years in February."

"Why did you separate?"

"Aha, now we're getting down and dirty." I started to respond, but Warren held up his hand. "It's okay.

Ask me whatever you want to. Selena made me swear I'd cooperate, and that's what I'm going to do. Even if it kills me." He flashed a high-voltage smile that quickly extinguished itself as a furrow crept across his forehead. "This is not easy for me to admit, you understand, but according to Selena, the magic was gone. I think I could have rekindled things. I had almost convinced her to come away for a long weekend at Montego Bay. But then, she met *him*." Warren's eyes turned cold. Stone cold. "The bastard!" He said the words so softly that I almost didn't hear them. It was as though they emerged of their own volition from somewhere deep inside him.

The intensity of the man's emotions shook me. I quickly changed the subject. "What do you know about a woman named Agnes Garrity?"

"Quite a bit," he replied, to my complete—and short-lived—surprise. "She's the old woman in Constantine's building who got herself killed a couple of weeks ago, isn't she?"

"That's right."

"I read all about it in the papers, and then Selena was talking about it just yesterday."

"But you didn't know her personally?"

"Oh, no."

It was time. "Now for the biggie," I said lightly. "Where were you on Monday night and, more specifically, during the early hours of Tuesday morning?"

"I was wondering when you'd get to that. On Monday night, I had dinner at home—alone. And then I watched some TV—alone. After which I went to bed—alone."

Later, when I was having a late snack at home—alone—I tried to crystallize my feelings about Jack Warren. He was intelligent and charming. And he was certainly a good sport. If someone had steamrolled *me* into getting together like that, I wouldn't have acted nearly as civilized. Still, something about the man disturbed me. Maybe it was the fact that he was *so much* in love.

Chapter 16

On Saturday morning, I phoned Sal Martinez at the store to update him on my progress. It wasn't much of an update, because I hadn't exactly made any progress. (Just the opposite, really, when you consider that I'd verified Louise and Alma Constantine's alibis.) But I felt I should keep in touch regardless. The man *was* paying the bills.

The only piece of news I had to discuss with him—Jerry's explanation of the fingerprints on the refrigerator—didn't do anything for Martinez at all.

"I know all about that, Deseeray. The boy tole me couple days ago, soon's he come back from havin' lunch wit' you. But it don' mean nuthin'. Who gonna believe Jerry, anyway?"

I said it was important to be able to present the police with a reasonable theory as to how Jerry's fingerprints *might* have gotten on the refrigerator door. "They may not place much credence in it," I explained, "but at least they won't be able to claim that there's no way the prints would have been on the door unless Jerry had killed her and stolen the money."

Martinez wasn't convinced. "It don' matter what you tell the cops. They don' wanna know what they don' wanna know."

I hung up thinking he was probably right.

After a second cup of coffee, I dialed the last name on my shrinking list of suspects.

Bill Murphy was unusually cordial, considering the reason for my call. He said he'd be home till about one if I wanted to make it that day.

*　　*　　*

My cab pulled up in front of the apartment house on West 84th Street precisely at noon. In the distance, I could hear church bells exultantly proclaiming the hour. It was a nice building, not elaborate, but clean and well-kept. Like so many other buildings on the Upper West Side, it probably had walls thick enough to protect noise-sensitive tenants from even the loudest, most inconsiderate, least talented piano-playing idiot neighbors in the world. Like mine.

Bill Murphy was short, not more than five-six or -seven, and skinny. One hundred thirty-five pounds, tops. He had prominent ears, a pallid complexion, and curly, dark-brown hair in the beginning stages of retreat. The man looked like he was in desperate need of some mothering. I liked what I saw.

He preceded me into the living room disguised as a den. Or maybe it was the other way around. It was furnished in leather and tweed, with a built-in floor-to-ceiling bookcase completely covering one wall and a gray brick fireplace dominating the second. Advertising awards and sports trophies decorated the walls and tables. The only art was a large print of a hunting scene—defintely not the work of the deceased—that hung over the gray tweed sofa.

The room said bachelor all over it, I decided with something very like glee. And then, on the cherry end table next to the sofa, among all the other memorabilia, I spotted a brass-framed eight-by-ten photograph. It was a picture of Bill Murphy with a dark-haired little girl not more than ten or eleven years old. They were at an amusement park, standing in front of a ride of some kind. The little girl had the remains of an ice-cream cone in her hand—and almost as much of it on her chin—while Murphy was lugging a huge stuffed animal (a hippopotamus, I think) that almost obscured his face. I picked up the photo.

"Your daughter?" I asked, trying to make it sound casual.

"My niece."

"She's very pretty."

"Yes," Murphy replied shortly, extending his hand

for the picture. I felt uncomfortable, as if I'd committed some sort of faux pas. But after he returned the photograph to the table, he said pleasantly, "Please sit down." And, when we were both seated, "Now, how can I help you?"

"You and Neil Constantine were formerly good friends, I was told."

"That's right—*formerly.* We'd been friends for more than twenty-five years. We met right after college."

"You were also business partners?"

"Until ten years ago, when Neil decided to devote himself full-time to painting."

"The end of the partnership didn't affect the relationship?"

"Not at all. In fact, after Neil left the agency, we started to see each other on a social basis more often, since it was the only way we could stay in touch. We'd have a couple of drinks together every once in a while or go out to dinner. We even had a weekly poker game up until two years ago. We'd meet either at Neil's or here—we were the only bachelors in the group—put away a few beers, and send out for pizza or Chinese or something. Those were good times." There was real nostalgia in his voice.

"What broke it up?"

"One of the guys moved to Jersey. Another became a high-powered exec who only had time for making big business deals." *What luminous gray eyes the man had.*

"Your friendship with the victim *did* sour, though. Because of money, wasn't it?"

His tone was dry but without rancor. "I guess *you* would say money."

I didn't miss the inference. "What would *you* say?"

"For me, it was a question of trust. I lent him ten thousand dollars when he needed it. He made no attempt to pay it back when *I* did."

"You'd gotten into financial difficulty?"

"I needed the money back so I could expand the business."

"It was last year that you made the loan to him, I understand."

"That's right. A year ago August." He shot me a gap-toothed smile. "Selena seems to have filled you in pretty well."

"Not really. She just gave me a couple of the bare facts."

"Nice girl—uh, woman—Selena."

"That's okay. She's a girl to me, too. She seemed to be very much in love with Constantine."

"She was. They had their problems, like we all do, but they were really crazy about each other."

The buzzer in my brain went off. "What sort of problems are we talking about?"

"Nothing that would lead to murder, I assure you. I shouldn't have said anything, but I don't see how Selena could possibly be under suspicion. She was in Chicago when Neil was killed."

"I didn't say she was a suspect. I'm just trying to get everything straight in my head."

"Their fights didn't really amount to a hill of beans, anyway. Mostly they were about her husband—or maybe ex-husband; I'm not sure what their status is these days. Neil resented the guy's constantly calling her."

"There must have been more to it than that," I prodded.

"Well, they also argued about getting married. Actually, *argued* is the wrong word; *squabbled* would be a lot more accurate. Neil wanted to rush off to a justice of the peace almost from the day Selena moved in with him, but she seemed to have some doubts. Also, she was still married to the other guy, as far as I know. But you don't kill a man for wanting to marry you, do you?"

"I have this feeling, Mr. Murphy, that you're holding out on me." I didn't have that feeling at all, but sometimes it pays to say it. This was one of those times.

"Call me Bill. And it's really nothing."

"Okay, Bill," I agreed. A warmth was spreading

inside me, and I had to remind myself I was here to investigate a murder. "If it was nothing, you shouldn't have a problem telling me."

"Selena was a spender, that's all. And Neil was always trying to get her to cool it a little. But listen, Neil and I didn't even talk for the last few months— except when I called to bug him about the money. Maybe they'd worked everything out in the interim."

"It's possible, I guess."

I was just about to phrase my next question when Murphy leaned forward. "Say, can I get you something? Some coffee? There's a little German bakery down the block that makes fantastic streusel cake, a sample of which happens to be right on my kitchen table."

I wasn't even tempted. If I hung around this man, I could wind up svelte and gorgeous!

He sat back in his chair, looking disappointed.

"What can you tell me about Louise Constantine?"

"She's a nice woman—on the reserved side. We weren't exactly close, but we always got along fairly well. She was pretty crushed when Neil left her, although she took pains not to let it show. That's how she is, a very private kind of person."

"Were there other women—before Mrs. Warren, I mean?"

"No one serious. Not that I'm aware of, anyway, and I think I would have known about it if there were." He paused for a second or two. "No," he said with conviction, shaking his head, "I'm *sure* I'd have known about it."

"How did Louise take it when Selena Warren moved in with Constantine?"

"I have no idea. Neil didn't talk about it, and I haven't seen Louise herself in . . . must be over a year." Murphy was looking at me shrewdly. "Believe me, Louise is not the type to murder anyone. She doesn't have that kind of *intensity*."

On the basis of a single meeting, it was obvious I was a lot more tuned in to Louise Constantine than her ex-husband's ex-best-friend was.

"What about Alma?"

"Basically, she's a good kid. I always felt very sorry for her. Neil moved out when she was only seven or eight. That can be rough on a kid."

"She resented her father?"

"Sure she did. Enough to rebel and become a hippie—if that's still the right term. But not enough to kill him. Besides, I think it had gotten to the point where he was no longer that important in her life."

"So far you've managed to eliminate almost every one of my suspects," I reproached him jokingly.

"I hope I can do the same for myself." The gap-toothed smile reappeared, lighting up his face. Suddenly this middle-aged executive looked like a mischievous little boy.

I became aware, then, that Murphy hadn't checked his watch since I'd arrived. Not once. Still, I thought I should mention that the end was in sight. "I just have a couple more questions," I informed him.

"No problem. I've got plenty of time."

Now, as you know, this is not the response I usually get. Either Bill Murphy was an uncommonly tolerant man, or there was something chemical going on for him, too. I opted for the something chemical.

"When did you last see the victim?" I asked, almost cheerfully.

"Sometime in July. That's when we had this big blowup about the money. After that, our only contact was by telephone."

"I hear you had another big blowup on the phone the night of the murder."

"Selena *does* go on," Murphy responded good-naturedly. "Yes. I called him at ten after eight or so. It was to keep up the pressure about the money. I wasn't about to let him off the hook." All at once, his expression turned grim, and his voice began to quiver with a fury he wasn't quite able to surpress. "Naturally, good old Neil insisted he didn't have it, that he was waiting to receive his inheritance."

"You don't believe the victim couldn't repay you?"

"Not for a minute. Not for one single, solitary minute. You know, Desiree, I've always been a total ass when it comes to judging people. Seems I have to learn what they're really about the hard way." He managed a smile, and the dark mood seemed to lift.

"What did you do after the phone call?"

"As soon as I hung up, I jumped in the shower. Then I got dressed, grabbed my coat, and headed for Shanahan's; that's this little pub on Eighty-sixth and Amsterdam. They make the greatest corned beef and cabbage you've ever eaten, and Monday is corned beef and cabbage night."

"How long did you stay?"

"Until closing time. I had a leisurely dinner and then relaxed with a few drinks."

"And closing time was . . . ?"

"Two a.m."

"Can anyone verify that?"

"The waitress can. Check with her. Name's Coral Carlisle. She's a good friend of mine."

I winced. I didn't like the sound of that "she's a good friend of mine." I didn't like it at all. Of course, I was aware that I was displaying all the emotional maturity of a teenager—a mentally deficient teenager. This dried-up little man might be a murderer, for all I knew!

Murphy misread my expression. "She's not a good enough friend to lie for me in a murder investigation, if that's what's on your mind."

I assured him it wasn't. "I was about to ask—and I promise this is my last question—"

"Don't apologize," he cut in. "I've enjoyed this interrogation; I really have."

"I was about to ask," I began again in a not-too-steady voice, "if you've ever heard of a woman named Agnes Garrity."

He thought for a moment. "I don't think so. Should I have?"

"Not necessarily. She's an old woman who lived in Constantine's building. She was murdered the week before he was."

"That's right! The name *did* sound familiar. I read about it in the papers."

"But you never ran into her when you went to visit Constantine?"

"I may have seen her in the elevator a few times over the years, but I'm not even sure of that. I wondered, when I read the newspaper article, if it could be the same old woman I was thinking of. I guess that doesn't help you much, does it?" he asked, his eyes full of sympathy.

I shook my head.

"I'm sorry. I wish I could have been more helpful to you all around."

Once I was on the street, I was able to think more clearly. And what I thought was that I was behaving in a totally unprofessional manner. Not only that. I should probably be committed. "It will serve you right if Bill Murphy turns out to be the murderer," I told myself severely. And, to make certain my message carried enough conviction, I added, "And blows your stupid head off."

Chapter 17

Stuart and I had made plans to have dinner together that evening. He called me at 3:30 to firm things up.

"Any idea where you'd like to go tonight?" he asked.

"Ever heard of a place called Shanahan's?" I answered.

A little while later when I was soaking in the tub—chin-high in fragrant bubbles—my mind kept returning to the name "Coral Carlisle." It was a name that conjured up all sorts of repulsive images. She was a blond; that much I knew. And she was probably in show business. No one's born a "Coral Carlisle." Undoubtedly, she was waiting tables just until her big break came along. Oh, she was definitely tall. At least three inches taller than Murphy—six in her spikes. And she was voluptuous, but without an ounce of fat on her incredibly perfect body. It goes without saying that she had legs all the way up to her neck. And, of course, she was under thirty.

What was it I'd told myself earlier in the day about getting my head blown off? I was obviously not one to heed a well-meant warning.

And this dumb infatuation wasn't at all like me. When it comes to my personal life, I am almost unfailingly level-headed. Yet here I was, jealous of a woman I'd never met over a man I'd met just once!

"Now, whose alibi are you checking in this place?" Stuart asked me in the cab that was about to deposit us at Shanahan's.

"The victim's former business partner. Constantine

owed him a lot of money, and Murphy—the partner—
seems to no longer have loved him, to put it mildly.
Look, if the place doesn't appeal to us, we can always
have a drink and go somewhere else to eat. Murphy
says they have the greatest corned beef and cabbage,
though."

"You've sold me. You know how nuts I am about
corned beef and cabbage."

"I certainly do. Unfortunately, they only serve it
on Mondays."

"Harlot!"

Shanahan's was small and very pubby, with red-
checkered tablecloths, dark wooden paneling, and
sawdust on the floor. It was also extremely crowded
and ear-shatteringly noisy. We had a reservation,
which entitled us to a tiny table in the back directly
opposite the kitchen.

The minute we sat down, an adenoidal little waiter
who looked barely old enough to drink rushed over
to take our order. "Two Perriers with a twist of lime,"
Stuart told him.

As soon as he scurried away, I checked out the help.
There were two other people waiting tables. Both
male. Then the door to the kitchen swung open and
a waitress came out balancing a large tray covered
wtih steaming dishes of hearty food. From where I
was sitting, her burden pretty much obscured her face.
All I could really see of her were bony legs extending
from beneath a worn, too-tight uniform stretched taut
across a short, too-plump frame. When she set the
tray down, I got the rest of the picture: faded blue
eyes, steel-gray hair, and a weary, lived-in face.

I took up my vigil again.

Our waiter came back a few minutes later. "Is Coral
Carlisle working tonight?" I asked as he was depos-
iting the drinks.

"Sure, that's her." He tossed his head in the direction of the woman I knew could positively no way be
Coral Carlisle. "Did you want her for something?"

"I'd like to talk to her when she gets a chance."

"She know you?"

His curiosity would have to go unsatisfied. "No. But I'd appreciate your giving her the message."

"No problem," he agreed reluctantly.

While I was sipping my Perrier and waiting for Coral, I looked into every plate on every table within looking distance. I liked the menu. I had also developed a ferocious appetite since the moment our waiter had identified that man-trap, Coral Carlisle.

"Well?" I asked Stuart after he'd finished his Perrier. "Feel like eating here, or should we just get another round?"

He came up with the right answer. "Let's be absolutely fearless and give the food a try. If my nose doesn't deceive me, we have hit pay dirt."

I ordered the shepherd's pie and Stuart chose the London broil. While we were waiting for our entrees, Coral stopped at the table. She was so harried she was almost breathless. "Herbie told me you wanted to talk to me," she said loudly, straining to be heard above the din.

"I'd appreciate it." I took out my license.

"Something wrong, Officer?" she asked tensely, obviously mistaking me for a cop.

"Oh, no," I yelled, pushing my vocal chords to their limits, "there's nothing to worry about. I'm a private investigator, and I just wanted to ask you one or two questions. It'll only take a minute."

She glanced around to make certain her customers were all being taken care of. They weren't. "Waitress!" some loudmouthed college kid in a University of Pennsylvania sweater shouted. "What the hell happened to our beers?"

A young couple sitting at the table next to loudmouth's was also vying for her attention, with the man impatiently signaling for the check.

Coral looked at me apologetically. "I'll be back soon's I can," she promised.

The shepherd's pie was delicious. So was Stuart's London broil (which I only sampled at his insistence). Ditto my pecan pie, slathered with fresh whipped cream, and Stuart's strawberry cheesecake (also sampled at his insistence). Coral returned just as we were getting refills on our coffee.

"I'm really sorry. Saturday nights the place is a zoo. This is the first chance I've had to take a bit of a break. Now what is it you were wantin' to know?" Even above the mayhem you couldn't mistake the brogue, which I found quite charming—now that I no longer regarded the woman as a rival.

"Bill Murphy tells me he's a pretty regular customer here."

"Murph? Oh, sure. He's been comin' in for years."

"Do you remember him being here Monday night?"

She pursed her lips. "Mondee, huh? I can't say's I do. But he's here so often, it's hard for me to tell one time from the next. For sure, though, if he *was* here Mondee night, he had the corned beef and cabbage. He's just crazy for Shanahan's corned beef and cabbage, he is. I remember the first time he brought in his fiancée, he—"

My heart stopped beating. "His fiancée?"

"Ex, I guess she must be." My heart resumed its pumping. "One day, he just started comin' in by himself again. Just like that. Never said a word about it, neither. And I didn't ask him anythin'. He'd tell me if he felt like, is how I saw it. Beautiful lady she was, too—tall and blond, with a real good figger." I thought Coral seemed slightly embarrassed after she'd mentioned the "figger," but sometimes I'm a little too sensitive.

"How long ago did she stop coming in with him?"

"Two, three months back, it was. Now, most nights, he sits down and has his dinner all alone. Sad, I'd say. And him such a lovely man."

"I believe Murphy was here Monday night until two, when you closed up, if that'll jog your memory."

"'Fraid not. But if Murph told you he came in Mondee, he came in Mondee. Only thing is, he's confused about that two o'clock business. We closed early Mondee night—a little after twelve, it was. Jim—the boss—his wife was sick, and he wanted to get on home."

Now my heart dropped completely out of my body. "You couldn't be mistaken about which night you closed early?" I asked too anxiously. I could feel Stuart looking at me quizzically.

"No, it was Mondee. I know, because—" She stopped abruptly. "Murph's not in any trouble, is he?"

"Of course not," I answered.

"I didn't say anythin' I shouldn't of, did I?"

"Of course not," I answered again. "It was Bill who gave me your name and asked me to talk to you."

"I guess it's okay, then." But she returned to her rationale still looking a little apprehensive. "I'm positive it was Mondee account of I remember thinkin' it was a good thing it wasn't Tuesdee, because Tuesdees my son picks me up after work. And I'da been hangin' around here for almost two hours, waitin' for Brian to show up."

Well, I'd found out what I wanted to know and then discovered I didn't want to know it. But if you'd like to hear something *really* stupid, try this: As upset as I was over Bill Murphy's lie—and its frightening implications—I was just as unhinged about the goddamn blond.

Chapter 18

I guess it sounds strange that I put Murphy's love life right up there with the possibility he might be a killer. But it was hard to conceive of that man murdering anyone. On the other hand, how did I know the blond was really out of the picture? It had been two or three months, Coral said, since he'd stopped bringing her to Shanahan's. That wasn't very much time. They could be getting back together again any day now. Or maybe they hadn't actually broken up at all. Maybe she'd just taken a job out of town. Hell, if she was that gorgeous, maybe she was in California making a movie, and they were carrying on one of those bicoastal things.

I forced myself to stop thinking about *that* mess and concentrate on the mess I called my apartment. Ellen, who had returned to her own place on Thursday, was coming over for dinner that night, and Charmaine, my every-other-week cleaning lady, hadn't shown up in over a month. I got out the vaccum, the squeegee, the brushes, the rags, and half a dozen different cleansers and went to work. I was scrubbing the toilet bowl, which ranks at the very top of the list of "jobs I can live without," when the case wormed its way back into my head. Which was okay this time, because it took my mind out of the toilet bowl.

I'm happy to report that I finally put things in perspective. To wit: I was being paid to conduct an investigation on behalf of Jerry Costello. And Jerry wasn't only my client; I was also extremely fond of him. More important, I was certain he hadn't been involved in either murder. Well, as of now, I was going to stop this obsessing about Bill Murphy and start devoting my efforts to finding the killer. No matter who it might turn out to be.

Ellen arrived at 7:00 with a bottle of zinfandel, and we began our small-scale festivities with some mushroom quiche and a glass of the wine. (When it comes to drinking—or not drinking—I'm easy. Most of the time, I just go along with the company I'm keeping.)

I'd managed to convince my Nervous Nellie of a niece, in the course of the couple of days she'd spent with me, that the murders were connected; ergo, she was safe. So it was a relatively calm Ellen who sat on the sofa next to me, bursting to hear about the latest developments in the investigation. I promised to bring her up to date after we'd eaten.

In the meantime, she filled me in on the Caribbean cruise she was planning for spring, complained about her job as an assistant buyer at Macy's, and laid out every nasty detail of a betrayal she'd suffered at the hands of her now former best friend, Gladys. Eventually, she got to the good stuff.

Ellen had met SOMEONE.

Turning pinker with every word, she confided how much she liked this man. And how much he seemed to like her. His name was Herb Saunders, and he was an engineer—but he wasn't boring, like most engineers. Just wait till I met him; I'd see! He was, of course, very good-looking—tall and dark and slightly balding, which was a real plus because she thought bald men were so much more virile-looking, didn't I?

I nodded, but Ellen was too caught up in her narrative to notice.

"It was a blind date, can you imagine? The first decent one I ever had. We went to the movies—one of those buddy movies. I forget the name of it. And then we had a late supper at the Brasserie. And then we went to this little piano bar, where the man sang songs from the forties and fifties. You would have loved it, Aunt Dez," she gushed.

(I *knew* she didn't mean anything by that.)

"We went out again last night, and he took me to

see *City of Angels*. I didn't tell him you took me for my birthday."

"Smart girl."

"I'm seeing him next Saturday, and you wouldn't believe how nervous I am."

Oh, yes, I would! What I wouldn't have believed was how nervous *I* was about this romance. But it had been a long time since there'd been anyone special in Ellen's life. And she's very dear to me. Which is why I was also pretty miffed.

"Why didn't you tell me about him before?"

"I was afraid of jinxing things. I still am, but I couldn't keep it in any longer. I had to tell *you*, at least."

That smoothed my feathers. "Don't worry, you won't jinx it." I was leaning over to give her a reassuring buss on the cheek when the timer sounded announcing that dinner was ready.

We were having roast loin of pork with sherry, which, nice Jewish girl that she is, happens to be one of Ellen's favorite dishes. With it, I'd prepared a sweet potato casserole and green beans with almonds. Dessert was Bananas Foster. If I say so myself, it was a very good meal. No. To be absolutely honest, and thoroughly immodest, it was a sensational meal.

Ellen hadn't wanted to talk about Herb during dinner—it gave her butterflies—so we chatted about a dozen other things. After the dishes were cleared away, we went into the living room with our coffee refills. As soon as we sat down, Ellen demanded I bring her up to date on the investigation.

I told her about Selena and how, apparently, she was in Chicago when Neil Constantine was murdered. And I told her about Louise and Alma being at the movies and about the doorman's confirming the time they'd come in. Then I told her about the two people who had no alibis.

When I wound down, Ellen eyed me knowingly. "You like this Bill Murphy, don't you, Aunt Dez?"

"Sort of. But I can't let that interfere with my job.

Besides, if the other alibis hold up—and it looks like they will—there's a fifty-fifty chance he's a murderer."

"Oh, I wouldn't say that," Ellen responded earnestly. "The husband—what's his name?—had twice as many reasons for wanting Mr. Constantine dead."

"Warren. Jack Warren. And how on earth do you figure that?" I'm ashamed to admit I was a little annoyed with her. But where did she get her crazy arithmetic from, anyway?

"Look, first off, he—Warren, that is—probably wanted Constantine dead because Selena was in love with him, right?"

"Right."

"Then, second, Selena would inherit all that money, so if they reconciled . . ." She didn't finish the sentence, but she didn't have to. "I think those are both much stronger motives than an unpaid loan, don't you?"

"Absolutely!" Ellen really *did* have a point there. I was angry with myself for not having realized Warren could benefit financially from Constantine's death. But after a minute or two of reflection, I had to throw a monkey wrench into Ellen's theory. "Uh-oh. Not so fast. Warren may not even have known about the inheritance."

"Ask Selena if she mentioned it to him."

"She wouldn't admit it if she did."

"You could try," Ellen urged. "And anyway, even if he *didn't* know about the inheritance, love is still a much stronger motive than a few thousand dollars."

"Ten," I reminded her.

"Than a *hundred* thousand dollars."

We sipped our coffee in silence for a few minutes. Then Ellen piped up with, "You *are* going to check out her alibi aren't you?"

"Selena's? You bet."

"How about that doorman? Maybe he lied."

"I guess it's possible. But why would he?"

"You never know," Ellen asserted stubbornly. "Maybe they bribed him. Wait a sec. Did you ask those two women anything about the movie to make sure they really saw it?"

"It wouldn't have done a bit of good," I retorted. "If *I* were going to lie about going to a movie, I'd pick something *I'd* seen before. And they could have seen this one anytime; it's a rerelease. I'll bet it's even out on videocassette."

"What's the movie?"

"A Star Is Born."

"With Barbra Streisand? I saw that years ago. You ever see it?"

"No, but I *did* see the Judy Garland version a lot *more* years ago. Say, would you like to listen to the album? It's really beautiful."

"Sure."

I hunted up the album and put it on the turntable of what is probably the oldest phonograph in the Western world. The magnificent voice of Judy Garland filled the room. We sat there, neither of us saying a word, until she'd finished her heart-stopping rendition of "The Man That Got Away."

"Now don't tell me Streisand sang it like that," I challenged, with no provocation at all.

"Huh?" Ellen replied.

"When *she* played that part." Sometimes you have to spell everything out for Ellen.

"Ohhhh." The dawn had finally broken. "I didn't understand what you meant. I thought you knew."

"Knew what?"

"The songs are entirely different in the Barbra Streisand movie. I think she wrote them herself."

"Are you positive—I mean about the songs being different?"

"I'm *very* positive."

Well, you can't get more positive than that. I reached over and hugged my darling niece hard.

Now that I'd reacquired two more suspects, the odds on Bill Murphy's being a killer had suddenly shrunk to one in four. And, in spite of the fact that this meant the murders were even further away from a solution, I was a lot happier about things.

I didn't think my feelings in any way violated the vow I'd made over the toilet bowl. Not really, that is.

Chapter 19

I spent all of Monday morning trying to reach Alma Constantine. I finally got Tess around 2:00.

"It's important that I talk to Alma. Any idea when she'll be back?"

"She has classes till after three. She should be home by quarter of four, unless she stops off somewhere," Tess informed me pleasantly.

"Please have her get back to me as soon as she comes in. It's important," I reiterated.

We hung up, and I steeled myself to make the call I'd been putting off for days.

Tim Fielding and I hadn't had any contact since the morning we'd gone to see Selena Warren. I knew he was furious with me, and I really couldn't blame him. But I wasn't to blame, either. I'd done what I had to do for my client.

After a brief rehearsal (in which I also played the part of a very forgiving Fielding), I picked up the phone and dialed. And—lionhearted soul that I am—promptly hung up. Retreating to the ladies' room in disgrace, I returned with renewed resolve.

"Sergeant Fielding," said this pleasant voice on the other end of the line. The pleasant voice turned brittle when I identified myself.

"I know you're angry with me," I began.

"You might say that," Fielding snapped.

This was not going to be easy.

"I'm really sorry for the way I interrogated Selena Warren. I was definitely out of bounds."

"I'd have to agree with you."

I knew any attempt to justify my actions would be fatal, so I stuck to remorse. "I was trying to help my client, but I had no business taking over the investigation that way. I can't tell you how rotten I've been feeling about the whole thing." I got my voice to crack just a little (thanks to a short stint in my high school drama club), and Tim started to relent.

"Well, I know you did it because you're so anxious to clear the Costello kid," he admitted grudgingly.

"I am. But I still had no right to—"

I guess he got tired of listening to me munch on all that crow, because he interrupted with, "Why don't we just forget it?"

"Would it be okay if I came by tomorrow? There are a couple of things I wanted to discuss with you. I'd really appreciate it."

"Well, you've got balls; I'll give you that." I wasn't sure, but I thought his voice reflected the beginning of a smile. "I won't be in tomorrow," he said, "but check with me Wednesday."

What a guy!

At 5:30, I still hadn't heard from Alma, so I tried the apartment once more before leaving for home. Tess sounded embarrassed when she told me her roommate must have been detained.

After dinner, I called again. And got Tess again. "Alma still hasn't come in. I can't imagine what's keeping her. She must have stopped at a friend's." To her credit, Tess didn't seem very comfortable lying.

"Look," I said, "I've uncovered some new evidence, and I'm giving Alma the courtesy of discussing it with her before I take it to the police. Please relay that message to her."

Alma returned my call ten minutes later. It was apparent she wasn't thrilled to talk to me. Under pressure, she agreed to meet me for lunch the next day at a coffee shop a couple of blocks from NYU.

I showed up five minutes early, at 12:25. Alma shuffled in a half hour later.

She was not a thing of beauty.

Her hair was as dirty and stringy as I remembered, her face as devoid of makeup—and as much in need of it. She wore a soiled raincoat over a matted blue sweater and torn black slacks.

As we sat facing each other in the booth, I noticed for the first time how good her features were—nice eyes (which a little mascara could do wonders for), a short, straight nose, and full, well-shaped lips. My God, with a little soap and water and some help from Revlon, the kid might actually pass for the issue of her good-looking parents!

"What did you want to see me about?" she demanded without preamble.

"Let's order first, okay?"

"I'm not hungry."

"Have something light, then."

She put on the wire-rimmed glasses, which traveled immediately to the tip of her nose, and gave the menu a quick once-over. "I'll just have an egg salad on white and a glass of water," she told the waiter.

"I'll have the same, but with a cup of coffee, please."

"Oh, and bring me a Coke, too," she added as the waiter started to walk away. He had only taken a few more steps when she brought him to a stop with, "Wait a minute. And some french fries." He managed to get a couple of steps farther before Alma called out again, "And some onion rings!"

There went my good intentions—which surface so rarely and which are always so terribly fragile. "Ditto!" I yelled to a rapidly retreating back.

"Well?" Alma said sharply when we'd finally completed our ordering.

"Why don't we eat first?"

"I don't have a lot of time." Unlike our previous meeting when she had been merely perfunctory—and maybe just the slightest bit unpleasant—her tone clued me in that she was now out-and-out hostile.

"Okay, then let's get down to it. You told me you

and your mother had gone to see *A Star Is Born,* right?"

"Right."

"With Barbra Streisand, right?"

"You're batting a thousand." The little twit had developed a real attitude!

"Do you remember our conversation about 'The Man That Got Away'?"

"The song? Yeah, I remember."

"Well, Streisand never sang it. That song wasn't even *in* the movie you claim to have seen."

"I don't believe this shit!" she retorted in a voice very close to a shout. "That's your idea of *evidence*? Now I've heard everything! I *knew* you were trying to trap me that day, and damned if you're not still at it!" Her belligerence took me aback. Frankly, I hadn't thought she was capable of that much emotion. And she wasn't through yet. "Listen, I never said Streisand sang your goddamn song! I just said Judy Garland didn't—for the simple reason that she wasn't in the goddamn fucking movie!"

Oh, how I wished I'd been carrying a tape recorder last Thursday, so I could throw this snotty kid's words right back in her face! I was seething, but I was able, somehow, to keep my voice even. "We both know you're lying," I said. Under the circumstances, what else was there *to* say?

At this point, I expected Alma to cut out of there, but she apparently had more of an appetite than she'd let on. She sat in silence, just glaring at me, until the waiter brought our order—which she literally pounced on.

I tried again to get her to level with me. "Just because you don't have an alibi doesn't mean you'll be accused of murdering your father," I told her between egg salad bites. "As a matter of fact, I'm pretty certain no one considers you a serious suspect. And just because you can't provide your mother with an alibi doesn't mean she has anything to worry about, either. Not if she didn't do it. But what could get you *both* in big trouble is sticking to this ridiculous story, when I've already established that it isn't true."

"You're full of crap, you know that? Why don't you check with my mother's doorman?"

"I did, and he's lying. Just like you are."

"Yeah? Why would he lie?"

"I don't know—yet. But I intend to find out."

"Look, I saw that movie, whether you believe me or not. And you're not going to get me to admit what I never said in the first place. Maybe you should start using a tape recorder."

Thanks.

The waiter came by then to ask if there'd be any- thing else. I was about to request the check when Alma jumped in. "I'll have a marshmallow sundae with Burgundy cherry ice cream and nuts," she said. "And lotsa whipped cream."

What the hell! "Make that two."

Alma left as soon as she'd demolished her dessert. She didn't bother saying good-bye.

Late that night, I went back to Louise Constantine's apartment building.

The uniformed gentleman who held open the door was tall and thin and unfamiliar to me. "Where's the regular doorman—the one who's usually here at this time?"

"Englehardt? He's out with the flu. Anything I can help you with?"

"No, thank you. I guess it'll have to wait for Englehardt."

"He'll probably be in tomorrow. You could try then."

"I will," I told him. "I certainly will."

Chapter 20

I overslept the next morning. When I got to the office a little after 10:00, Jackie greeted me with a mildly disapproving look and a couple of phone messages. Both messages were from Blanche Lovitt.

Blanche and I had been friends in college. Not really close friends—I guess friendly acquaintances would be more accurate. But we'd always been fond of one another and, up until just a few years ago, had kept in contact via an exchange of Christmas cards and a very occasional phone call. It had been almost five years, though, since I'd last seen her. And that was by accident.

I'd stopped in at a jewelry store in Short Hills, New Jersey, at which establishment my client suspected her (allegedly) dallying eighty-year-old husband of purchasing some costly little trinkets for his (alleged) chippie. Anyway, the clerk was waiting on someone else when I got there, and when the someone else turned around, it was Blanche Lovitt.

We wound up having lunch together, and Blanche told me she had moved to Short Hills about a year earlier, because Alan, her plastics-manufacturer husband, had purchased a new plant in the area. "Only a few months later, Alan skipped out on me," Blanche said, looking inordinately pleased, "so he could take up residence with a forty-inch chest." Her husband's departure, she informed me, not only freed her from a smug, self-important little hypocrite who constantly belittled her—a low-life she should have dumped years ago—but also made her an extremely wealthy woman.

We left each other that day solemnly promising to stay in touch. Blanche vowed to call me for lunch in a few weeks, when she expected to be in the city. But it never happened. And two or three years later, even the Christmas cards stopped.

Now, after all this time, she was so anxious to talk to me she'd phoned twice within an hour. Well, if it was that important, it wouldn't be nice to make her wait. (Okay, so I was also burning with curiosity.)

"Dez! Thank God! I've been going crazy waiting to hear from you!" Blanche exclaimed when she heard my voice.

"I just walked in and got your message," I told her, a little defensively.

"Oh, I realize that, and I appreciate your calling back right away."

"Is something wrong, Blanche?" I asked, knowing how stupid that sounded the minute I'd said it.

"I'm afraid something's very wrong. I should have called you weeks ago, but I kept putting it off. And now that I finally made up my mind to do it, I'm jumping out of my skin. You know—actually, I guess you don't know, but I remarried last year. I'm Blanche Newman now."

I was wondering whether or not to offer congratulations, but she didn't give me a chance. "I can't even tell you how happy I was with Mark, my husband. He's—he used to be, I should say—so thoughtful and loving, so much fun to be with. Everything Alan wasn't. I really thought I'd lucked out and found myself the perfect man this time. I should have known better!"

"What happened?"

"About a month and a half ago, Mark started coming home late from work a couple of times a week. I'm talking *really* late. Like two or three in the morning. He always had an excuse, of course—tons of paperwork, client meetings—he always came up with something. And for a while I believed him. Not because he was so convincing, but because I wanted to.

It had all been so wonderful that I refused to admit to myself that things had changed. You understand?"

I understood.

"But lately he doesn't even act like himself. I don't mean he's turned nasty or anything. I don't exactly know how to explain it." She paused, groping for the words. "It's like he's *preoccupied* all the time; like his mind is somewhere else. I think there must be another woman. It's the only thing that makes sense. But I've gotten to the point where I have to *know*. Will you look into it for me, Dez? Please?"

I explained about the double homicide I was working on and how it was consuming virtually every second of my waking life.

"Please. I'll pay you whatever you say."

Blanche was close to tears, and I felt like a louse. But I honestly didn't see how I could take on anything else. "I'm so involved with these murders right now that I'm not doing justice to my other cases. I wouldn't be able to devote the time I should to this, and I know how important it is to you. Look, let me give you the names of some top-flight investigators, really good people who'll be able to handle it properly, all right?"

"I guess it'll have to be, but I'd feel so much better if *you* were handling it." She was sniffling now, and I felt like an even bigger louse. But what could I do? I recommended three P.I.s who in addition to excellent credentials had fairly sympathetic natures and told her I'd be talking to her soon.

I really wish there were some way to amputate a conscience. Mine has been causing me grief almost from the cradle. I spent ten guilt-ridden minutes justifying to myself why I could not possibly have taken this case. Then I spent another ten minutes justifying my decision to Jackie, who agreed that, under the circumstances, I had had no alternative. Then I called Blanche back.

"Have you spoken to any of those investigators yet?"

"Not yet. I've been trying to get myself up for it."

"Well, forget it. I'll look into this for you myself. I

just have to figure out the logistics. But don't worry, I'll work something out. I'll drive over to see you tomorrow, and we can talk. Okay?"

"Thanks, Dez. Thanks a million."

I phoned Tim Fielding next, which was something *I* had to get myself up for. In spite of our reasonably cordial conversation two days earlier, I knew it would be a while before our relationship got back to normal.

Tim was civil, which was as much as I could hope for, considering. He agreed to let me come by late in the day.

It was just before 5:00 when I arrived at the station house. For the first couple of minutes, things between my old friend and me were pretty awkward. But I drew upon all my chutzpah and plunged in anyway. "I've been investigating the Constantine murder pretty thoroughly," I stated, then added hastily, "as I know you have, too. And I thought it could be beneficial to both of us if we pooled our information."

"You are really some piece of work, you know that, Mrs. Shapiro?" The words might not have sounded too encouraging, but they were said with a kind of reluctant admiration. "Okay. What is it you want to know?" He was using the same exasperated tone he'd always affected with me.

"The last time, you mentioned you'd checked out Selena Warren's alibi."

"We did. American confirms that a Mrs. Selena Warren flew to Chicago with them on the afternoon of the twenty-first. She returned the thirtieth on the seven a.m. out of O'Hare, which landed at LaGuardia just after ten-thirty New York time—hours after her boyfriend got himself dead. You're barking up the wrong tree with that lady, Dez. She really loved the guy."

"Seems so. By the way, do we know anything more about Constantine's estate?"

"We know it was pretty healthy. Aunt Edna did okay by him—left him a little over four hundred thousand dollars. So even if that's all there is, that's two hundred thou for Mrs. Warren, and the same for the daughter. But listen, you're barking—"

"I know. But look at it this way. The more mistakes I make, the more superior you can feel."

"You got something there," Fielding replied, smiling broadly.

"Say, did you ever find out if anything was stolen from the apartment?"

"We did, and it wasn't."

"I'm not surprised. I suppose you looked into everyone else's alibi?"

"Yep. The mother and the daughter were at a movie, and the kid spent the night at her mother's. The doorman confirms they got home around midnight and neither of them went out again. Incidentally, what did you think of little Alma?"

"I know she doesn't act too heartbroken about her father's murder, but you've got to remember that Constantine walked out on his family when she was only about eight years old. She grew up feeling he'd abandoned her."

"I'm not talking about that. I'm talking about what a little slob she is. If she was my kid, I'd throw her in a tub of water and use a can of Ajax on her."

"You checked out the other alibis, too?" I prodded, anxious to get him back on track. I had to find out what he knew that I didn't.

Fielding responded by cowering theatrically. "Okay, okay, Simon Legree, sir. Let's see. The business partner claims he was at some local restaurant until two a.m. But that doesn't hold up, since the place closed at twelve. Which means he's a possibility. And Jack Warren says he was home alone all night. So he's also a possibility."

"That's pretty much where I am, too." I wasn't about to disillusion Tim on Louise and Alma. At least, not until I was a little further along with that angle myself. "What about the ballistics report?"

"What *about* the ballistics report?" he countered.

"Was it the same gun that killed Mrs. Garrity?"

"Negative. But you know, Dez, it's not out of the question that we have two unrelated murders here."

"You don't really believe that any more than I do."

"I don't know *what* I believe at this stage of the investigation. We'll just have to wait and see how everything shakes out, won't we? Say, you did mention *sharing* information, didn't you?"

"Yes, I did."

"Well?"

So I proceeded to tell Fielding about Jerry and our new fingerprints-on-the-refrigerator-door theory.

"You call that sharing? You're really a pisser, you know that?"

"You have to admit it's plausible, don't you?"

"You want to know what's plausible? It's plausible that your client—who isn't too swift anyway—spent all his time in the cooler trying to come up with some shit he was hoping would get us off his back."

"But it *is* possible, isn't it?"

"Sure. *Anything* is possible, including the kid offing the old lady, just like we figured in the first place."

"Oh, come on."

"Don't 'come on' me, Dez. So far, I haven't learned anything to make me change my mind. As far as I'm concerned, your client is still the number one suspect in the Garrity killing. And he'll continue to be number one until a tie-in between the two murders is established. If there *is* a tie-in."

"You're not serious, are you?"

"You better believe I am. And another thing, the next time you come in here with the proposition we share information, I'm gonna make sure you go first."

I was walking out the door as Walter Corcoran was coming in. Judging from the spots on the brown paper bag he was carrying, my favorite cop had just dropped a few bucks at the local greasy spoon.

"Well, if it isn't Desiree Shapiro, the world's A-number-one pain in the ass."

"Happy Wednesday to you, too. And may your supper provide you with all the heartburn you so richly deserve."

Chapter 21

As soon as I left the precinct, I went looking for a working pay phone, which in New York City can be like the quest for the Holy Grail. After four clunkers—two of which ate my quarter—the search paid off.

I dialed Louise Constantine's apartment building. Somebody named Arthur told me Englehardt would be taking his regular eleven o'clock shift that night. At least, as far as Arthur knew.

It was only a little past 6:00—five hours to Englehardt. I took a taxi to my apartment, picked up my shopping cart, and headed for D'Agostino's. An hour later, I was back home with a cartful of survival essentials: eggs, milk, juice, coffee, soda, tuna, chicken, three kinds of cheeses, two kinds of pasta, salad fixings, ground round, frozen pizza, and Häagen-Dazs macadamia brittle.

Just as I'd finished unpacking everything, my neighbor Harriet came in to borrow some cornstarch. She wound up staying for close to an hour so she could fill me in on how great her kid was doing in college, then ran across the hall to get some recent snapshots that were supposed to show me how handsome he'd gotten since the summer. When she finally left, I decided I'd better not waste any time in appeasing my stomach, which had become embarrassingly demanding during Harriet's visit. I wasn't in the mood to even make myself a sandwich by then, so I went downstairs, intending to grab a bite at this neighborhood coffee shop I often frequent when I'm too tired or too lazy to fend for myself.

A charming-looking little Italian restaurant came between me and my coffee shop.

I'd noticed the place in passing for a couple of months now, but this time I stopped to read the menu. The prices appealed to me. Then, when I peered inside, so did the homey checked tablecloths and the Chianti-bottle candleholders. Somehow—maybe because I was so hungry—I didn't take much note of the fact that the place was almost empty. Only that the four people eating there were all smiling.

It must have been gas.

After a wilted salad, rubbery veal piccata, and leaden cheesecake, I was prepared to take on the formidable Englehardt.

He favored me with a frosty smile when I presented myself at the building and held the outer door open for me. "How are you tonight, ma'am?" he recited disinterestedly, tipping his hand to his cap.

Now, whoever came up with that dumb adage about words—or was it names?—never hurting you didn't know beans. A word like *ma'am* can make a woman shrivel up inside. (Vow: I would *not* go home tonight and scrutinize my wrinkles.)

I managed a smile that had about as much warmth as Englehardt's. "I don't know if you remember me," I said.

"Sure, I do. You asked me some questions about Mrs. Constantine last week. Is she expectin' you tonight?" He started to turn toward the house phone, then hesitated, no doubt because of the hour.

"No, she isn't. I came to see you."

If he was at all disturbed by this revelation, it didn't show. "What can I do for you, ma'am?"

"You can tell me why you lied to provide Mrs. Constantine and her daughter with an alibi for the night of her husband's murder."

"I didn't lie. What I said's how it was. Mrs. Constantine and the young lady come back here around midnight and stayed in the whole night. That's how it was," he reiterated, setting his jaw firmly in place and looking me straight in the eye. I had to give the man credit; he was a damn good liar.

"I don't know what she's paying you, but—"

Englehardt broke in, his eyes flashing and his face turning a shade very close to magenta. "Now, just a—"

"I don't know what she's paying you," I repeated loudly, overriding his protest. "Whatever it is, though, it couldn't possibly be enough. Do you know the penalty for obstructing justice?"

"I didn't do no such thing." His tone retained its authority, but his gaze waivered. He opened the doors for an elderly couple entering the building and, as soon as they were out of earshot, continued his denial. "She didn't pay me nuthin'. What I told you's the Gospel truth."

"I have evidence that says different. Which means you could be in very serious trouble."

"How many times I got to say it? I'm not lyin'."

"You could even be held as an accessory after the fact."

"It was the way I said," Englehardt maintained in a voice that was rapidly losing its bravado.

I wracked my brain for another legal threat to cement my advantage and, after a brief pause, came up with, "At the very least, if there should be a trial and you're called on to testify, you could be slapped with a perjury charge."

"For Chrissake," he mumbled, more to himself than to me. "I don't need this." Then he swallowed hard. "All right. Maybe what I said wasn't exactly one hundred percent the way it was. Then again, maybe it *was* the way it was. I'm not exactly sure."

"I have no idea what you're talking about."

"This won't go no further, will it? I mean, I wouldn't want to lose my job."

I told him my only interest was in finding Neil Constantine's murderer. "Unless you killed him, you won't get in any trouble. At least, not because of me."

So after a lot of preamble—consisting mainly of his insistence that he was only trying to keep his job and the extraction of numerous assurances from me not to betray him to management—Englehardt finally admitted to a little drinking problem. His boss, he told me between sucks on his lower lip, had threatened to fire him if he came to work "under the influence" one more time. That was months ago, and he swore he'd been watching his step ever since.

"Then, last Tuesday, Mrs. Constantine comes down to talk to me. She looks terrible, you know? I could see right away somethin' was wrong. I ask her, 'Anything wrong, Mrs. Constantine?' And she tells me as how her ex was murdered last night—in the early mornin' it was, really. And she says it's lucky for her I was on duty then. 'Why's that?' I ask her. Because, she says, the police are checkin' everyone's alibi, even hers. But seein' hows I got such a good memory and was so reliable, I'll be able to tell 'em how she was back here with her daughter by midnight and how neither of 'em set foot out of the buildin' again all night.

"I tell her I'm real sorry, but I didn't remember seein' her or her daughter last night. Well, she kep' insistin' I must of and I keep sayin' I'm sorry. 'Alma even spoke to you,' she tells me, 'and you asked her how's school.' Finally she says to me, 'You must of been drunk again or you'd remember. I'm gonna have to have a word with management,' she says, 'unless your memory improves.'"

"So you let her blackmail you?"

"What was I supposed to do, huh? I got a wife just got laid off and bills up the kazoo."

And to think I'd felt sorry for that manipulative bitch! "You know you should have told the police about this right away, don't you?"

"I guess so. But, like I been tryin' to explain—and I got your word you won't report me—I'm not one hundred percent positive it didn't happen like she said. I *did* take one drink before I came to work that night. Only one, and it was the first time since I don't know when, honest to God. But it was a healthy one, if you know what I mean. So I said to myself that maybe, now that I'm not real used to the stuff anymore, it could of affected me just a little, and I forgot about seein' the two of 'em. It could of happened that way, couldn't it? Besides, I was sure she wasn't the kind of lady who'd go around killin' people, so there didn't seem to be no real harm in helpin' her out some. Listen, you *did* promise—about not reportin' me—right?''

I assured him again that he had nothing to worry about from me. His coconspirator, however, did not share Englehardt's immunity.

Chapter 22

At 9:30 the next morning, even before my first cup of office coffee, I called Louise Constantine.

No answer.

Damn! I was itching to have a talk with that charming lady.

The rest of the morning was spent in going through the mail—which was mostly bills—and pushing papers around the desk. At a quarter to 12:00, I grabbed a hamburger at the luncheonette downstairs, after which I retrieved my Chevy from the garage around the corner and headed for Short Hills, New Jersey.

I pulled up in front of Blanche Newman's house a little before 2:00.

Actually, *house* is a misnomer. This was a mansion. A stately white Georgian-style building three stories high, it was set back on what must have been acres of beautifully groomed lawn. I followed a long circular driveway and parked to the left of the house, behind a new red Mercedes. Even farther to the left, at the rear of the place, I glimpsed the tennis courts. I wondered if the swimming pool was back there, too. I had no doubt there *was* a swimming pool.

"Dez!" a voice called just then. Blanche was standing in the open doorway, looking anxious. "I was afraid you'd get lost."

"Not with your directions." We hugged at the door, and I got a close-up of my friend's light brown eyes with their dark blue circles and the deep worry lines that pinched her mouth and creased her forehead. Five years ago, she looked ten years younger.

We walked into a huge two-story entrance hall that

had pale green marble floors and sculpture and arti-
facts set into wall niches. I followed Blanche down a
long central corridor until she stopped at an open door
and motioned me inside.

The room was large—maybe twenty by thirty feet—
and unbelievably elegant. It was, in fact, the most elegant room I'd ever seen, with Louis XVI furniture
(probably the real thing, too), painted wood-paneled
walls, and Aubusson carpeting. It was all done in soft
pastels of rose, cream, and green. Even the fireplace
had a rose marble mantel.

"I thought we'd be more comfortable in this room—
I call it my sitting room. It's more intimate than the
living room or the library."

I damn near choked.

"Have you had lunch, Dez?" Blanche asked when
we were seated, her hand reaching for a bellpull behind the sofa.

I assured her I'd taken nourishment.

"A drink, then?"

"Thanks, but I'm fine."

"Okay. Now, what can I tell you?" I knew she
didn't require any prompting, so I just let her talk.
Which she did for about ten minutes, reiterating what
she'd said during our phone conversation and going
into a lot more detail about Mark Newman's lost vir-
tues. "I can't believe this is happening," she murmured. "If you had known him then . . ."

It was time to give Blanche's narrative some direction. "I think you'd better tell me how Mark sets up
these late nights of his. I mean, does he just not show
up a couple of nights a week? Or does he call you?
Or what?"

"He always calls, but not until around five, to tell
me he won't be home for dinner that night."

"Where does he work?"

"Martin and Newman. He's a partner. It's in Livingston, which is only a few miles from here. Wait. I'll
get you the address. She stood up and walked over to
a small leather-topped desk in front of the window at
the far end of the room. For the first time, I took a

really good look at the whole Blanche. And I was stunned.

A tall woman—almost five-eight—she'd always been, well, not really heavy, but sort of full-blown. Now she was rail-thin. Her gray wool slacks could almost have accommodated two Blanches. And in the light from the window, I noticed the prominent bones above the vee of her white silk blouse, along with the now less-than-prominent chest.

"Mark's a stockbroker. Did I tell you that?" she asked, handing me his business card and resuming her place on the sofa.

"No, you didn't. Not that I remember, anyhow."

"I know what you've probably been thinking," she blurted out suddenly.

"What?"

"That Mark married me for my money—for all this." She waved her arm, a gesture meant to take in not just the room or the house, but all of her other financial assets as well.

"I wasn't thinking that at all, Blanche," I said, not entirely honestly.

"Well, I wanted to make things clear. Mark is a very successful broker. He has plenty of money of his own."

"I'll need a recent picture of him. Will that be a problem?"

"Oh, no." She almost smiled as she yanked on the bellpull.

In two or three minutes, there was a knock on the door. A short, chunky middle-aged woman entered.

"There's a photo album in the library. It's on a shelf to the left of the fireplace as you walk in—the second shelf from the bottom, I think it is. Could you bring it in here please, Lila?" Blanche commanded politely.

Lila was back in less time than it took me to open my bag, dig out my wallet, and slip Mark Newman's business card into it.

"As you can see, we take a lot of pictures," Blanche informed me as we leafed through the album. She stopped at a snapshot of a rounder, happier Blanche gazing adoringly into the pleasant face of a man about her own age. He was maybe an inch taller than she was and stocky, with thick, wiry blond hair. She stared at the picture for a few seconds, absently caressing it with her fingertip. "This was our honeymoon. Barbados," she said in a quivering voice. Her olive complexion seemed to have been drained of its pigment.

"I'll need a really good likeness of him," I put in quickly, in an attempt to move her on to more neutral shots and, hopefully, ward off the tears.

"This looks just like him. But maybe it's a little small?"

"Bigger would be better," I agreed.

She continued to thumb through her mementos, dabbing at her eyes and pausing often to explain where a particular snapshot had been taken and how happy the two of them had been then. I was about to settle for less than the ideal photo in order to spare Blanche—and myself—further anguish, when she came across a head shot of Mark that was obviously the work of a professional. "How's this?" she said triumphantly, already disengaging the photograph from the album. "Mark sat for this only about three months ago. He was chairman of some charity function, and they wanted a decent picture for a brochure they were mailing out. It's the kind of thing you were looking for, isn't it?" she asked, handing me the portrait.

"It's perfect," I replied, relieved to see Blanche closing her memory book.

"Listen, you *will* be able to handle this for me? I know how busy you are...."

"I wouldn't have agreed to it if I didn't feel I could manage. I think I've figured out a very efficient way of conducting the surveillance. I'll let you know the details just as soon as I've got everything all nailed down. Don't worry. You'll have your answers soon."

She looked so stricken at the prospect that I felt compelled to ask, "Now, you're *sure* you want to go ahead with this?"

"Of course I don't want to; I *have* to."

"Okay, I'll get back to you soon," I promised, preparing to leave.

"Do you have to go just yet? Can't you stay and talk for a few minutes? We haven't seen each other in such a long time. How long has it been, Dez?"

"About five years."

"Stay for a while," she pleaded. "I promise I won't get maudlin. Say, do you remember Carl Figeroa, the jerk Claire Wiley had such a crush on? He was in our French class, remember? Well, I ran into him at the Livingston Mall last year, and guess what?"

And so I let Blanche guide me on an excursion through our college days, which actually I thoroughly enjoyed. Then the desk phone rang.

Both Blanche and I automatically glanced at our watches. Mine said 5:08. There was only one ring, the call evidently having been answered somewhere else in the house. A short buzz followed a few seconds later. Blanche walked slowly over to the desk and, hand shaking, picked up the receiver of the dainty white and gold instrument. "Thanks, Lila," she sighed into the mouthpiece. She pressed a button on the phone, said hello, and proceeded to listen. Her entire contribution to the brief conversation consisted of a numb recitation of ". . . I'm fine . . . nothing much," and ". . . all right, see you later, then."

When she was seated alongside me again, Blanche relayed what I'd already gathered. "Mark won't be home for dinner. He has this important client flying in from Michigan who won't get here much before ten, so there's no telling what time the meeting will be over. I'm not to worry, though, he'll wind things up as early as he can." It was said with frustration. And anger. And utter despair.

I wanted to respond with something comforting, but I knew that whatever I came up with would sound impossibly Pollyanna-ish. So, for a change, I kept my mouth shut.

After a few minutes of silence and a lot of eye-blotting, Blanche was able to eke out a smile. "I'm sorry," she said, her voice normal again. "I guess I should be used to it already, but I'm not a very quick study."

"Don't apologize, for heaven's sake. I understand."

"Have dinner here, will you, Dez?"

"Thanks, I'd really like to, but I've got a ton of paperwork waiting for me at home."

"Please. This is the first time in weeks that I've been able to get my mind off things even for a few minutes."

I couldn't find the strength to say no again.

We ate in the breakfast room, which was larger than most dining rooms. The table was a festive one, set with a beautiful ivory linen cloth and colorful pottery dishes. The meal, served by the indispensable Lila, consisted of watercress soup, a soybean casserole that I will only describe as a fitting companion to the soup, and, for dessert, an Indian concoction called *galub jamon* that tasted like rose petals.

"Mark and I have been into healthy eating lately," Blanche stated proudly. (Now she tells me!) "Except for the *galub jamon*, that is. Tons of butter! But what would life be like if we didn't do a little indulging once in a while, right? You didn't finish yours, Dez. What's the matter? Didn't you like it?"

"Oh, it's not that. It's just that I had an enormous lunch today. But what about you? You've hardly eaten a thing," I countered, staring meaningfully at her plate. The dessert, like the rest of Blanche's dinner, was pretty much intact. "If you keep this up, you're going to get yourself sick," I warned.

"I'm okay. Or I will be. Once this thing is settled."

I left Blanche's around 7:00. As soon as I came out of the Lincoln Tunnel, I headed for Nathan's on 34th Street—and *my* idea of indulging.

Two hot dogs and an order of fries later, I was back in the apartment phoning Harry Burgess.

Harry's a semi-retired P.I. from Fort Lee, New Jersey, and an old friend. Through the years, I've always been able to count on him for a little assistance when

I wasn't feeling well or on those rare occasions when my less-than-flourishing business happened to flourish.

I explained about the investigation, and Harry jumped at the chance to help out. "Means Midge won't be at me for a couple hours," he said. "Don't get me wrong. She's a wonderful woman—the best. But Christ, that woman can find something for me to do every friggin' second of the day. She's got me painting walls and scraping floors and fixing things that aren't even broken. But you don't want to listen to an old fart's marriage problems. You just tell me what you want me to do."

We worked it out so Harry would cover Mark Newman's office Mondays through Fridays from 4:30 on. Blanche would contact him on the car phone if she heard from her husband. If she didn't get in touch with him by 5:30, Harry could pack it in for the day. However, if she *did* call, he was to alert me immediately before following Newman to wherever—and whoever. Then he was to phone me again from the stakeout, and I'd take off and relieve him.

With Harry doing the legwork, I'd still be able to devote practically all of my time to my murders. Of course, it meant some restrictions as far as scheduling appointments. But I didn't anticipate any difficulties. I'd set things up early enough so I'd be free by 4:30, and I'd wait until the last minute to firm up any later meetings. Unless, that is, I got the green light from Harry.

The surveillance was to begin the next day, so I told Harry I'd fax Newman's picture to him first thing in the morning. He thanked me profusely for giving him the job, and I thanked him profusely for taking it on, and we hung up.

I went to bed as pleased with myself as if I'd mastermined a strategy of global significance.

Chapter 23

I faxed the photo to Burgess on Friday as promised. Then I called Blanche to fill her in on the arrangements I'd made.

"I'm so afraid of how this will turn out," she said when I'd finished explaining things to her.

"I know," I responded gently. "Look, who was it that said you have to pray for the best but expect the worst? Something like that, anyway." I reconsidered the advice I'd just tendered. "Well, never mind that. Let's just pray for the best."

"That's what I'm doing. And Dez, thanks again for spending the day with me. It helped a lot. I have the feeling the dinner menu wasn't exactly to your liking, though. You hardly ate a thing."

"Don't be silly. I had more than enough to eat last night," I replied truthfully, remembering with fondness the good stuff I'd wolfed down at Nathan's.

My next call was to Louise Constantine. This time I got her in. "We have to talk," I said, trying not to let the hostility seep into my voice.

"We've already talked. I've told you all I can tell you."

"This time I have something to tell *you*."

"Look, if it's about Alma and some song, then—"

"It's not about any song. But it is about Alma."

"What about Alma?"

"It's nothing we can discuss on the phone. We have to talk in person."

"I see." Long pause.

"Can I come by tonight?"

"I won't be home tonight." Another long pause.

"You can stop in tomorrow afternoon. About four-thirty."

"I'll be there."

As soon as I replaced the receiver, I started to psyche myself up for the call I should have made four days ago. The one to Bill Murphy.

As you may have guessed by the agonies I went through on Monday over getting in touch with Tim Fielding, the telephone is not my milieu. (Which can be something of a trial, considering how important phone contact is for a P.I.) I sat there frozen for five minutes, then decided I'd give myself a reprieve and put off the ordeal until I'd had lunch. But after half an hour of trying not to think about it—and being able to think of nothing else—I couldn't wait to get the damn call over with.

Murphy sounded delighted to hear from me. Which did not exactly reinforce my avowed objectivity.

"I have a few more questions I'd like to ask you," I said after some brief amenities. "Would it be possible for me to stop by your office later this afternoon?"

"I'll be tied up in meetings most of the afternoon, and then I'm off to see a client on Long Island at four. Say, do you like Italian?"

"Italian what?" I asked stupidly.

"Food. Italian *food*. There's a wonderful Italian restaurant I'd like to take you to. If you don't have other plans for lunch today, you could interrogate me over a good meal."

"I'm sorry, but I *do* have other plans." I was, I thought, firm without being rude.

"How's tomorrow, then?"

"Tomorrow's Saturday," I reminded him.

"I don't know about you," he responded, obviously amused, "but I even eat on Saturdays."

Couldn't the man figure out that I was trying to avoid seeing him in any kind of a social setting? I stiffened my back—and my determination. I was going to retain my professionalism no matter how enticing the carrot. I'd have to get him to talk to me in his office. Lunch was simply out of the question.

"What time Saturday?" I was apalled to hear this strange voice ask.

I got off the phone as disgusted with myself as I'd ever been in my life. I had to be a total dimwit to even consider having lunch with Bill Murphy! *Anything* I did to further my personal interest in another suspect could seriously jeopardize my commitment to my client. And do I have to mention that—intellectually, anyway—I wasn't really too gung ho about fooling around with a possible murderer? So why did I accept Murphy's invitation? Don't ask *me*.

I woke up at 6:30 on Saturday morning and tried for hours to will myself back to sleep. I finally threw in the towel at 9:00.

After a cup of coffee, which was all I could manage, I figured I might as well start getting ready for lunch. It was way too early, of course, but I just couldn't work myself up to doing anything else. As it turned out, I barely had enough time to put myself together.

I look a long, luxurious bath. Following which I splashed myself generously with Ivoire, applied my makeup—and proceeded to my first crisis.

It began with having to grapple with the same momentous decision millions of other women all over the world were undoubtedly wrestling with at that very moment: what to wear.

I finally settled on a gray A-line skirt with a coordinating gray and green floral blouse—and loathed myself in them. I changed to a navy silk V-neck shift, accessorizing it with the strand of seven-millimeter pearls Ed had given me for our second wedding anniversary. I just couldn't handle wearing the pearls that day, so I swtiched to a thick gold choker. It took an intense five-minute struggle to hook the thing. Then I came to the conclusion that it made my neck look too stubby. At that point, I decided it would be better to wear something that didn't call for any jewelry. So, what did I do? I put the gray outfit back on, cursing my insecurity. And Bill Murphy for being the cause of it.

But all this was nothing compared to crisis number two.

A small wayward clump of hair on the left side of my head refused to lie flat. Even after being bombarded with what, in my windowless bathroom, was an almost lethal dose of extra-extra-hold hair spray. In desperation, I combed some plain water through my hair and wound up with a headful of something very much resembling red mucilage—completely flat, except for that one miserable clump, of course. I got out my wig, which also required a bit of taming but which, praise the Lord, eventually responded to the persuasion of extra-extra-hold.

It was 10 to 12:00 before I left the apartment, which gave me exactly ten minutes to make it from East 82nd Street to West 51st by noon—normally close to a half hour cab trip. Fortunately, I was able to hail a taxi as soon as I got downstairs, and—because it was Saturday and traffic was light—I showed up at the restaurant only about five minutes late.

Murphy was already at the table, having a glass of beer. He stood up to greet me, and for a breath-catching split second I got the idea that he was going to kiss me. But either he had second thoughts or I was engaging in a little wishful thinking, because we ended up shaking hands. (Mine, I'm afraid, was disgustingly clammy.)

Bill Murphy looked—as the kids would say—"hot." He was dressed casually, but not *too* casually, in a handsome camel-hair sport jacket, dark brown slacks, and a white dress shirt, open at the throat. If I'd had any hope that this meeting would straighten me out, I could forget it.

"I'm glad you came," Murphy told me when we were seated opposite one another in the comfortable, leather-upholstered booth.

I could feel myself flush. "Have you been here long?"

"A few minutes. I made sure I was here a little early. I didn't want you to have to wait."

Did he have to be so *considerate*?

He ordered a glass of chablis for me, then abruptly declared, "You want to talk to me about the time I left Shanahan's."

"That's right."

"That's what I thought. The police have already paid me a second visit."

"What did you tell them?"

"The truth. It was an honest mistake. I'd just taken my watch in for repairs that day, so I had no idea of the time. And when Coral said they were closing soon and asked if I wanted another drink, well, she does that every night. It never dawned on me they were closing so much earlier that night."

"Did you see anyone you knew after you left Shanahan's? Maybe someone in your building?"

"Afraid not. There wasn't a soul around."

"What about the doorman?"

"We only have one part-time. There was no one on then. But I give you my word, I went straight home—and stayed there all night. And honestly, Dez, until the police so kindly informed me of my error, I was under the impression it was two a.m. when I left Shanahan's. Just as I told you." The gray eyes probed for a clue to my reaction. "You don't look like you believe me."

No matter how it was phrased, I knew Murphy was asking me a question. And I didn't have an answer for him. I hadn't even had time to think about it.

"Did the police believe you?" I asked noncommittally.

"They didn't say, but I doubt it. The two cops that came to see me both had your look on their faces—the one you're wearing now. But what *they* think isn't that important; I care about what *you* think."

I felt the blood rush to my face again. And I wasn't too pleased with the way some other parts of my anatomy were behaving, either. I covered up my embarrassment by assuming my most professional voice. "And later, when you came home, didn't you notice the time then?"

"No. I went into the kitchen, made myself some

coffee, and sat down to take a quick look at the newspaper—which I hadn't had time to read during the day. I don't have a clue how long I sat there. To tell the truth, I'd had a couple of beers too many at Shanahan's, and I fell asleep at the kitchen table."

The shamefaced grin that accompanied this admission made Bill Murphy look ridiculously young. And very dear.

"All I *do* know," he added, "is that it was close to four a.m. when I woke up and went to bed." The grin faded, and his voice grew soft. "Listen, Dez, I have proof about my watch being repaired that day. I didn't bother showing it to the police, but the next time we see each other, I'll bring along the receipt." He put down his drink and leaned forward, looking at me intently. "Tell me something. What motive do you think I could possibly have had? With Neil dead, how could I expect to get my ten thousand dollars back?"

"Maybe you figured you'd have a better chance of collecting from the estate."

"That's not very likely. I never had him sign anything. Neil and I were best of friends, remember? And you *should* be able to trust your best friend," Murphy pointed out, his face beginning to cloud over with what I would come to think of as his Neil Constantine look.

"There's still a possibility of collecting. Selena knew about the loan. Maybe she'll feel she should honor Neil's debt. Even if she doesn't, if other people knew about it, you might be able to sue the estate for payment."

"Those are good thoughts. But my lawyer—who's an extremely competent man—tells me my chances of getting the money back now are piss-poor. Fortunately, it doesn't matter that much anymore. Not that I'm happy about getting stiffed, you understand. But I just don't have the same urgent need for funds that I did a few months ago."

"You had another motive, too," I reminded him. "You hated the man."

"You've got me there. But I didn't hate him enough

to kill him. Besides, I'm just not the killer type. That's something I'd like you to accept on faith." Murphy's Neil Constantine look had vanished, replaced by a kind of wistfulness that made him seem as vulnerable as I felt.

He suggested we order lunch then, and the nature of our conversation changed. Murphy talked about his agency and related a hilarious anecdote about one of his more eccentric clients. And I entertained him with this case I once had in which this woman hired me to find her missing Siamese cat, which led to my discovering that her crippled husband—he was in a wheelchair—had been cheating on her with the woman who abducted the cat. It was really wild! But I'll tell you about that later. . . .

The lunch—as I'd been promised on the phone—was delicious. But I was too nervous to do it justice. (So nervous, in fact, that I skipped dessert!) Over coffee, I learned that Murphy had been married once years ago. He didn't say whether he was a widower or the marriage had ended in divorce, and somehow I managed not to ask. *Plus* I refrained from trying to work his girlfriend into the conversation. Which, believe me, took a lot of refraining.

When I left Murphy that day, I was even more attracted to him than I'd been before. And even more conscience-stricken about allowing it to happen.

I had to do *something* to reaffirm my responsibility to Jerry, *something* to remind me whose side I was on. So from the restaurant, I took a cab to Martinez's store.

It hurt to see all that hope reflected in Sal Martinez's face when he saw me coming through the door.

"You got some news?" he asked eagerly.

"Nothing we can bank on yet, but I wanted to let you know what's been happening. Is Jerry around?"

"You jus' miss heem. He got three, four deliveries to make."

"You bring him up to date for me then, okay?"

"Yeah, sure."

I tried to make things a little rosier than the reality. "I've managed to break the alibis of three of the suspects in Neil Constantine's murder. Which means there are at least four people who had the motive and the opportunity to kill him. And there's not a doubt in my mind that the person who shot Constantine killed Mrs. Garrity, too." I didn't mention—and I was hoping Martinez wouldn't realize—that by increasing the number of suspects, I had complicated my job considerably.

"The cops think it was the same one, too?"

"I'm not sure *what* they think. They claim that until a connection between the two deaths is established, Jerry's still the prime suspect in the Garrity killing. But frankly, I don't believe they really feel that way."

"Yeah, well, anyhow, Deseeray, you gotta fin' them that connection, right?"

"Right. But look, Sal, there's something you should know. As of now, I have absolutely no idea who committed the murders. None. I don't know how long you expected the investigation to go on—these things *do* take time. . . . What I'm trying to say is, if you're not satisfied with how things are going and you'd prefer to have someone else handling it, I'd understand."

"Hey, why you talkin' like that? Nobody say you hab to fin' the killer the firs' day. I don' wanna get no other P.I. I know you workin' hard on thees an' that you care about Jerry, jus' like me, an' that you gonna fin' the one who done it. Maybe you not gonna fin' heem tomorrow, but you gonna fin' heem."

Well, this was a switch—Martinez reassuring me. I was very touched.

To be honest, though, I'd have continued my investigation even if he'd taken me off the case. Even, in fact, if it cost *me* money.

Chapter 24

On the way up in the elevator, my anger at Louise Constantine replenished itself. I tried hard to supress it. I thought about how much in love she'd been with her ex-husband. (I had no doubt she was leveling with me about *that.*) If she wasn't his killer—and maybe even if she was—she had to be genuinely distraught over his death. And apparently she was also fearful she'd be accused of his murder. Plus, it was only natural she'd want to protect her daughter. But as much as I could sympathize with the woman's trauma, I despised her methods. She'd actually terrorized that poor soul downstairs!

I rang the doorbell with the zeal of an avenging angel.

Louise was dressed in a plain light yellow shift that did absolutely nothing to enhance her pale blond good looks or her slim figure. I wondered that her artist husband hadn't had more of an influence on her sense of color and line. "Now, what's this about Alma?" the flat voice demanded before I'd even settled myself into the sofa.

"Your doorman has admitted that you blackmailed him into confirming the alibi you concocted for her and, of course, for yourself." I said it quietly, making a superhuman effort to conceal my antagonism and avoid getting thrown out.

"He's a liar."

"I don't think so. Not about that, anyway. At any rate, he no longer supports your story."

"The man's a drunk. I'm surprised he even remembers to show up for work, which, incidentally, he hasn't bothered to do very much of lately."

"I understand he had the flu."

"What would you expect him to say—'I was at some bar tying one on'? It doesn't matter, though. Alma and I were together all night, and we don't need some drunk vouching for us."

"Alma told you we had lunch the other day." In view of what Louise had said on the telephone, I didn't have to make that a question.

"She told me. She said you accused her of not having seen the movie, which I really resent. If you accuse *her* of lying, you're also accusing me."

I wanted to shout *Bingo!* but settled for, "Your daughter doesn't seem to know very much about a picture she's supposed to have just seen."

"There was some misunderstanding about a song, she said."

"There was no misunderstanding," I stated flatly.

"Well, I don't know the explanation, but I know there is one. Why don't you ask *me* about the movie?"

"That won't be necessary. I'm sure you saw it." I clamped down on my tongue to keep from finishing my thought with, *At some time or other.* I was equally sure she'd filled her daughter in on whatever she could think of. But obviously she hadn't thought of everything.

"We *both* saw it a week ago this past Monday at the Biograph. Just as we've been telling you over and over again. And anyway, neither Alma nor I had any reason for killing Neil. He was Alma's father. She loved him."

"Not according to her. She informed me herself that she'd always felt he abandoned her."

For once, Louise Constantine's voice reflected her emotions, becoming—for her, at least—almost impassioned in defense of her daughter. "For God's sake, how can you take anything kids that age say at face value? These kids all think being negative is 'in.' Besides, after all these years, why would she suddenly want to kill him?"

"Aunt what's-'er-name's inheritance doesn't seem too shabby a motive."

"Alma doesn't care a thing about money," Louise retorted quietly, her usual controlled self again.

"So you both say. And what about you? With your daughter inheriting, I imagine you'd have access to the money, too."

"I told you the last time. I wasn't aware that Neil had come into an inheritance. And it wouldn't have mattered if I did know. I don't need the money. When Neil dissolved his business partnership ten years ago, he walked away with a nice cash settlement, and he supported Alma and me very well. Of course, 'artiste' that he was, he couldn't be concerned about maintaining a decent lifestyle himself." The evenness of her delivery contradicted the unmistakable bitterness of the words.

Neither of us said anything for a few moments and then she put in, "And if you think I'd murder him because he got involved with another woman, you're way off base. I'm one of those cretins who never knows when to give up. Believe it or not, I still hoped to get him back." Two bright pink spots appeared on her cheeks. As in our previous meeting, Louise Constantine had exposed her feelings, and, as I'd seen before, her candor was short-lived. "Look, you're not the police. I don't understand why I'm even talking to you."

"Because you're concerned about what I might know. I'll tell you one thing I know. Your ex-husband had been somewhat short of funds lately, so you and Alma must have felt the pinch, too."

"For your information, Mrs. Shapiro, I made some wise investments when Neil left me. Between the income I receive from them and my accounting work—I became a C.P.A. a few years ago—Alma and I manage quite nicely, thank you. In fact, I haven't taken a dime from Neil in more than four years."

"Did you know that Neil gambled, Mrs. Constantine?"

"I knew. But he wasn't what you'd call a big gambler."

"He borrowed ten thousand dollars from Bill Murphy last year to cover a gambling debt."

"Ten thousand? Neil? Are you sure?"

"Yes, I'm sure."

"Why didn't he ask me for the money? I would have given it to him."

I didn't have an answer for her. But she didn't expect one.

"We were still friends," she continued sadly. "He could have asked me." For a moment, she seemed to forget I was in the room. I reminded her.

"Mrs. Constantine, I'm going to give you some advice that I'm positive you don't want, but I hope you'll consider. For your sake—and for Alma's. It's the same thing I told her; maybe you'll see the wisdom of it. Just because you have no alibi for the night of your ex-husband's murder doesn't mean you'll be accused of it. There would have to be a lot more than that to tie either of you to the crime. A *lot* more. But this phony story could get both you and Alma in big trouble. Especially with the doorman now admitting that he lied—that *you blackmailed* him into lying."

"I'll repeat this just one more time. Alma and I went to the movies that night, and by midnight we were back in this apartment, where we both remained until morning. Whether that drunk downstairs corroborates it or not."

I could see I wasn't budging her, so I left a minute or two before Louise Constantine would have gotten around to requesting it.

Chapter 25

It looked like I'd gone about as far as I could with this doorman thing. For the time being, at least. Maybe Fielding would have better luck with the Constantine ladies than I did, although I seriously doubted it. But, anyway, it was my turn to share.

As soon as I got back to the apartment, I tracked Tim down at home. (It wouldn't exactly endear me to him if he found out about the phony alibis from anyone else.) He wasn't what you'd call ecstatic at my news, though.

"So what you're telling me, Dez, is that I got two more suspects than I had yesterday. Great."

"I thought you'd want to know," I responded, a little petulantly.

"You're right, I do. Sorry. It's just that I liked things better narrowed down. But thanks for letting me know. I really mean that." There was a pause. "I guess," he added with a chuckle before hanging up.

Well, with all that had happened that day, I was too keyed up to be interested in dinner. But if I go without eating for very long I usually wind up with a miserable headache. So why ask for trouble?

I made myself an omelet, tossing in whatever I came across in the refrigerator—green pepper, tomato, scallion, Swiss cheese, Genoa salami, and a few sprinkles of parmesan. It wasn't half bad. Either that or I was hungrier than I'd thought.

It was only after I'd finished eating and was working on my second cup of coffee that I permitted myself to think about whether or not I believed Bill Murphy's explanation.

I had no problem accepting as fact that he'd taken his watch in to be repaired that day. But to lose a full two hours that evening and not be aware of it? And not to notice the time once he got home? Come on!

But, on the other hand, when you're out having dinner and then sitting around and tossing back a few—and probably solving world problems with some of the other regulars in the place—it's not inconceivable you'd forget about the time. And just because I have a clock in *my* kitchen does not mean its de rigueur for the rest of the world. At any rate, that was easy enough to check. Wrong! What was I thinking? I was not going to go *near* Murphy's apartment again. Anyway, who says that if there's a clock in the room, you have to look at it? Still, it's a natural thing to do....

The man was definitely lying to me. But then again, maybe not. Could be I was bending over backward *not* to believe just because I wanted to believe so badly. If that makes any sense at all.

I felt the headache I'd tried to avoid creeping up on me, so I turned to the television for a little distraction. The pickings were pretty crummy, and I settled for *The Golden Girls*. The raunchy ladies were, as usual, talking about sex, with Blanche spouting something positively outrageous and Sophia coming back with a gem that, even these days, I didn't know you could get away with on TV....

I woke up at 8:00 in the morning with the television blaring away. Half of me was hanging precariously over the sofa, and my neck was twisted at a ridiculous angle and hurt like hell when I tried straightening it out. I couldn't believe I'd slept through the entire night like this! Especially since I hadn't felt the least bit tired. I guess I'd been pretty desperate to escape for a while and keep myself from driving myself crazy. No doubt I'd also had it with *The Golden Girls*.

After a warm shower and some breakfast, I decided there was a good chance Ellen would be up by now. Anyway, I'd waited as long as I could.

"Well?" I demanded when she picked up the phone.

"Aunt Dez?"

"Mm-hmm."

"I was just going to call you. I wasn't sure you'd be up yet."

"And I was afraid I'd wake *you*."

"Oh, no. I didn't sleep too well last night. I've been up for hours."

"Well, tell me."

"It was wonderful. *He's* wonderful."

"Where did you go?"

"First, we had dinner in the Village, a *really* nice Italian place—Ennio and Michael's, it's called. They have the best Veal Sorrentino. That's veal with—"

I cut her short. "Okay, you can tell me the menu later. Get to the good part."

"Aunt Dez!" Ellen admonished.

"Just kidding. What did you do after dinner?"

"We went to see *Pretty Woman*. You should go one day. It's adorable."

"And then?"

"And then we went back to Herb's place for a little while. He has the most gorgeous two-bedroom co-op on East Seventy-second Street."

"Uh-*huh*."

"No, I *did not*."

"Did I ask you that?"

"Well, that's what you meant."

"When are you seeing him again?"

"Wednesday night. We're going to Caroline's. You know, the comedy club. What's been happening with the investigation?"

"You were right about the doorman," I said, bringing her quickly up to date. "But I'm still absolutely nowhere," I finished, whining in my most unattractive manner.

"Don't worry, Aunt Dez, you'll solve those murders."

The really special thing is that Ellen believes what she says.

I spent the rest of the morning typing up my notes of the last couple of days and most of the afternoon cleaning up the apartment. (Charmaine was AWOL again.) In the evening I had dinner with Stuart, after which we rushed downtown to catch an off-Broadway show that is very likely the worst play I've ever almost seen. We both knew it was a disaster within the first ten minutes, but in deference to the actors, we hung in until intermission.

There was a coffee shop around the corner from the playhouse, and since we'd skipped dessert in order not to be a second late for this glorious evening of theatuh, we stopped in for some pie and coffee. For almost an hour, we sat around discussing the mental aberrations of the playwright, the incompetence of the director, and the stupidity of the producer. Then Stuart asked how the investigation was going.

"It's not," I said, a little annoyed at being reminded of my albatross on one of the few occasions I was actually managing to ignore it for a couple of hours.

"You know what I find, Dez? Sometimes it really helps to get away for a few days. Lets you clear your mind and get a different perspective on things. You're just too close to everything right now."

"You may be right. But I can't afford the time. Besides, I wouldn't know where to go. And even if I did, I'd just take the whole mess right along with me."

"You're hopeless," he said, his voice revealing just a trace of annoyance. "Look, my brother and sister-in-law have a little place upstate they're not using right now. If you change your mind about getting away, I'm sure they wouldn't mind your staying there. I could certainly ask them. I wish I could go along and keep you company, but I'm involved in straightening out a very crooked estate right now."

"Thanks. I appreciate the offer. I really do. But the only way I'd be able to distance myself from this thing would be to leave my head back in the city."

"You might surprise yourself. It's so peaceful up there you almost have to relax. You could get in some reading. . . ."

"I don't have the patience."

"You could do some fishing. . . ."

"Yecch."

"Okay, then rowing."

"I can't swim."

"So take nature walks!" Stuart shot back, very close to shouting. Then, resignedly, "All right, you win. But I wish you'd at least think about it."

I promised I would.

I didn't go to his apartment that night. Somehow, I couldn't. I told him it was because I was just too frustrated and uptight about my lack of progress with the investigation. He said he understood, but I could see he didn't quite buy it. So, in addition to everything else, I laid a guilt trip on myself about hurting Stuart.

Chapter 26

I slept pretty badly that night. The last time I looked at the clock it was 4:30, and it was quite a while after that before I finally dropped off.

I guess I forgot to set the alarm. Or maybe I slept right through it. A wrong number woke me at quarter to ten. I literally dragged myself to the office, and I don't know why I bothered. I wasn't just tired; I was numb. I seemed to have the attention span of my neighbor Harriet's retarded Pekingese. By noon, I gave up even trying to accomplish anything resembling work.

"I'm going to a movie," I informed Jackie, whose eyebrows shot up almost to her blondish-brown hairline. "See you around three."

Pretty Woman was, I am sure, a very funny movie. But you couldn't prove it by me. Sitting there and trying to lose myself in the picture, I was more tense than ever. All I kept thinking was that I had absolutely no business being there.

When I got back to the office, there were a few messages to return and four walls to stare at. But, while I was still being totally unproductive, at least I wasn't trying to enjoy it.

Then, promptly at 5:00, the phone rang. "It's a go tonight," Harry Burgess said, plainly excited. "Newman's wife just called. She heard from him a few minutes ago, and he's got a late dinner with a prospective client."

"Good. Get back to me as soon as you can. I'll wait here for your call."

"Right. Talk to you soon."

Burgess's message brought me to life. Suddenly I could function again. I had a job to do, and, what was even more important these days, it was one I was definitely equal to. I sent downstairs for a quick sandwich. This could be a long night.

The next installment came at 6:45. "He just walked into a pretty swanky-looking restaurant not far from his office," Harry informed me. "I had a look-see, and so far he's alone at the table. I'll keep an eye peeled and let you know what develops."

At 8 o'clock, Harry phoned again. "Newman had dinner by his lonesome. He drove off a few minutes ago, and I'm right behind him."

The final call came at a little past 9:00. "We hit some traffic. But it looks like we're finally here."

"Where's here?"

Harry gave me an address in Brooklyn Heights.

I picked up my car, and forty-five minutes later I turned into a residential street in Brooklyn Heights. It was lined with well-kept middle-class homes, a mix of large one-family houses and multifamily brownstones. There wasn't an inch of parking space, so I pulled up alongside Harry's black Datsun. He got out of the car and joined me in the Chevy.

"That's the place." He indicated a one-family across the street, diagonally opposite the car. All the windows were covered with closed venetian blinds, but I could see bright lights peeking out between the slats. "A woman opened the door for our boy. Fairly young, I think, maybe thirty. She was all decked out in a long skirt. Since then, I've seen about six or seven other guys go in there, all of 'em pretty well dressed. The last guy, he had a woman with him. A real good-looker, too."

"Same woman always open the door?"

"A couple times I couldn't be sure; my view was blocked. But all the other times, it was the same one."

"Got any ideas?"

"I'm thinking maybe a high-class whorehouse. I was real tempted to check it out. You know, go over there and ring the bell and ask if I could use the phone. But I didn't want to do anything until I got your okay."

"I think it's a fine idea. Go to it."

Harry was back in three minutes.

"Same woman answered the door. I say my car broke down and ask if I can call the AAA. She says she's real sorry—very apologetic about it, she was— 'But,' she says, 'our phone's out of order.' Tells me there's a pay phone on the corner."

"Did you see anything?"

"Not a thing. I think she must have been in the vestibule. But I did hear plenty of noise. Nothing I could make out. But the place is really jumping. Want me to hang out with you till Newman leaves?"

"Thanks, Harry; I can take it from here."

"I really wouldn't mind. To tell you the truth, I'm kinda curious."

"I'd love your company, but I need your parking space."

"Yeah, I guess you do. Say, Dez, I didn't even have a chance to tell you how good you're lookin'."

"Aggravation must agree with me. But thanks. You look good, too. You put on some weight, didn't you?" Harry is so small and thin that when he worked for the police department half a lifetime ago, his nickname was "Splinter."

"I guess I gained about fifteen pounds this past year. I'm so bored, all I do is stuff my face. And you, my friend, look like you dropped a few since I last saw you."

"I wish," I said, leaning over and kissing his stubbly cheek. "Now get going so I can pull into your space before a cop comes along."

After Harry left, I put on a Bette Midler tape, adjusting the volume so it was just about audible. A while later, I poured myself some strong black coffee from the thermos I'd brought along. Not because I needed the jolt; I didn't. Every nerve in my body seemed to be standing at attention. But it was something to do. The car was warm and cozy, and after a few minutes I began to worry about falling asleep (although I hadn't felt this energized since God knows when). Just to be on the safe side, though, I shut off the heater. Even if I turned into a solid block of ice, there was no way I'd allow myself to screw this thing up.

During the next couple of hours, it grew bitter cold out. And at some time or other I completely lost contact with my extremities. Meanwhile, traffic to and from the house across the street was pretty heavy, with a lot more people coming than going. A distinguished-looking business type wearing a homburg pulled up in a cab. Ditto two younger men. A middle-aged couple arrived by limousine. And a number of people, evidently looking for parking, circled the block a few times before apparently settling for a less convenient space somewhere else. After a while, even Harriet's Pekingese could have figured out what was going on in that house.

Still, I needed definite confirmation. I got it a few minutes before midnight.

Two men were leaving the place, so I slid down in my seat and opened the window a crack—just in case. Fortunately, they walked directly past the car. "Like I keep telling you," the taller of the two lectured his friend, "craps is a lousy game. Why don't you listen? You have a much better chance of winning with black-jack. Do you have any idea what the percentages are?"

By then they were out of earshot, so I didn't get to find out the percentages. But I did hear—practically from the horse's mouth—what Mark Newman had been up to.

I wondered how long I'd have to wait before Newman called it a night. I was turning blue and my buns were sore. Also, I'd given up on the tapes quite a while ago, which left me with nothing to do but think. Something I hadn't been too successful at lately.

I went over my four suspects again—Louise, Alma, Jack Warren, Bill Murphy. There were reasons for all of them to want Constantine dead. And none of the four had an alibi. Of course, it was just luck—and Ellen—that had helped me see through Louise and Alma's phony story.

Which brought me to Selena Warren.

Some time back, I'd unconsciously removed her from my list of suspects, or at least from the "A" list. Which was dumb. Maybe the police had confirmed her whereabouts to their satisfaction, but, after all, they'd accepted the alibis of the Constantine ladies, too. As for Selena Warren, the only thing they'd bothered to verify was that she'd flown to Chicago the Sunday before the Garrity murder and returned home nine days later, on the morning of Neil Constantine's death. But how did they know she didn't sneak back to New York a couple of times in the interim? And, more to the point, how did *I*?

Sure it was far-fetched. But people have gone to much greater lengths with a lot less incentive. I put the girl back on my "A" list, where she would be staying until I checked things out myself.

Say, maybe Stuart *did* have something there—about a change in scenery giving you a new perspective. Of course, I wasn't exactly certain that freezing to death in a car in Brooklyn Heights would really qualify.

I thought about Selena again. Something she'd told me that morning at Frannie Eppinger's began to work its way into my consciousness, then retreated before I could grab hold of it. I remembered how, at the time, I'd made a mental note that it could be important. But I'd never committed the note to paper. And now, of course, I'd lost it somewhere in my head.

I felt like hitting that head on the dashboard, but I was so anesthetized from the cold I probably wouldn't have felt it. "Don't worry, it'll come to you," I assured myself. But I wasn't convinced.

Mark Newman left the house a little before 1:00. He was, thank God, alone.

It wasn't until after 2:00 that I finally got back to the apartment. I threw off my clothes and crawled into bed, too exhausted to even consider brushing my teeth. It didn't take long for me to fall asleep. Just long enough to torture myself for a few more minutes, trying to recall Selena Warren's words.

I woke up with a start. It must have been around dawn; the early morning light was already crawling in under the shade and insinuating itself into the room.

I opened my eyes wide. I could feel the corners of my mouth curve up in a smile. Now I remembered what Selana Warren had said.

Chapter 27

Blanche was positively ecstatic over the news that her husband was an inveterate gambler.

"To tell you the truth," I said, "when I saw him walk out of there alone, I felt like somebody had given me a present."

"You're a good friend, Dez."

"Friend has nothing to do with it. I'm a coward. If he'd been with another woman, I wouldn't have wanted to be the one to break it to you."

When we hung up, I remember thinking that there were times—although not nearly enough of them—when being a P.I. can be a very satisfying job.

A few mintues later, I made a call to a contact of mine at the phone company. She promised to get back to me soon with the information I asked for. I heard from her right after lunch. What she told me was enough to convince me it was time for another talk with Selena Warren.

I reached Selena at the art gallery. There was no problem in getting her to see me that evening.

She answered the door wearing navy blue slacks and a powder blue sweater that did wonderful things for her deep blue eyes and dark, shoulder-length hair. Outwardly, at least, the girl seemed to be well on the way to recovering from her lover's death.

"Let's go into the kitchen," she suggested. I followed her through a living room that looked really schizoid. New emerald green chairs flanked a tattered olive sofa. And a richly burnished sideboard sat on top of a threadbare, mud-brown carpet. The paint on the once-white walls was dirty and peeling, an unfortunate background for the many exquisite Neil Constantine florals decorating the room. "We were in the middle of redoing the place when Neil . . . when Neil was murdered," Selena explained, sorrow etched in her voice.

We sat at the kitchen table and, over freshly brewed coffee and an Entenmann's pecan Danish ring, I all but accused Selena Warren of murder.

"Maybe you can clear something up for me," I began.

"Sure."

"Do you remember your mentioning to me that you telephoned Neil from Chicago every night at nine?"

"I don't remember saying it, but it's true."

"*Every* night?"

"That's right."

"The phone company has no record of a call to this number from Chicago on Monday the twenty-second."

"They must have made a mistake," Selena said slowly as the color left her face. "Oh, I remember now," she amended brightly. "Neil told me on Sunday that he would be going out Monday night, so I didn't call then. I'd completely forgotten about that."

"Did he tell you where he was going?"

"I didn't ask him."

I decided to take a flier. "You were seen in New York that Monday," I improvised, with all the sincerity I could dredge up.

"That's not true!"

"I'm afraid it is. Look, Selena, I haven't said anything to the police about this. I wanted to give you a chance to explain first. I'm hoping it's something that won't have to go any further."

There was a pause before she replied. "Okay," she conceded. "I had some personal business to attend to in New York, so after I saw that my mother was all right, I arranged with one of those services to have a home health care aide come in and look after her until I got back on Tuesday. But what's all this about, anyway? Neil wasn't killed until the following week."

"Yes, I know. But Agnes Garrity *was* killed that week—between midnight and two a.m. on Tuesday morning."

"Agnes Garrity? I didn't even know the woman."

"Maybe not. But whoever shot Neil shot her, too."

"It doesn't make sense. I'm sure Neil didn't know her, either. What could her death possibly have to do with Neil's?"

"That's what I'm trying to find out. I'm going to have to ask you the nature of the personal business that brought you back to New York, Selena." I could see her bristling, so I quickly added, "I'm not being nosy. I'm trying to see if we can keep this just between the two of us."

"You won't go to the police?"

"Not if I'm satisfied your coming back to New York had nothing to do with the murders."

"All right. I came back to get an abortion. Don't look so shocked. Sometimes it's the only thing you can do."

"I'm not shocked, and I'm not judging you. Honestly, I'm not. But why didn't you just wait until you got back—or have the abortion in Chicago?"

"I'd already been to a private clinic here in New York. When the doctor examined me at that time, he said the fetus was too small for the procedure, so we set up the appointment for the twenty-second. I didn't want to reschedule. Not if I could possibly help it. I wanted to get it over with, and I wanted Dr. Peters to be the one to do it."

"How long were you at the clinic?"

"A few hours."

"And then?"

"Then I spent the night at Frannie's. She's the one who got the name of the clinic for me, and she went with me when ... when I had it done."

"So you called Neil from Frannie's that night, and he assumed the call was coming from Chicago?"

"Yes." It was almost a whisper.

"The baby was his?"

"Of course it was!" Selena snapped, furious now.

"I'm sorry. I didn't mean anything by that. I just wanted to understand."

"Even if I told you why I had the abortion, you probably wouldn't understand."

"Try me. It just could be important."

"I don't see how. It had nothing to do with the murders, either of them." She looked at me searchingly, as if my expression could help her make up her mind. "Oh, what's the difference?" she said with a sigh, directing the question at herself. After a second or two, there was another sigh. "It really doesn't matter anymore." Then she began.

"You see, Neil was always pressuring me to get a divorce and marry him. I loved him more than I've ever loved anyone in my life, and I think we would have gotten married eventually. But I wasn't ready to get married right *then*. And I certainly wasn't ready to be a mother. I knew if Neil found out about the baby, he'd insist we had to get married. And I just couldn't—not *yet*. So I did what I had to do." She swallowed hard. "You must think I'm terribly selfish and shallow."

"I don't think that at all. It must have been a very difficult decision for you," I murmured, my voice filled with compassion.

"It was," the girl replied, fighting to contain her tears—and losing. She put both arms on the table and buried her face in them. Her body shook with near-silent sobs.

"Are you all right?" I asked after a couple of minutes.

"I'm okay," she sniffed. "Sometimes I just get this way." She lifted her head and absently accepted the tissue I was holding out, mopping up the tears and delicately blowing her nose. "It's bad enough that Neil was murdered," she said when she'd composed herself. "And believe me, that has to be the most horrendous thing you can imagine—someone you love dying like *that*. But I have to live with this other terrible thing, too—something *I* was responsible for. The truth is, I haven't been happy with myself since I had the abortion. And I feel so much worse about it now that Neil is gone."

"Don't blame yourself. You—"

She didn't let me finish. "It's okay. It takes time, that's all."

"I'll have to talk to your friend Frannie, and I'll need the address of that doctor," I told her softly.

"I'll write it down for you," she agreed.

I pressed on, trying to be as gentle as I could but knowing there was really no way she wouldn't be upset by my questions. And no way I could avoid asking them. "There's one other thing I'd like you to straighten out for me."

"What's that?"

"On Monday the twenty-ninth, the night before Neil died, you made your call to him a lot earlier than usual—seven forty-one. And it wasn't placed from your mother's."

"I went grocery shopping that night. For my mother. I wanted to make sure she had everything she needed before I left for New York the next day. Afterwards, I had plans to meet a friend of mine for coffee. Anyway, I was concerned that I might not be near a pay phone at nine, and I didn't want Neil to worry—he was always worrying about me. So when I saw a phone outside the supermarket, I decided to make the call then."

"Were you anywhere near the airport?"

"I was at least three quarters of an hour away from it. Why are you asking me that? I came back to New York on Tuesday morning. You can check with American Airlines."

"I'm not disputing that you were on the seven a.m. out of O'Hare on Tuesday. But it's possible—and I'm just talking *possible*—that you also flew to New York on Monday night. If, for example, you got the eight p.m. flight to New York, it would have brought you into LaGuardia about eleven-thirty our time. You could have grabbed a cab to the apartment—which is a thirty-minute ride, max, at that hour—and, after . . .

uh . . . a confrontation with Neil, caught the one a.m. back to Chicago."

"And then what did I do? Turn around and come back to New York again?"

"It could have happened that way, Selena."

"That's crazy. You've got me flying back and forth all night. And for what? I loved Neil. You have no idea how *much* I loved Neil. The whole thing's ridiculous."

"I admit it would have taken some planning. But you yourself told me about all the trouble you had to go through for the abortion. It's not inconceivable you decided that two hundred thousand dollars was worth some trouble, too."

"But I didn't! I *couldn't* have killed Neil. He meant everything to me!"

"I'm not saying you killed him. I'm just saying that, logistically, it's a possibility. I can't in all conscience eliminate you as a suspect until I've checked everything out. I hope you understand."

"I guess you have to do your job," Selena responded grudgingly. "But in the meantime no one has to know any of this, do they?"

"No, they don't. Not unless it becomes necessary. I promise. I have only one more question to ask you. . . ."

She took it like a stoic. "Go ahead."

"Was Alma aware that her father had come into all that money?"

"I imagine Neil would probably have told her, but I can't say definitely. He didn't do it in front of me. Alma made it plain that she wasn't overly fond of me, so our contact was pretty minimal."

"And what about your husband? Did you ever mention anything to him about the inheritance? I'm talking about before Neil was killed."

"No, of course not. Why would I?"

"Are you sure?"

"Yes, I'm positive."

In view of Selena's loyalty to Warren, it was the answer I expected.

Chapter 28

Morton Peters, M.D., looked exactly like the Pillsbury Doughboy—round and soft and huggable.

"What can I do for you, Ms. Shapiro? I'm afraid I can only spare you a few moments," he informed me, the cherubic little face mirroring his contrition.

"That's all I need, Doctor. I understand you recently performed an abortion on a Mrs. Selena Warren. I just want to confirm that."

"I'm afraid I'm not at liberty to help you. A matter of patient confidentiality, you know. I'm really very sorry." The lively eyes looked down, too embarrassed to meet mine. "Believe me, I *am* sorry," he reiterated, staring at his pudgy, well-manicured hands primly folded on the desk.

"You don't understand. Mrs. Warren herself gave me permission to speak to you. I'm here at her suggestion."

"No offense meant, Ms. Shapiro, but I have no way of knowing that for a certainty, now, do I?"

He was right, of course. "Suppose I call her, and then you can talk to her and verify it."

He hesitated. "I guess that would be all right." He seemed to be turning something over in his mind. "Yes. That would be fine."

Luckily, Selena was in her office. I explained that Dr. Peters wanted her permission to give me any information and handed the phone over to him.

"Hello, Ms. Warren, how are you?" He listened, nodding. "Glad to hear it." A pause. "Well, fine. But I'm going to have to ask you a few questions, if you don't mind, just to make certain you're you." He tittered a little at how absurd the statement sounded, then added soberly, "There's nothing more important than protecting a patient's right to privacy, now, is there?" He picked up a pencil and began jotting down Selena's answers. "Your full name and date of birth, please.... Uh-huh. Address? ... Just a moment, please. No, I have it. Social Security number? ... What was that? ... And just when did we perform the procedure? ... Uh-*huh.* All right, thank you very much, Ms. Warren. Now, you take care of yourself, hear?"

Peters pushed back his chair and stood up, notepad in hand. "I'll be back in a moment." He returned three or four minutes later carrying a manilla folder. "It all seems to check out. So exactly what is it you want to know?"

"Just whether Mrs. Warren was here on Monday, October twenty-second."

"She was," he responded, without opening the file.

"Thank you, Doctor."

"That's it?"

"That's it."

"I hope you don't mind my being cautious. But I do think a physician must be extremely careful not to betray his patient's confidence."

"As a matter of fact, I respect you for it. I should have brought an authorization from Mrs. Warren."

The pinchable face was beaming. "Thank you for understanding, Ms. Shapiro," said the rosebud mouth.

Frannie Eppinger was expecting my call. She confirmed everything Selena had told me, adding, "I swear she never left the apartment Monday night. Besides, after what she'd just been through, you don't think she was in any condition to go out and murder someone, do you?"

I had to admit it was most unlikely.

Well, if Selena didn't kill Mrs. Garrity, then—according to the theory I'd been propounding for two weeks—she didn't murder Neil Constantine, either.

I mentally crossed her off my list of possibles. I was back to the same four suspects. Now, given my convictions, I probably should have found out right at the beginning where all these people were when Garrity was killed. I rationalized that I was very new at this.

Then something else occured to me.

I should preface it by telling you that Sam Spade is not the only detective I fail to emulate. I have also never been able to utilize my "little grey cells" in the manner of the great Hercule Poirot.

I thought about how the resourceful Poirot always advocated having a dialogue with everyone connected with a crime, the idea being that, sooner or later, something important was bound to slip out.

Well, it was certainly worth another try. After all, who was I to argue with Hercule?

The next day, I dropped in on Fielding.

I started off by asking how he'd made out with Louise and Alma Constantine. Just as I figured, they were still sticking to their alibi. Then I worked my way around to wheedling a copy of the least gruesome photo he had of Agnes Garrity out of him—which was the real reason for my visit. The picture would be my pretext for establishing contact with the suspects again.

I called Louise Constantine first. I told her I'd appreciate her taking a look at the photo to see if she recognized the old woman, because, I explained, Garrity's murder was connected to her former husband's.

"I'm sorry, Mrs. Shapiro, but I have no intention of allowing you to interrogate me a third time."

"It won't take long, and it might provide a lead to Mr. Constantine's killer. You *do* want the murderer apprehended, don't you?"

"Certainly I do. But I saw the woman's picture in the newspaper. And I'm positive I never set eyes on her before."

"Those newspaper photos are terrible. You

wouldn't be able to recognize your own sister from most of them."

"I don't have a sister. And I never met that old woman. Even if I did, how in the world would that help you?"

"Maybe you noticed her with someone else," I suggested. "Or maybe she made some remark that seemed very unimportant at the time but would have a different significance now, in light of her murder. Just let me come up and show you the—"

"Absolutely not."

"All right, then. But I'm sure you wouldn't mind telling me where you were between midnight October twenty-second and two a.m. on the twenty-third."

"I assume that's when the woman was killed?"

"That's right. It's just routine. We're asking everyone with a tie-in to Mr. Constantine." Fortunately, she did not question who I meant by *we*.

"I don't remember where I was. But more to the point, I don't see why I should have to account to you for my whereabouts."

"I only—"

"Listen, you've wasted enough of my time. I think I've been very patient with you. Probably a lot more than I should have been. But that patience has worn thin. Don't contact me again, or I'll be forced to go to the police and file a harrassment charge." All this without raising her voice even a decibel.

"Could you—"

"Good-bye, Mrs. Shapiro." She hung up in my ear. It was a good time to take a break and call Ellen.

"How was last night?"

"Oh, Aunt Dez ..." was the rapture-laden response.

"You've really flipped for this guy, haven't you, Ellen?"

"I think I may be in love with him," she admitted softly.

"How does *he* feel? Has he said anything?"

"Not yet. But I know he cares."

"I'm really happy for you. But promise me you'll take it slow. I don't want to see you get hurt."

"I will—take it slow, that is."

"Good girl."

"And no, I haven't," she said emphatically.

I made three other calls that morning, all to Alma Constantine. No answer. It was Tess who finally picked up late in the afternoon.

"Alma knew you'd be calling, and she won't see you," Tess told me pleasantly.

"I'd like to speak to her anyway. Just for a second. Is she there?"

"Umm ... it ... umm ... won't do you any good." She lowered her voice to an almost conspiratorial whisper. "Her mother's lawyer advised her not to talk to you. I'm sorry." For the second time that day, I heard the same infuriating click.

Jack Warren was, at least, willing to meet with me. "You can stop by the office and run that picture by me, if you want to," he suggested. "I'll be here till six or so."

I didn't think that would give me much of an opportunity to engage him in conversation, so I said I had appointments all afternoon. "But I could come by your apartment later. Would that be convenient?"

"I don't dare say no." He laughed. "I tried it once, remember?"

That evening, Warren was every bit as friendly and cooperative as he'd been during my previous visit. For the most part, anyway.

He looked at the old woman's picture and shook his head. "Nope," he told me, "but I was only in the building that one, very regrettable, time."

"I know. It was a long shot, but I was hoping."

"You said on the phone that the two deaths were connected? It's hard to see how they could be."

"Tell me about it," I responded wryly. "But I know there's *something* linking them together. I just don't know what it is."

"Yet," Warren amended gallantly.

"Thank you. You're right. *Yet.* I wonder if you re-member where you were between midnight on Monday, October twenty-second and two a.m. on the twenty-third."

"Is that when the old woman was killed?"

"Yes."

He screwed up his damned attractive face. "I'm sorry," he said, "I just can't think. It was weeks ago, you know, and I'm lucky if I remember what I did yesterday. Chances are, though, I was right here. I don't go out very much—just dinner and a couple of drinks with a friend once in a while."

"Well, if it should happen to come to you ..."

"I know. Give you a call," he finished for me genially.

He seemed to expect me to leave then, and I wasn't quite ready. "Could I trouble you for something cold to drink? Then I promise I'll get out of your life forever."

"You've got it," he replied, flashing that megawatt smile, "as long as you promise."

He went out to the kitchen, returning with Cokes for us both. As soon as I'd taken a few obligatory sips, I tried getting him to talk about Selena. It didn't require much effort. I opened with, "I saw your wife the other day, and she seems to be doing very well."

Warren was off and running. "She'll be all right. Selena's got character. I know you can't tell by looking at her, but she's a strong lady."

"You've seen her since the murder?"

"No. She told me she wanted time by herself. I've been trying to convince her to at least have lunch with me. But she keeps saying she's not up to it yet."

"It takes a while."

"I know, but I just want to help, if I can."

"How did you two meet, anyway?"

"We were college sweethearts. She sat two rows in front of me in Adolescent Psychology. I'd dated other girls before—lots of them; in fact, I was going with someone when we met. But the minute I saw her, that was it. I broke off with Mary Ellen the next day."

"Selena's going to be quite a wealthy young woman now."

"Yes, she told me."

There was no way to be delicate about what I wanted to ask next, but I did try going in the back door. "I guess that's the kind of thing she'd have mentioned to you even before the murder. I mean, to let you know that Cosntantine wasn't just using her."

"No, she never said a word about it until a few days ago." His eyes narrowed. "Wait a minute! I see what you're getting at."

"I'm not getting at anything. Really. It was only an offhand comment."

"Let's forget it, then," Warren said agreeably enough. But he got to his feet.

I'd about shot my load, anyway. "Thank you very much for your time," I told him. "I really appreciate your seeing me."

That night, Murphy phoned. "How do you like Chinese—and don't ask me, 'Chinese what?' "

I called up all my pathetically meager resources. "I love Chinese, but I won't be able to have lunch with you again, Bill. Not until this investigation is over."

"Don't be so presumptuous. I had no intention of asking you to lunch."

"Oh, I thought—"

He was laughing now. "Dinner was what I had in mind."

"I'd really like to. But I can't. I shouldn't have accepted your last invitation." My mouth felt like it was crammed full of cotton.

"I can't understand how your having dinner with me would compromise your investigation. But maybe it's because I don't want to. Tell you what. I'll call you the night you nail the killer, and we'll make those dinner plans. Deal?"

"Deal," I replied shakily. "Uh, I was going to get in touch with *you* in the morning." I gave him my theory about there being a connection between the two murders. "You mentioned that you might have seen Agnes Garrity at some time or other. Would it be okay if I came by your office tomorrow and showed you a picture of her? It's much clearer than the one that was in the papers."

"You sure *that* wouldn't compromise you? Sorry," he added quickly, "I'm being stupid. It's just that I was really looking forward to our getting together. Look, tomorrow's a pretty full day, but I can spare a half hour or so if you could be there by ten."

"I'll be there."

"There" turned out to be small but attractively appointed quarters in lower Manhattan. A young receptionist with an ample chest and a skimpy skirt showed me into a good-sized corner office. Murphy was seated at a handsome mahogany desk, his jacket off and tie askew. As soon as I walked into the room, he rose and hurried around the desk. "I'm glad to see you," he told me, imprisoning my extended hand in both of his.

"It's good to see you, too," I responded, hastily pulling away. Sitting down on a chair alongside the desk, I busied myself with digging the photograph out of my attaché case.

I'd expected Murphy to resume his seat, but he perched on a corner of the desk, not more than a foot away from me. As I handed him the photo, I could feel that insidious, telltale flush of mine creep across my face, sabotaging my valiant attempt at professionalism.

"Mrs. Garrity, huh?" he asked, examining the photograph.

"Yes."

"I'm not sure, Dez. I think this was the woman I saw, but it was a long time ago, and I only saw her once or twice. And only for a few minutes in the elevator. Is it important?"

"I guess not. I was hoping the picture might trigger something, that's all. By the way, would you happen to remember where you were on Monday, October twenty-second, say between midnight and two a.m.?"

"I need an alibi for the first murder, too, is that it? Let me check something." He walked around to the front of the desk and, sitting down, flipped through a large blue leather agenda book. "Here it is," Murphy announced, pointing to an entry in the ledger and turning the book around so I could see it. "I was on the coast—L.A.—from Thursday, October eighteenth, through Monday, October twenty-second. Trouble is, I was back in New York by eleven-thirty Monday night."

"That's when your plane landed?"

"That's right."

"Where did you go from the airport?"

"I took a cab straight back to the apartment. I remember the traffic being particularly heavy that night—an accident just outside the tunnel. I didn't get home till almost one. And, before you ask, I'm afraid nobody saw me. I guess that makes me a prime suspect in *two* murders now, huh? One where I didn't even know the victim." He smiled his silly, gap-toothed smile, and I noted with some sort of perverse satisfaction that you could drive a truck through the space between his teeth. But it didn't help at all.

When I got back to my own office, I reached the epic conclusion that life stunk.

It's really no picnic being incredibly attracted to someone you yourself might prove to be a murderer.

Chapter 29

Saturday night was a lulu.

My good friend Pat Martucci, formerly Altmann, formerly Greene, formerly Anderson, had insisted I join her and her most recent significant other for dinner.

We met at a Bangladesh restaurant in the East Village that had only one decent thing on the menu: the price. It was reassuring to know that although I was in imminent danger of getting ptomaine, at least I wouldn't have to pay a premium for it.

The company did nothing to encourage my appetite. While Pat happens to be an exceedingly nice person—caring and bright and forthright and loyal—she is also a colossal pain in the butt whenever she finds true love. Which, as you may have concluded, is a fairly regular occurrence with her. And tonight she was really outdoing herself.

This big, robust woman—who, if you stuck a blond braid on her head, would have been a perfect prototype for Brunhilde or Isolde or some other Amazonic Wagnerian heroine—was dribbling baby talk! Even worse, she and Roy, her cigar-chomping consort, were all over each other. Between them and the food, I had an almost overwhelming desire to throw up.

I kept telling myself the meal would be over soon. But when at long last it came to a merciful conclusion, I let Pat talk me into going somewhere else for a drink. I have no idea why.

The liquor, if anything, made the two of them even more amorous. I excused myself right after Roy put his hand down the front of Pat's dress to show me where she kept her mad money.

Now, normally I might have been a little uncomfortable in a situation like that. It's even conceivable I might have been amused (at least some of the time). But, that evening, I was truly mortified. I mean, where did an otherwise intelligent, both-feet-on-the-ground-type middle-aged woman come off letting herself get so completely gaga over a pair of pants!

I was upset for hours after I got home. But I refused to examine why I was taking my friend's romantic folly so personally.

That night, I dreamed that Jerry Costello was on trial for murder. The scene was like something out of an old British movie. The judge and both attorneys were dressed in powdered wigs and flowing black robes, and the defendant—poor Jerry—was seated in the dock.

The trial itself was short and disturbing. The prosecutor, to whom I did not bother to assign a face, contended that Neil Constantine was actually Jerry's father and that Agnes Garrity was his mother. Well, even in my dream, I knew this was completely ridiculous, so I kept waiting for the defense attorney, who looked suspiciously like Walter Corcoran, to make some objections. But, like Corcoran, he was totally useless. The judge passed sentence in no time. For his crime, whatever that was (and the only thing I could figure was his unfortunate parentage), Jerry was sentenced to hang.

At the hanging, the dream turned into a western. I can still see Jerry on the muddy knoll of this stark, endless plain astride a huge brown horse. His hands are tied behind his back, and the outsize animal dwarfs him, making him look heartbreakingly small and defenseless. A crowd of people is standing a few feet away, the men in Stetsons and chaps and faded jeans, the women dressed in ankle-length gingham with matching bonnets. There is a rope dangling from the one growing thing on the plain: a barren, misshapen

oak. A large man in a black hood fastens the free end
of the rope around Jerry's neck. Then I notice that
Tim Fielding is part of the silent, watching crowd. He
steps forward and comes over to Jerry's horse. He
strokes the animal's face and feeds it lumps of sugar.
After a while, he circles the horse, tenderly patting its
flank. He stops, and I think he is about ready to rejoin
the others. Suddenly he brings back his hand and slaps
the horse hard. It bolts from underneath the boy.
Leaving Jerry's feet dangling in the air.

I woke up with a start. My cheeks were wet with
tears and my hand was over my mouth, as though
stifling a scream. I promised myself that under no circumstances would I ever have Bangladesh food again.

I couldn't fall asleep after that. I guess I was afraid
I'd go back into the dream, and the last thing I wanted
to do was attend Jerry's funeral.

I got out of bed around eight and made myself a
large and satisfying breakfast—orange juice, apple
pancakes with bacon, and the kind of perfectly perked
coffee I am rarely able to produce. Then I moped.

The more work I did on this investigation, the less
I seemed to be accomplishing. I had eliminated one
suspect, but I'd reactivated two others. And my record
on the Garrity murder was even more pitiful. There,
I'd concentrated all my efforts on trying to get something on the wrong man!

Jerry would be better off with another P.I., someone
who knew how to get results. I had no business taking
this on in the first place. What did I know about murder anyway?

I would go and see Martinez Monday and tell him
I had to resign from the case. And, this time, I'd go
through with it.

Wait a minute. . . .

The police weren't any further along in this mess
than I was. In fact, I'd been the one to tell *them* that
Louise and Alma's alibi didn't hold water. And they
hadn't found out about Selena's returning to New
York the day before the Garrity murder, either. (And
I didn't see any reason they ever should.) When it

came right down to it, maybe I wasn't all that terrible at this.

But I still had to decide what to do next.

Unfortunately, I'd already tried Hercule's advice and come up empty. (And, to tell the truth, I was a bit put out with him for neglecting to provide instructions on what to do if two of your prime suspects refuse to talk to you.) But I wasn't ready to abandon him yet. There was one more area to explore.

I was going to speak to everyone in the victims' building. Maybe someone would tell me something they hadn't told the police. An image popped into my head of the finicky Poirot—with his luxuriant "moustaches," his sartorial grandeur, and his prissy little mannerisms—sitting down for a friendly tête-à-tête with that shining example of elegance and gentility, Sean Clory.

I laughed for the first time in days.

I decided I'd better get my hands on some photographs. I called Selena Warren. Did Neil have any recent pictures of Louise and Alma in the apartment? She said there were quite a few of them. And Bill Murphy? Selena was certain she'd seen some somewhere; she'd check. What about Jack? Did she have any good pictures of him? Only a couple of albumsful, she informed me.

I explained why I wanted to borrow the photos and persuaded her to go through them that afternoon and select a few of the best likenesses for me. "I could stop by later and pick them up, if that's all right."

"Why should you bother? I can drop them off at your office in the morning, on my way to the gallery."

At a little after 6:00 that evening, Stuart called. "I know it's last-minute, but I've been working at home all day—that estate matter I told you about—and I could use a break. If you haven't eaten yet, and you're free, maybe we could get a bite together."

"As long as you don't have Bangladesh in mind."

"I was thinking more of deli, if that's okay with you."

"You're on."

We went to the Carnegie Delicatessen, where we shared knubblewurst and pastrami sandwiches and ate all the kishka, cole slaw, potato salad, pickles, and sour tomatoes we could find room for.

After dinner, Stuart asked if I wanted to go back to his place for a drink. We wound up spending the night together.

While I didn't feel completely comfortable about it in view of my feelings for Murphy, I hadn't wanted to offend my good friend again. Besides, I considered my lovemaking with Stuart to be therapeutic. It was the only exercise I ever got.

Chapter 30

When I walked into the office on Monday, the pictures were already on my desk waiting for me. Selena had included three pretty decent photos of Louise and Alma Constantine, four of Warren, and two of Bill Murphy. I picked out one of each.

After that, I called Tim Fielding.

"*Now* what can I do for you?" he bantered.

"You can tell me what's new."

"I wish there was something to tell. How about you?"

"Ditto."

"Wait. I *do* have a piece of news that'll interest you. The D.A.'s office refuses to bring your client up before the grand jury."

"Don't tell me you're still after Jerry."

"You amaze me, Dez. You really do. I told you the last time that right now he's still our prime suspect in the Garrity homicide. But you seem to have a problem with your hearing."

"It's just so silly that I couldn't believe you actually meant it. And I certainly didn't think you were ready to look for an indictment. It's a good thing the D.A.'s got more sense than the police department."

"Whoa! I didn't say he thinks your kid is innocent. He just feels Constantine's death clouds the issue. Rosen—the A.D.A. I was talking to—says the grand jury will be looking for a tie-in between the two murders. Since they won't be getting it, we've got to come up with some very hard evidence against the kid on the Garrity thing. Which means your client's off the hook."

Before I could respond, he added ominously, "For now."

"You really can't see that the murders are interrelated?"

"I'm from Missouri. I gotta be shown. Remember, there were two different weapons."

"What does *that* prove?"

"It doesn't *prove* anything. But it *could* indicate two different perps."

"It could also indicate that the murderer was afraid to be caught with the weapon after shooting Garrity, so he ditched the gun. It's even possible that he—or she—had no intention of killing Constantine at that time."

"It's just as likely—maybe more likely—we have two *different* murderers. And, as of now, the Costello kid is our number one suspect in the Garrity case. And I'm not discounting that he could have blown Constantine away, too."

"Oh, come on. What motive could he possibly have had for shooting Constantine?"

"Let me ask *you* a question. You're sure there's a connection, right?"

"Absolutely."

"So what motive could the suspects in the Constantine murder have had for offing the old lady?"

"That's what the police should be trying to find out," I sputtered.

"Oh, no. Since you're the one who's so sure of a connection, we've decided to leave that job to you. *Especially* since you've had so much experience with homicides."

"Hey," I reminded him, "you weren't born to the purple, either. I knew you when you were refereeing domestic disputes and collaring turnstile jumpers."

Fielding laughed good-naturedly. "Touché. Listen, Dez, I gotta get back to work. But do me a favor, huh?"

"What?"

"Call me the minute you got this thing wrapped up." He hung up before I had time to zing him back.

I tried to concentrate on the positive aspect of that conversation. At least my client wasn't in any immediate danger of being indicted. But since I hadn't seriously considered that he would be, I wasn't terribly relieved to learn he *wouldn't* be. On the flip side, it seemed as though Fielding would be spending all his time trying to gather evidence against Jerry instead of searching for the real killer.

I shuddered. It looked like my dream could prove prophetic.

Just then, Jackie brought in the mail. There was an envelope imprinted with Murphy's business letterhead. Inside was a short note: "Forgot to give this to you on Friday. Bill." Clipped to the back of the note was a receipt dated October 29 from a local jewelry store. It was for the repair of a Movado watch.

Of course, the receipt wasn't exactly evidence of anything. Except that Murphy was definitely telling the truth about *something*.

In the afternoon, I began my canvassing of the murder building.

I started with Sean Clory. It took a while for me to convince the son of a bitch to even let me into the apartment house. "Get lost!" the well-loved voice shouted over the intercom.

"I don't have to remind you of my client's family connnections, do I?" I shouted back.

"Up yours. That shit's not gonna work this time."

"Will five bucks do it?"

"Twenty."

"You're out of your mind!"

Clory quickly aborted our negotiations. I buzzed again, but he was playing it cute. I kept my finger on the button until he picked up. "Get the fuck outta here, lady," he growled.

"Twenty," I conceded disgustedly.

He buzzed me in.

Even the $20 was no assurance of Clory's hospitality. "A double sawbuck gets you into the building, not my living room," he told me, blocking the entrance to his apartment with his large and dirty person.

I finally had to up the ante to twenty-five so I could gain entry to the inner sanctum.

Once he'd gotten himself a beer and sprawled out in his favorite chair, it wasn't hard to draw Clory into conversation. Not when the topic was Neil Constantine. "He was somethin', that guy," he said admiringly. "Ya gotta hand it to him. A middle-aged guy like that gettin' hisself a piece a ass like that Warren chick. Ya gotta hand it to him," he said again, his voice close to reverent.

I asked Clory if he knew the murdered man's ex-wife and daughter.

"Not exactly to talk to, but I useta see 'em when they come to visit. The wife, now, I ain't seen her in must be more'n six months; the daughter I seen maybe two, three months back." I got out Bill Murphy's picture. "Maybe. But I can't say for sure." I shoved Warren's photo under his nose. "Nah. Don't look familiar. The kid, though, she useta be here a lot. She was kinda cute when she was young, too. Hard to believe now, ain't it? Turned into a real slob, she did." He made this pronouncement solemnly, his bare belly hanging out from under his filthy white T-shirt. "Wife's not bad, though. A course she was a helluva lot better lookin' when she was younger. I'll tell you sumpin' about them real cold, stuck-up types. You get 'em in the sack, and bam!" His right arm shot straight out, fist clenched. Then his voice grew soft, reflective. "Could be she's hotter'n that Warren chick," he mused, his eyes glazing over with secret thoughts. I expected that any second he'd begin to drool. He belched instead.

"What time will Mrs. Clory be home?" I asked, trying to ignore the sound effects.

"She can't tell ya nuthin'."

"What time will she be home?" I repeated.

"Around five-thirty, same as last time," he informed me grudgingly, punctuating the information with another loud, foul-smelling belch.

"I'll be back. And don't try hitting me up for any more money for tonight."

"I don't operate like that. A deal's a deal." He was actually offended.

After Clory, I decided to see what I could learn from the tenants on the fourteenth and fifteenth floors. But the few who were at home had pathetically little to tell me. As I'd anticipated, even Agnes Garrity's immediate neighbors said they rarely saw her. And, while Neil Constantine had been a familiar figure in the building, contact with the dead man seemed to have been restricted to an exchange of the usual pleasantries. And only a handful of people recognized his family. As for Murphy and Warren, the photos of both men drew blanks.

Things looked more promising once I began talking to Dr. Max Ellison.

Ellison, who lived directly opposite Constantine, had known the victim fairly well. He had met Louise and Alma many times. And he was even acquainted with Bill Murphy, who, he told me, used to visit Constantine frequently. "That goes back a while, though. I haven't seen Murph in a long time."

"Murph?"

"Oh, we got to be pretty friendly," he said, smiling. "Up until two or three years ago, they had this regular poker game, and whenever someone couldn't make it, I'd fill in. Nice group of fellas. I enjoyed those evenings very much."

I spent about fifteen minutes chatting with the elderly doctor, who, I suspect, was lonesome enough for the company not to mind my incessant questions. But in the end I really didn't learn a thing.

At 6:15, I rang Ellen's doorbell—just in case. It turned out it was her day off, and she was home and hungry. We went to a little coffee shop in the neighborhood. An hour later, I was back, gently questioning Erna Clory. For once, though, her husband had been right. She couldn't tell me nuthin'.

I took the elevator to the fourteenth floor again and

spoke to one of the tenants who hadn't been home earlier. No luck there, either. Then I came to apartment 14B.

The doorbell was answered by a tiny, white-haired woman in her late seventies or early eighties. She asked me in, and when we were seated at the kitchen table, I spread the photos out in front of her.

"I know this face!" Mrs. Chartoff exclaimed, grabbing up Alma's picture. "I saw her leaving Mr. Constantine's apartment real late the night he was murdered. It was maybe twelve or maybe even one o'clock."

"You were coming home from somewhere?" I asked, my adrenaline going haywire.

"Oh, no. Just taking the garbage out to the incinerator. I don't sleep so good, so sometimes I get out of bed and have a cup of tea and a little piece of cake. I don't like to leave even a crumb around for the roaches," she explained, "so I always take everything out to the incinerator when I'm through. That night, when I was going back to the apartment, I heard a door open. I took a look, and there she was, coming out of Mr. Constantine's place. Big as life." She stabbed at Alma's photograph with her finger, her eyes shining with triumph.

"Have you told the police about this?" I demanded excitedly.

"No, she hasn't," said a thin, raspy male voice.

I turned around, startled. I hadn't been aware there was anyone else in the apartment. But standing in the doorway was a frail, wizened little man, a look of distress on the deeply wrinkled face.

He reached into his shirt pocket for his glasses, adjusting them carefully as he shuffled slowly over to the table. "Could I have a look at that?" he asked quietly, standing behind his wife's chair. She handed him Alma's picture, and he studied it intently for a few seconds. "Must be Sara's got this young lady mixed up with Mrs. Wilkerson's granddaughter—fourteen-F. She—the Wilkerson girl—comes here all the time to visit her grandmother."

"Oh, I don't see how it could have been a mistake, Lou," Mrs. Chartoff contradicted hesitantly, shifting around in her chair and peering up at him. "When I was coming back from the incinerator, I—"

"Sara, Sara," the old gentleman broke in, shaking his head sadly from side to side. "Don't you remember? You weren't even home when that artist fellow was killed." He turned to me. "Our daughter had another baby, and Sara and I flew down to Virginia to give her a hand with the older ones. We were down there the last two weeks in October." He placed his hand gently on his wife's hair and added so softly it was an effort to make out the words, "Sometimes she gets a little confused." A few minutes later, he walked me to the door. "I'm sorry, miss," he said. "She was just so anxious to help."

I took the elevator up to fifteen, where I enjoyed a touching reunion with the king of the canine foot fetishists. Philip, it seemed, was as enamored of my sensible, beat-up oxfords as he'd been of my gorgeous Italian-leather pumps. When, with a little help from the doting Mr. Lambeth, I finally managed to wrench my right shoe (which still contained my right foot) from Philip's mouth, I read it as a sign that it was time to go home.

By Wednesday night, I'd talked to everyone in the building and learned absolutely nothing. I was so tired, I was ready to drop. Worse yet, I had no idea where I could possibly go from here.

Thursday was Thanksgiving. Ellen had flown down to Florida the night before to spend the holiday with her parents. She'd invited me to join her a few weeks earlier. "I'd really love for you to come with me," she'd urged. "So would my parents. Mom wanted to know should she call you herself, but I told her you and I don't stand on ceremony, that I'd ask you."

"Thank you, Ellen. And thank your mom. But I'd better pass. I'm really so caught up in this case right now that I'd be lousy company."

"Ohhh, Aunt Dez . . . it'll do you good to get out of the house and be with family."

"Next year. If I'm invited, that is."

Monday night, at the coffee shop, Ellen had brought it up again. "I hate to see you spend Thanksgiving by yourself. Please change your mind."

"Remember when you first asked me?"

"Sure."

"Well, I was practically a human being then. I've degenerated rapidly. Honestly, Ellen, this thing has really gotten to me. I'll be better off by myself."

"Okay, if I can't convince you. . . . I'll talk to you on Saturday, then."

"Saturday?"

"I'm flying home late Friday night. I have to work on Saturday, and I've got a date with Herb Saturday night. And Sunday you're coming over to my place for dinner, okay?"

"I honestly don't think—"

"Okay?" she'd persisted in this don't-mess-with-me tone.

"Okay." I had figured it would be fruitless to argue. Besides, in the event I didn't slash my wrists after three straight days of my own unbearable company, I might be extremely grateful for Ellen's.

Now, I'm not saying that if I hadn't said yes to Ellen that night, I wouldn't have solved the case eventually, anyway.

But you never know, do you?

Chapter 31

Somehow I managed to survive the holiday and my own miserable disposition.

Ellen called early Saturday afternoon.

"How was Thanksgiving?" I asked.

"Good. It was wonderful seeing the folks again. And, of course, Steve and Joan and Aunt Minna and Uncle Sam. Everyone sends their love. What about you? Did you wind up doing anything?"

"Just sat around feeling like a total incompetent."

"Ohhh, Aunt Dez, how can you—"

I interrupted so poor Ellen wouldn't have to go through the tiresome business of reassuring me for what must have been the hundredth time over the past few weeks. "It's okay. I'm only kidding," I said, trying to sound cheerful as much for myself as for Ellen. "Sooner or later I'm gonna nail this scum," I vowed.

"Of course you will."

I smiled into the receiver. It was good to have her back.

"I'm so sorry you were alone on Thanksgiving. I was hoping Stuart would call at the last minute and drag you out for dinner."

"He probably spent the day with family."

"Well, did you fix yourself a nice dinner, anyway?"

"I sure did."

"What did you have?"

"A lovely ham." I didn't bother mentioning that the ham came in a package and went between two slices of bread. Before she could get around to requesting the rest of the menu, I changed the subject. "Are you excited about tonight?"

"I'm jumping out of my skin."

"Any idea where you're going?"

"Uh-uh. But it doesn't matter. I'll talk to you Sunday morning, okay?"

"You better believe it. And have a fantastic time tonight."

"I will," she replied wistfully.

I slept till after 10:00 on Sunday, and the call to Ellen took precedence even over my morning coffee. "How did it go?"

"It was great. Perfect."

"What did you do?"

"Some friend of Herb's who's with the U.N. had a small party, so we went over there for a while. I met the most interesting woman from Syria. She was telling me . . ."

Now, I'm afraid I'm not always as patient as I should be with Ellen's stories, so this time I forced myself to shut up and listen. Which probably served me right. I proceeded to learn everything I would ever not want to know about a woman I'd never met. And never would meet. But I kept quiet right up until Ellen began to go into detail about the Syrian lady's Lebanese escort. At that point, I felt totally justified in breaking in. "Did you go back to Herb's place after the party?" I asked without much subtlety.

"No, we came here for a while. I opened up that bottle of Grand Marnier you brought me a couple of months ago, and we had some of that and talked until almost three in the morning."

Before we hung up, she answered the question I hadn't asked. "No, I did not."

I decided to spend the rest of the morning catching up on my household finances. I was in the process of motivating myself to pay a few bills when the phone rang.

"I just went down to get a newspaper, and by the time I came back, the elevator was broken," Ellen apprised me. "I stopped in to tell Mr. Clory, and he said he'd already heard about it and the repair people would be here soon. But it *is* Sunday, so I thought I'd better let you know in case they don't show up. I wouldn't want you to have to climb all those stairs."

"Much as I'd like to come over, I'm with you."

At 4 o'clock, Ellen called again. "It's working!" she informed me happily. "See you around six?"

I quickly got myself dressed. On the way to the subway station, I picked up some Italian pastries, which Ellen and I both adore and which, therefore, neither of us considers inappropriate for Chinese take-out. (Knowing Ellen, I had no doubt the cuisine du jour *would* be Chinese takeout.)

It was just after 6:00 when Ellen buzzed me in.

I got on the elevator thinking—like the true masochist I am—about the same thing I always thought about these days. What was it I'd missed? There must be something. . . . The door clanked shut. I reached out to press the button, and my hand froze. Of course! How could I have failed to realize it in all this time? And if *that's* true, why, then . . .

By the time the elevator creaked to a stop on the fourteenth floor, I knew why Agnes Garrity had been killed.

Chapter 32

Ellen was waiting for me at the door to her apartment. "I know why Mrs. Garrity was killed!" I blurted out.

"No!" she shrieked, dragging me inside. "Tell me!" she ordered, gently pushing me onto the sofa.

I was bursting to oblige her.

"It makes sense. It *really* does," she said when I'd finished sharing my conclusions. "But who do you think did it?"

I had to confess I didn't have that little detail worked out yet.

"But you *will,*" insisted my one-person fan club. "I know you will. Look what you just figured out about Mrs. Garrity. But try to relax for now; I want you to enjoy your dinner. It should be here any minute."

Sure enough, within five minutes the food arrived. It was agreed that while we ate we'd talk about everything but the murders. Over the won ton soup, spare ribs, egg roll, and sweet and pungent shrimp, Ellen prattled on about Herb. He was merely the nicest man in the world. And one of the brightest. And, my God, was he sexy! (This last attribute accompanied by a giggle so kittenish that if it had come from anyone but Ellen, I would certainly have gagged.)

The more she went on about her Herb, the more alive she seemed to become. Until that moment, I had never believed that anyone could actually glow. But there was no doubt about it; my niece glowed.

After finishing every last morsel on our plates, we moved on to the moo shoo pork. "You didn't say a word about your niece and nephews yesterday," I remarked while trying to roll a serviceable pancake.

"Did someone do the world a favor and disappear them?"

"Ugh. No such luck. They were there, all right. You know, not because he's my brother, but Steve's a *really* nice guy and Joan's a sweetheart. I can't figure out how the two of them could be the parents of three such despicable little monsters."

"Careful," I warned. "You keep this up and you'll never get the 'Aunt of the Year' award."

Ellen laughed and went on to complain about how the kids had disrupted the Thanksgiving holiday. I swear I heard every word she said.

"Kimmie kept ramming the breakfront with her tricycle," she related. "Well, Steve and Joan were both out of the room, so I told her—very politely, too— that the living room was no place for a tricycle, but if she really wanted to ride it, then she should be careful of the furniture. The little brat hauled off and punched me in the stomach! Can you imagine? And Justin! I honestly think he's gotten to be as impossible as his brother. Can you believe he actually took a bite out of Neville? That's Aunt Minna's shih tzu!" She proceeded to describe the events that led up to the shih tzu's becoming her nephew's midafternoon snack.

Now, those kids may not have been good, but they were certainly fun. At least from a safe distance. What I'm trying to make clear is that I was really paying attention to Ellen's anecdotes. Which makes what happened next all the more astonishing.

"And wait till you hear what Josh pulled!" she was saying.

I never did hear what Josh pulled. Because—in spite of the fact that I'd been listening to Ellen and, at the same time, concentrating on catching the pork filling as it leaked out of a spreading tear in my disgustingly sloppy pancake—some tiny corner of my brain must have been reserved for other things.

"I know who did it," I announced.

Chapter 33

The proclamation was delivered quietly, which had the effect of making it all the more dramatic.

Ellen reacted expectedly. "Oh, my God!" she screeched. And, a second later, "Who was it?" And, without waiting for an answer, "See? I *told* you you'd do it!"

My heart was pounding so hard it threatened to break through my rib cage. "The only person it *could* be," I said in a surprisingly steady voice.

"Well?"

"I'll explain everything after we finish dinner," I promised, suddenly remembering I was holding a pancake when it fell apart and the entire filling plopped onto the kitchen floor.

"Oh, Aunt Dez. . . . Don't be like that."

"I've got to take a few minutes to calm down." I didn't add that, with all my insecurity and after so many false starts, I desperately needed to savor my success. Even if it was only for a little while.

We ate our cannoli and rhum babas and drank our Chinese tea in silence. (Which is to Ellen's lasting credit, since it is a terrible trial for her not to talk at *any* time, and, just then, the strain must have been almost unendurable. When, after about ten minutes, I pushed aside my empty cup, Ellen had clearly had enough of this temperamental little display of mine. "Okay," she said firmly.

So I filled her in on what had led me to the identity of the murderer.

"It certainly seems to fit," Ellen concurred.

"It couldn't have been anyone else, don't you see?" I demanded, anxious for her confirmation.

"Of course I see."

"It's so obvious, I can't understand why I didn't spot it right away."

"Because it *is* so obvious, that's why. You, the police—all of you—were looking for a complicated explanation. That's why everyone missed it at first. But I knew you'd be the one to finally figure things out."

"That's true, I guess—about our looking for a complicated explanation. I guess it *was* a case of not seeing the forest for the trees. You know, Ellen, I'm absolutely sure I'm right about this. But the trouble is, I don't know how I can prove it. . . ."

When I got home that evening, my mood kept zigzagging between elation and desperation. I sat at the kitchen table for hours, mostly staring into space, trying to come up with a way to convince the police of the validity of my theory.

And then it hit me: an absolutely foolproof plan for trapping the murderer!

I began working out the details. By the time I had everything doped out, it was past midnight. I tried the Twelfth Precinct—just in case—but was informed that Fielding had left at 6:00. I was too keyed up to wait until the next day to contact him. Suppose it was his day off? Suppose he was going on vacation? Supppose . . . I dialed his home number, hoping his wife wouldn't be the one to answer.

"Yeah?" said a male voice, gruff with sleep.

"Tim? It's Desiree."

"What's wrong?" he asked sharply, suddenly wide awake.

"Nothing's *wrong*. In fact, everything's finally *right*. I know who committed the murders."

"Sure you do. Look, do you know what time it is? Couldn't this have waited until morning?"

"I'm sorry. I was afraid you might not be in."

"I'll be in at eight. But I'll have to go right out.

Come by around three, and tell me about it then. Now hang up so I can get some sleep."

I was a little more considerate of Ellen. I didn't call her until 6:30. I could tell I'd awakened her, but she was gracious enough to deny it.

"Can you meet me for lunch?" I wanted to know. "I have an idea, but I'm going to need your help. I'll also need a key to your building."

"I'll have one made up this morning. Where do you want to meet and when?" she asked excitedly.

We met at a deli near Macy's at 1:15. It took a few minutes for us to get a booth, and as soon as we were seated, Ellen placed the key on the table. "Now, what do you want me to do?" she demanded, cheeks flushed and eyes shining. It was obvious she relished the adventure.

I laid out my plan, emphasizing the importance of her part in it. "Look, you're sure you want to do this? I don't see how you could be in any danger, but there's always a possibility something might go wrong."

"Oh, don't worry about *me*. Nothing's going to happen to me. It's *you* who's really taking a chance."

"I'll be fine. I told you about the backup I'm arranging for."

"Ye-e-s," she replied, not sounding too convinced. "But still, you're putting yourself on the spot. And like you said, something could go wrong."

"Hey, I'm an old pro," I countered, smiling.

She didn't smile back. "Just be careful," she warned when we parted, kissing me on the cheek. "I don't know what I'd do if anything happened to you."

On that cheerful note, I headed downtown to the station.

"You're early," Fielding pointed out when he saw me.

"Give me a break. It's ten minutes before three."

"Okay, sit down and tell me what brilliant conclusion you've reached."

At that moment, Corcoran walked by. "*This* I gotta hear," he remarked in his grating, high-pitched voice. He took a seat at the desk in front of Fielding's and pushed his chair back, swiveling it around to face us. "So give, Einstein," he commanded.

I looked at Fielding pleadingly. "Could we go somewhere for coffee?"

"Yeah." Then, to his partner, "Listen, I'm gonna cut out for a little while. Be back in about half an hour."

Corcoran snickered. "Damned if Miss Chubbette here hasn't got you on a string."

"Cool it, Walt," Fielding warned. He stood up and shrugged into his jacket. "C'mon. Let's go."

We were sitting in an uncomfortable booth in a shabby luncheonette about a block from the precinct. I ordered my fifth cup of coffee since the morning and Fielding asked for tea. "I've already had four coffees today," he said almost apologetically.

He waited patiently, not saying a word, while I spent a couple of minutes collecting my thoughts and (I admit) building up the suspense. If Fielding was chomping at the bit for my news, though, it didn't show.

"It was the damnedest thing," I said at last. "I was visiting my niece Ellen—you remember Ellen, don't you?—when the whole thing suddenly became clear to me. I mean, I figured out why Mrs. Garrity was killed and why one person—and only one person— had to have been the one who killed her."

"And who *is* this alleged killer?"

"I can't tell you that yet."

Tim's face, I saw, was changing color, and these little blue veins at his temples were bulging out. "You are absolutely unbelievable!" he exploded. "And I have just about had it!"

Well, I'd done it again: perturbed my almost unperturbable friend. But I'd really had no choice. It seemed I was forever saying I was sorry to the man. "I'm sorry," I said. "Honestly. But I'll be able to explain everything soon. Very soon."

"Just explain this. Why in hell did you wake me at almost one in the morning? Was it to get me here and tell me that you couldn't tell me?" The little blue veins were becoming more prominent by the second.

"No, of course not. I called because I need your help in trapping the killer."

"You need my help, but you're not going to say what it is you found out or who you suspect. Now, have I got that straight?"

"Yes," I replied shamefacedly.

"You got balls, Shapiro. Anyone ever tell you that?"

"I think you may have."

"Okay," he growled. "Let's hear it."

So, divulging as little as possible about the plan itself, I enlightened him as to the role I hoped he'd play in it. "I'm afraid to do this without you, Tim. I need you to back me up."

"That's beautiful. You don't trust me enough to let me in on the thing, for God's sake, but you're relying on me to maybe save your life." He shook his head wonderingly.

"It's not that I don't trust you, Tim. It's just that if I tell you who I suspect, and if for some reason the plan doesn't come off, you'll decide I was wrong; that this person I *know* is the perp must be innocent. And after that, I'll never be able to convince you otherwise."

"You're so sure you've got it nailed?"

"Yes, I am."

In the end, Fielding agreed to help. Just as I knew he would. Not only that, he offered to draft Corcoran into service as well.

I left Tim with the key Ellen had duplicated for me. After which I roamed the neighborhood until I found a working pay phone and had a brief conversation with Selena Warren.

Then, with wet hands and a dry mouth, I made my call to the killer.

"I've come across an important piece of evidence," I said. "And I'm reasonably certain it will help us discover the identity of Neil Constantine's murderer. Everyone who had any connection with the case is being asked to meet in the Constantine apartment at midnight tomorrow."

"Is this a joke?" The voice was both wary and impatient. "It sounds like something out of a late-night movie."

"It's no joke, believe me."

"But midnight? Aren't you being a little melodramatic?"

"I know it seems strange, and I wish I could say more. But all I can tell you is that I'm sure you'll be interested in what I have to say, and there's a valid reason for the lateness of the hour. Just be there at twelve, and I promise to clear everything up."

"All right," came the reluctant reply. "But this better be good."

Chapter 34

Tuesday was a miserable night, as rotten, I recalled, as the night of Agnes Garrity's murder. The rain was coming down in such torrents that I got completely drenched—even though the cab had pulled up just a few yards from the door of the building and I was carrying the one umbrella I owned that didn't have a single broken spoke. I rubbed my feet on the torn carpet remnant in the outer lobby and shook myself out as energetically as Brewmeister, my much-loved and long-departed German shepherd, used to do. After which a waiting and by now extremely jittery Ellen held the door open for me. It was 11:20.

I handed Ellen the envelope she'd need for her small but vital task. Then I got on the elevator and pressed 15.

There were a couple of bad moments on the way up when the car started to bounce around and then jerked to a stop between floors somewhere. But I pressed the button again, and the decrepit old relic got its second wind and made it to my floor.

I headed straight for the utility room and slipped inside, leaving the door ajar a crack so I could see out. Fortunately, one of the few lights in the poorly lit hall was only a couple of feet from my hiding place, so I'd have no trouble making out the killer when the time came. I opened my king-size shoulder bag, groping around until I rested my hand on the .32-caliber gun nestled reassuringly at the bottom. Not that I felt I was in any real danger, you understand; the killer would never know I was here until I was ready to reveal myself. Besides, Tim would be showing up pretty soon, so there was absolutely nothing to worry about.

Still, as the minutes passed, I became increasingly edgy. I shifted from one foot to the other just to keep myself occupied. And I constantly looked at my watch. Which made no sense, since the tiny room was pitch-black. Once, I felt something brush against my ankle. *A rat!* I thought, terror-stricken. Then, when I became aware that whatever it was hadn't moved, I took a deep breath, bent down, and felt around me. I had been attacked by a pile of old newspapers!

My relief lasted all of a second or two. What had happened to Tim? He should be here by now! I estimated I'd been closeted in my dirty little hideaway for at least an hour. Probably it was more like fifteen minutes.

Soon I came up with something new to worry about. Maybe I'd left a trail of water in the hall, which the killer could follow straight to the utility room. "You *are* an ass," I informed myself. Half the people on fifteen must have been caught in that downpour; the floor was streaked with mud. Besides, hadn't I wiped off my boots downstairs and then shaken myself till my brains rattled?

I can't tell you how many other things I thought of that scared me silly. All I *can* tell you is that I succeeded in making myself so crazy that, like the coward I am, I actually considered abandoning my post.

Then, suddenly, I heard a door open and close— the door to the stairwell, I knew. Footsteps came quickly down the hall. Moments later, a figure entered my line of vision, then moved on. The sounds stopped. With a sick feeling, I pictured the killer ringing the bell to a vacant 15D and waiting. And waiting. . . .

This was going all wrong! Where the hell was Fielding?

The footsteps echoed again, then halted abruptly directly opposite to where I stood quaking behind the door.

I pressed my eye tight up against the crack. I could see the puzzled expression on the face. I watched, mesmerized, as it quickly changed to a look of comprehension and, finally, to fury. The killer had figured it out!

But something else was happening, too. *The killer seemed to be sniffing the air!* I stared in cold-sweat panic as the figure looked cautiously around, then turned and strode purposefully toward the utility room.

Never have I experienced such undiluted terror. I backed away from the door, struggling, at the same time, to pull the gun out of my handbag. But it had gotten tangled up in the hairnet I carried in the bag! I could hear the doorknob twisting slowly, quietly. Very carefully, the door was being coaxed open. A heartbeat later, the killer stood in front of me, framed in the half-open doorway.

I looked into a face contorted with menace. "What is this all about?" the deceptively soft voice demanded. I was too terrified to answer. Or move. Or even think. Icy fingers gripped my arm and pulled it—along with the hairnet-wrapped .32—from my bag. "You think you're pretty smart, don't you?" the killer accused, wresting the gun from my grasp.

With that, I sprang to life. I swung the ponderous handbag into the killer's midsection with a force that sent my would-be assailant reeling. The weapon went flying. Flinging the door open wide, I started to run from the closet. "Help!" I yelled in that empty, tomblike hall. The killer, still off balance, lunged forward, grabbing for me.

Can you imagine the look on Jack Warren's face as he stared down at the full head of hennaed hair clenched in his fist?

Everything went into fast forward after that. I took off like a bloated road runner, shrieking "Call the police!" to the invisible tenants who were, I'm sure, peeping fearfully through their peepholes.

I'd almost reached the end of the short hallway when a bullet—from my own damn .32—went singing past my ear. That's when I realized I'd gone the wrong way; the stairwell was in the opposite direction!

I stood there frozen, my back to Warren, waiting for the next bullet, the one that would speed me off to a better, happier world.

Then I heard a loud, familiar creak, followed by, "Police! Drop it!" I whirled around to see Fielding and Corcoran coming off the elevator, guns drawn and aimed in the vicinity of Jack Warren's heart.

"Are you okay?" Fielding cried, rushing toward me. I nodded weakly as he put a steadying arm around me.

"Sorry, Dez, we got into this little traffic accident," he told me sheepishly. Right before I passed out.

Chapter 35

When I came to a few minutes later, I was sitting on the floor, my head cradled in someone's lap, a cold compress pressed against my forehead. I opened my eyes and lifted my head, bending it back. It was Fielding who was providing the lap. His worried face peered down at me. "How do you feel?" he asked gently.

"I don't know yet," I told him, curving my lips in what I hoped would pass for a smile. I realized then that a small group of people—most of them in night-clothes—was gathered around us.

"Are you all right, darling?" said a voice I'd heard before. I looked up. Mrs. Chartoff broke free of the restraint of her husband's arm, which was encircling her waist, and bent down to take my hand.

"I'm fine, Mrs. Chartoff, thank you. I'm alive," I marveled.

Someone else offered to call an ambulance.

"No, I'm fine. Really," I insisted, just as the elevator door opened. Two uniformed policemen got off, weapons extended. Corcoran signaled to them, and they sheathed their revolvers and walked over to where he stood guard over a handcuffed Jack Warren. After a brief conversation, the newcomers left, a tight-lipped Warren in tow.

"It was my Lou that called them," Sara Chartoff informed me proudly.

A short time afterward, we were all gathered in the Constantine apartment. Selena, Ellen, Fielding, and

Corcoran were in the living room. I was in the bathroom, throwing up.

It was a brief, but thorough, purge. After which I repaired my makeup and did the best I could with the ravaged hairpiece that Fielding had kindly retrieved for me. Then I joined the others.

"Can I get you some tea?" a concerned Selena asked as I settled myself into one of the new emerald chairs.

"Thanks. I'd love some."

"Good. How about something with it?"

"I couldn't." I was still a bit rocky. After all, it's not every day that's nearly your last.

Selena got up, and Corcoran immediately put down the cup he was holding and sprang to his feet. "Let me help you," he offered, trotting after her. As he passed my chair, I noted with disgust that not only was he wearing the same besotted expression he'd displayed around Selena before, but this time he'd removed his wedding band.

"You sure you're up to this?" Fielding asked me when the two returned moments later.

"I feel much better now."

"It's almost one o'clock; we *could* do it in the morning," he offered.

"The one thing I'm not is tired; I'm too hopped up. Besides, I thought you'd be really anxious for an explanation."

"To tell the truth, I am," he confessed, breaking into a wide grin.

I began with, "I don't know if you're aware that this building has no thirteenth floor."

Three faces stared at me blankly. Ellen just sat there looking smug and nibbling on Oreos.

Corcoran spoke first. "What's *that* got to do with the price of toilet paper?" he demanded belligerantly. (The man obviously had no respect for the almost-dead.)

"*That* has everything to do with it," I countered in a decidedly superior tone.

Selena got up again in response to the whistle of

the tea kettle, and Corcoran followed suit. "Walter, please," she said, visibly annoyed. "I think I can manage to carry a little teacup by myself." She turned to me as a chastised Corcoran resumed his seat. "How do you take your tea, Desiree?"

"Plain is fine, thanks."

"Talk loud," Selena called as she went into the kitchen.

She was back with my tea just as I finished pointing out that the elevator had been out of order the night of Agnes Garrity's murder—which was also the first time I visited Ellen. "I walked up fourteen flights of stairs, and I wound up on the fifteenth floor," I said meaningfully. "But, since the numbers on the stairwell are so faded you can't even make them out anymore, I just assumed I'd miscounted." I paused to take a long, satisfying sip of the hot tea. Which may not have had any actual therapeutic value but made me feel nurtured.

I glanced up and, after noting that the three previously blank faces still showed no sign of harboring any intelligent life, set down my cup and continued. "It wasn't until I was coming up in the elevator this past Sunday that I happened to look at the panel— the one with the buttons—and realized there was no thirteen. Of course, it should have occurred to me long before. I mean, how likely is it that when you're walking up the stairs with your very last breath you're going to overshoot your floor? Besides, that business with the thirteenth floor is pretty common, especially in older, prewar buildings. Anyway, once I *did* figure it out, I knew why poor Mrs. Garrity was murdered."

Fielding's expression had undergone a change. I could see a glimmer of understanding there now.

"I was certain," I said, directing my words to him, "that the killer had done the same thing I did. He allowed for a thirteenth floor! So instead of breaking into fourteen-D, he ended up in the apartment directly above it. The police photos showed Mrs. Garrity lying in bed, almost completely covered by blankets. The only thing the murderer could see was that head of gray hair illuminated by the nightlight. And remember, Neil Constantine's hair was silver!"

"I still can't believe Jack would murder anyone," Selena said. "He has always been the kindest, most giving man. Even when I left him—which hurt him very badly—he was never anything but wonderful to me."

"I know, Selena, and I'm sorry," I sympathized. "I think he would have died for you. He certainly killed for you."

"But he isn't a violent person, honestly," she argued meekly, her eyes moist.

"I'm afraid your husband has another side to him. I got a little preview of it the first time I called and asked if he would see me."

"What brought you to Warren as the killer?" This from Fielding.

"Well, as I said, that revelation in the elevator convinced me that the first murder had been a mistake. But I didn't know *whose*. It took a little more time to figure that out. And it shouldn't have. Because it couldn't have been anyone *but* Warren."

"I don't follow you," Selena said simply.

"Look, this elevator is always malfunctioning, right? And everyone else involved with Neil had been coming here for years. They'd *have* to know there's no thirteenth floor. But your husband was only in the building once before, and that time the two of you took the elevator."

The only sound in the room came from Ellen and her Oreos.

"Later on, of course, Warren became aware that he'd killed the wrong person. Probably when he read the newspapers. So he got another gun—having, I'm sure, disposed of the first weapon—and, taking the elevator this time, rectified his error. But he was still under the impression that he'd miscounted the flights the previous week."

"So . . ." Fielding murmured thoughtfully. I could almost see him mentally connecting the dots.

"So tonight I tried to set up a situation where we'd

catch him repeating the mistake that got Garrity killed—a mistake only *he* would have made."

Now, I have to confess that unraveling the murders like this for my little audience had sent me on something of an ego trip. I felt such pride! Such power! In spite of the fact that less than two hours ago I'd nearly been splotched all over the fifteenth floor—and was still feeling a bit queasy from the experience—just then, I was on a real high.

Until Ellen inadvertently brought me crashing down.

"It's lucky the elevator wasn't on the blink the night Warren killed Mr. Constantine," she observed. "Because if he'd had to take the stairs again *that* time, he'd have ended up at that poor old woman's apartment first. And I'm sure he'd have figured the whole thing out—don't you think?—and your wonderful plan would have been ruined!"

My God! She was right! It had never occurred to me that Warren might have used the stairs when he killed Constantine. But as disturbed as I was that I hadn't thought of this possibility (which is pretty inexcusable), what bothered me even more was that Ellen *had*. With all of her artlessness and gullibility, she sometimes exhibits a shrewdness that could make me hate her.

Mercifully, everyone began to talk at that moment. Selena asked why it was necessary to set my trap for so late at night. I pointed out that it was less likely there'd be other people around then. "Also," I said, "I wanted to make sure he'd show up, and there's something almost mystical about the witching hour. By the way," I added, "I want you to know I wasn't very happy about involving you in this, even minimally, because of your feelings for Jack. But I had to have you buzz him in when he got here."

"I understand. And it's all right. If he did kill Neil, I want him to be punished."

Fielding was pursuing his own mental agenda. "I should have caught on," he grumbled self-deprecatingly, "as soon as you told me to ignore the 'out of order' sign on the elevator door. At least it should have got me thinking in the right direction."

"I don't know how you could have deduced anything from that. I just mentioned it because I didn't want you to have to walk up so many flights of stairs for no reason."

"Aunt Dez brought over a whole handful of those signs tonight," Ellen put in. "She had me tape them to the elevator door on every floor."

"Wasn't it enough just to tack one up in the lobby for Warren's benefit?" Corcoran asked me. "Why plaster them all over the place?"

"Look," I explained, "once I got Warren to take the stairs, I couldn't afford to let him get suspicious; I had to make sure no one else used the elevator, either."

"One more thing," Fielding said. "How in hell did he know you were in that little room?"

"I figured that out almost as soon as I saw him heading my way. I was really stupid. I know enough not to douse myself with perfume when I'm going on a stakeout, but I completely forgot about using a scented hairspray." As I spoke, I found I was self-consciously patting the sticky, disreputable hairpiece that covered my even less attractive hair.

"What was that damned thing doing in the middle of the floor, anyway?" Corcoran wanted to know, indicating the wig.

I told him how "that damned thing" was the reason I was still breathing. "And if it hadn't been raining tonight, I probably wouldn't have worn it," I concluded with a shudder.

Ellen evidently felt this required clarification. "Aunt Dez's own hair is just impossible when it rains," she informed the others.

"And thank God! That's what saved my life. At least the first time." I shot a grateful smile at Fielding, remembering a split second later to include his partner in the gesture.

"Even though I'm not very happy with how things

turned out, I really admire your bravery," Selena told me. "You put yourself in terrible jeopardy."

"Well, I didn't exactly plan for it to go down like it did," I admited. "The way I had it worked out, Tim, here, would join me in the utility room at eleven-thirty—a half hour before Warren was due. The whole idea was that when Warren tried to gain access to the wrong apartement, we'd confront him together. In the meantime, Corcoran was supposed to wait on the four-teenth floor, next to the stairwell, and watch for War-ren to come upstairs. Then he was to follow behind him and conceal himself on the landing. That way he'd be right there in case of trouble.

"But," I finished with a sidelong glance at a pain-fully embarrassed Fielding, "things got a little screwed up."

Chapter 36

The New York Times buried me.

But if the *Times* was less than impressed with my derring-do—relegating their coverage to a thumbnail-sized article way back in the second section—the other New York papers more than compensated for the snub. The story made page 4 of the *Daily News,* page 7 of *Newsday,* and page 3 of the *Post,* all of which devoted considerable space to my adventure.

I particularly liked the headline in the *Post*: LADY P.I.'S HAIR-RAISING ESCAPE FROM KILLER. To illustrate the point, there I was smiling inanely and holding my wig in front of me at arm's length as if it were a dead rodent. (And, given newspaper reproduction quality, unless you looked pretty carefully, that's probably what you thought it was.) There were slightly smaller pictures of Fielding and Corcoran, who were referred to as "hero cops," and another of Jack Warren captioned "alleged killer of two."

At my suggestion, the story we gave the papers was that I had been following this double murder suspect and that, when he discovered it, a confrontation ensued, during which he tried to eliminate me with my own gun. Only my trusty wig, plus the timely intervention of Sergeant Timothy Fielding and Detective Walter Corcoran, foiled his dastardly intent. Questioned as to how they happened to be in the building, Tim told them—also at my suggestion—that the police, too, were suspicious of Warren and had been keeping him under surveillance.

Now, before someone marks me as a candidate for

canonization, let me assure you that this seemingly selfless version of the events suited me just fine.

In the first place, I figured I owed Tim (and, okay, Corcoran, too) for the fact I was still breathing. Second, I was building a little goodwill with the police, which in my profession is not a dumb thing to do. And third, and maybe most important, I was not trying to establish myself as the kind of hotshot P.I. you'd call on for the scary stuff. (Murder being the scariest stuff there is.) Once was definitely enough, thank you.

Anyway, I was getting a big enough kick out of my fifteen minutes of fame the way things were.

By 10:00 p.m. Thursday, I'd heard from all my friends, a whole lot of aquaintances, and a woman I hadn't seen since high school. It seemed, in fact, like I'd heard from everyone I'd ever known except Bill Murphy. And hadn't he said he'd call me the night I solved the murders?

"I can't understand it," I told Ellen on the phone. "He was going to get in touch with me as soon as the investigation was over."

"Don't worry, he will," Ellen replied. As I knew she would. "In the meantime, enjoy being a celebrity," she added.

And I did. Until 11:00 p.m. Thursday, by which time the euphoria had worn off. When I went to bed that night, the only thing on my mind was the phone call I hadn't received.

The next day, Tim and I had a date for lunch—his treat. We met at a very good, very crowded steakhouse downtown, and after my second Bloody Mary, I completely forgot about Bill Whatchamacallit.

"I want to thank you for letting us have this one, Dez. I owe you."

"I think it's the other way around. You *did* save my life, you know."

"Barely," he retorted with an uncomfortable little smile. He paused for a second, then suddenly brightened. "But listen, it's a damned good thing Warren tried to off you."

"Thanks a lot."

"Think about it. If things had gone down as planned, there'd be no real evidence against the guy. What would we have, really? Just that he showed up at the wrong apartment."

"There's a good chance we could have gotten him to confess if we'd confronted him," I argued. "The surprise factor alone could have worked in our favor."

"I hate to say this, but you're kidding yourself. That guy's too slick a customer."

"I know how slick he is, but we would have caught him completely off guard."

"So-o-r-r-y. No sale."

"Well, at the very least it would have convinced *you* that Warren was the killer. And once you realized that, you'd have started to concentrate on getting some evidence against *him* instead of trying to put away an innocent kid."

"Maybe," Fielding reluctantly conceded, as a way, I suspect, of ending the debate.

The appetizers came. And I dug into five of the largest, tastiest, most un-iodine-y shrimp I've ever eaten, accompanied by a sauce that had exactly the right amount of bite to it. We both devoted ourselves wholeheartedly to our food. Then, when the dishes were removed, we went back to less pleasant things.

"You want a laugh? The perp still hasn't confessed. Swears it was so dark in the hall he could hardly see. He claims he thought it was a mugger hiding in the utility room."

"What?" I exclaimed so loudly that everyone around us turned to stare. Tim looked mortified. I lowered my voice. "He even spoke to me," I sputtered. "And there's a light right outside the utility room. I could see the expression on his goddamn face, for God's sake!" The redness in Fielding's cheeks signaled that I was getting louder again. "Sorry," I said more quietly, "but I can't get over the colossal chutzpah of the slime."

"Yeah, I know. But there's nothing to get excited about. Hey, I thought you'd get a laugh out of it. After all, I was there, too. I can testify about that light.

Besides, he shot at you while you were running *away*. Uh-uh. No chance even a two-year-old would buy that garbage. We're gonna get a conviction on this one. Don't you worry about it for a minute."

Just as the waiter set down my prime ribs, Tim brought up the subject I'd been trying, with some success, to push to the back of my mind. "Arraignment's today. The D.A.'s requesting that Warren be held without bail. And since it's a double homicide, he tells me he has every reason to believe the judge'll go along with it."

It wasn't until I realized how relieved I was that I knew how worried I'd been.

That night, I had dinner in Little Italy with Jerry, his mother, and Sal and Yolanda (Mrs.) Martinez. In spite of my substantial lunch, I managed to put away a five-course dinner with very little effort.

When I got home, there was a message on the machine. "Hi, Dez, Bill Murphy. Congratulations! I just heard. I've been at a convention in Chicago for three days. It's only nine o'clock now, but I'm bushed. Call you tomorrow."

I went to bed with a predictable pain in my stomach. And a big smile on my face.

Chapter 37

"Hi, Sherlock. Bill Murphy. I am so proud of you!
Are you okay?"

It was a little after 10:00 in the morning, but I'd
gotten up at 8:00, had some coffee, and gone back to
sleep about 9:00. I was, however, instantly awake at
the sound of that voice. "I'm fine," I said. If I'd
wanted to be completely truthful, I'd have added the
word *now*.

"I only found out about what happened yesterday;
my secretary saved a copy of the *Times* for me." (He
would have to read the stingiest version.) "You're
going to have to tell me all about it, you know, over
the dinner you promised we'd have when this thing
was over."

"Sounds good to me."

"Are you free tonight?"

I was going to lie about already having made other
plans so he wouldn't think my social life was as dull
as it actually was, but I was too anxious to see him.
"I'm free."

While we were making our arrangements, Murphy
said something about bowling, which I hadn't done
since college. And even in those days, when I was
getting in plenty of practice, I was so atrocious that
my very closest friends left me for dead last when
they were choosing sides. I didn't see any point in
mentioning this to Murphy. "Oh, I love to bowl," I
lied.

He called for me at 7:00. It didn't take more than
five minutes at the alley to convince me that I was

still the undisputed Queen of the Gutter Balls. Which, for once, didn't matter at all. We spent as much time laughing as we did bowling. Murphy, I discovered, had a marvelous sense of humor. Besides, he seemed to be getting quite a kick out of the fact that I was, as he put it, "the worst bowler on seven continents."

Appropriate to our activity, dinner was a burger joint. That's when we discussed the outcome of the case for the first time.

"The paper said Warren tried to shoot you," Murphy said, concern all over that dear, almost homely face.

"He came damned close. If Fielding and Corcoran had showed up even a couple of seconds later ..." I let the sentence go unfinished and put on a brave smile to milk it just a little.

"That son of a bitch!" Murphy muttered, his jaw set so tight he barely moved his lips. "They should have blasted him to hell!" Then he gave me a look that warmed my soul. "Thank God you're all right!" he said fervently. "What exactly happened?"

Which led to my telling him the whole story, the one that didn't get into the newspapers.

Murphy was obviously impressed. "Looks like I wasn't so off base, after all, when I called you Sherlock."

Then, for some dumb reason, the admiration I'd been hoping for made me blurt out a confession. "My 'foolproof' plan was a joke," I confided. "If it had come off as I'd anticipated, and Warren hadn't taken a shot at me, the police wouldn't have had a thing on him."

"I don't know about that. If he'd met up with you and this cop in front of the old woman's apartment, it would have been bound to throw him. You can't tell what he might have said."

He was sounding like me with Fielding, and I was now as skeptical as Tim had been. "And that's not all. I didn't even think to check on whether or not the elevator was working the night Constantine was killed," I admitted, going on to explain what Ellen had pointed out during the postmortem at Selena's.

"No one thinks of everything. And you were the only one who figured out how the two killings were related, remember that."

"Yes, but—"

"Never mind the 'buts.' You were the one who came up with the identity of the murderer."

You know, he was right. I'd solved a double homicide! That was something I should be feeling really good about. Okay, so I'd made some mistakes. But it *was* my maiden homicide investigation. And also, I promised myself, my final one.

That night, Murphy and I got around to more personal topics, too. I told him about Ed and how good things had been when we were together. And he told me about marrying at twenty-one and divorcing three years later. "We were like two little kids playing 'married,' " he said sadly. "I'm surprised it lasted as long as it did."

Just as I was wondering how I could get him to talk about his recent engagement, he brought it up himself. "Served me right," he said of the apparently short-lived romance. "Lisa's twenty years younger than I am. I must have been going through male menopause or something. Trying to recapture my lost youth. I met her at an agency shoot—she was in a cold medicine commercial—and she really came on to me. I was flattered as hell. It turned out that she thought I had a lot more money than I actually did, and I thought she had a lot more character than *she* actually did. Like I said, it served me right."

We must have sat there opening up to each other like that for almost two hours. After the first forty-five minutes, I caught the manager scowling at us every time I looked in his direction. I mentioned it to Murphy. "Don't let it bother you," he told me. "The place is practically empty. We're doing him a favor sitting here; it's better for business."

Eventually the manager, undoubtedly pushed to his

limit, came over to the table. "Will there be anything else, folks?" he asked pointedly, forcing a smile.

"I'd like some coffee, thank you. You, Dez?"

"The same."

That wiped away the smile, and the man walked away muttering nasty things under his breath. When the coffee came, neither of us took more than a sip or two. But it bought us another fifteen minutes, anyway.

It was after one when Murphy brought me home.

"Would you like to come in for a drink? Or," I added facetiously, "maybe another cup of coffee?"

He grinned broadly. "Not this time," he said, kissing my cheek. "But hold the thought."

Chapter 38

In the morning, Murphy called to tell me what a great time he'd had. "I don't remember when I've enjoyed myself that much," he said.

"Me, too."

"I'm flying to the coast Monday. We're shooting two commercials out there next week, but I'll be home by the weekend. How about coming up to my place for dinner Saturday and letting me whip up one of my irresistible specialties for you?

Somehow, I had a tough time picturing this man in the kitchen. "You're a cook?" I asked skeptically.

"A chef," he corrected. "And one of the great ones. Prepare yourself for a truly religious experience."

As soon as the conversation ended, I called Ellen. I couldn't wait to tell her about my evening and this morning's phone call. I was also eager to find out how things had gone with Herb last night.

She was ecstatic about both our dates. "I'm so glad you've met someone you care about. Not that Stuart isn't a *wonderful* man," she put in hastily, "but I know you don't have *that* kind of a relationship. Maybe the four of us can go out sometime. I'm dying to meet Bill. And you still haven't met Herb, and I'm *so* anxious for you to get to know him."

"Not any more anxious than I am. But it'll have to be after next week, since I can't very well inform Murphy that his dinner for two will be turning into dinner for four."

"Not unless you want a little cyanide in your soup," Ellen said, giggling.

Significantly, this time she hung up without offering her usual answer to the usual question I didn't ask.

On Monday morning, I showed up at work for the first time since the preceding Tuesday. Jackie hugged me. Elliot Gilbert and Pat Sullivan hugged me. And their almost inanimate law clerk looked like he *wanted* to hug me. Again, I realized how pleasant it was not to be dead.

Four things happened during that week that stand out in my mind.

First, on Monday afternoon I got a new, and much-needed, client. It was an extortion case, a referral from—are you ready?—Louise Constantine! Well, nothing surprises me anymore. But if anything *could have,* that certainly would have.

Then there was this problem of Ellen's. Herb hadn't made plans on Saturday night—as he normally did—for the following week. But Ellen had attributed it to their relationship's having entered a new stage. She didn't explain what she meant by "new stage," but she didn't have to. By Tuesday, however—when I met her for lunch—she was almost a basket case. "He hasn't called," she told me softly. The words only confirmed what I could read very clearly in her expression.

"Why don't you call him?"

"I wouldn't want him to think that because of what ... um ... because we ... um ... got closer that I'm acting as if I own him."

"Don't be silly. Just call and say 'Hi, how are you?' and see what develops. Maybe he's been sick. Or busy. It's also very possible that he's nervous about getting involved, so he's taking a little breather." She looked at me doubtfully. "Listen," I continued, "he'll probably be glad to hear from you."

"What if he's not?" she challenged.

"Then you either ask him what gives or, if you're not ready to deal with it, you say you have to get back to work or there's someone at the door or whatever and that it was nice talking to him and you hang up."

She looked so stricken that I felt compelled to reassure her. "I doubt very much that it will happen like that. But if it *does,* at least you'll *know.*"

"I guess you're right."

A few minutes later, when we were deep in a discussion about our waitress's purple hair, Ellen suddenly blurted out, "I'm definitely going to call him," repeating it three more times during the meal. The commitment, I decided, was her way of girding herself into action. But I wasn't at all sure she'd manage it.

Then, on Wednesday, she phoned me at the office to say she'd left three messages with Herb's secretary, who always placed him at a meeting, and one on his answering machine at home. She sounded so awful that I wondered if I'd given her the right advice after all. But, on reflection, I realized that sooner or later she'd have to resolve this thing. So I abandoned the inclination to flog myself and settled for keeping my fingers crossed.

Later that afternoon, just as I was getting ready to leave for home, Fielding capped off a lovely day. "I've been deliberating with myself since yesterday on whether to call you," he said, his voice guarded. "I'm sure you have nothing to worry about; it has absolutely nothing to do with you. But I knew if you heard it from someone else, I'm a dead man. So I figured it would be better to tell you myself."

"Thanks so much for enlightening me."

"Don't be cute. I just wanted to let you know that Warren made bail Monday."

"Bail! I thought there wasn't supposed to *be* any bail!"

"Yeah, but we got ourselves some tight-assed, bleeding heart judge who didn't see it like that. No previous record, roots in the community, and all that crap. He did set it pretty high, though. Two hundred fifty big ones."

"But we're talking about a *double homicide.*"

"I know, I know. The D.A. hit the ceiling. But look, Warren's not going to come after you or anything. He's too smart for that. It would be like an admission of guilt."

He was probably right. I mean, the man would have to be a complete idiot to try anything with me. And Jack Warren was no idiot. So how come, in an eighty-degree office, I suddenly felt this terrible chill?

My fourth red-letter event was Thursday's dinner with Stuart. He'd been calling regularly since Wednesday of the previous week, but I kept putting off our getting together. I wanted to see him, and I wanted to postpone seeing him. Which is what happens when you're a coward. You see, I had made up my mind to tell him about Murphy.

Stuart picked me up at the apartment at 8:00. He wouldn't say where we were going, so I was flabbergasted when the cab pulled up in front of Lutece.

The food was as marvelous as I remembered from my one previous experience at the restaurant. Ten years earlier, Ed and I had had dinner there as a double celebration—for my birthday and the resolution of a very lucrative case he'd been working on.

Now, while Stuart usually takes me someplace pretty nice, Lutece is more than pretty nice. I mean, it's truly elegant. And Stuart's pulling out all the stops like that made it even harder for me to let him know about the new man in my life. Anyway, from the minute we sat down, he had a million questions about the case, so I was able to table any discussion of Murphy for a while.

In fact, I took my last sip of coffee and my last bite of an absolutely unbelievable frozen raspberry mousse with almond meringue—and I *still* hadn't said anything. Then Stuart asked if I'd like an after-dinner drink.

"Will you be having one, too?"

"You know, I think I will. After all, this is an occasion."

It was over the Grand Marnier that I finally worked my way around to Bill Murphy.

"I can't say I'm exactly shocked," he said when I got through telling him how taken I was with another man. "You haven't really been yourself lately. At first I thought it was because you were so preoccupied with the investigation. But then I began to suspect there might be someone else in the picture."

"Look, Stuart, you know how I feel about you. I mean, you've been such a wonderful friend for so many years and, of course, even more than a friend." I fumbled in the wilderness of my brain for the right words. "What I'm trying to say is that this really doesn't have anything to do with our friendship, except when it comes to spending the night together. I mean, not that it hasn't been terrific—it has—but I just wouldn't feel right about it, under the circumstances. Uh, not that I think I'm so irresistible that it should make a big difference in your life, but I *did* want to explain about things and, uh, about why I can't stay over at your place anymore. At least, not as long as I'm involved with another man. Oh, I didn't mean I expect you to be waiting around for me . . ." I broke off in confusion. "Damn! I'm really making a mess of this," I finished lamely.

Stuart smiled. "You did fine, Dez, and I understand completely. Let me just say that our friendship is very important to me, too. I would hate like hell to lose it. And while I've thoroughly enjoyed the physical side of our friendship, if you feel uncomfortable with that part of it, I can live with it. Not happily," he added gallantly, "but I'll have to adjust."

I don't know whether it was the relief at finally getting the thing off my chest or because Stuart was being so characteristically thoughtful, but I started to cry. Not loudly, you understand, but noticeably enough for him to hastily take care of the substantial check and hustle me out of there. "C'mon," he said, with a firm hold on my elbow. "We wouldn't want André Soltner to think you're critiquing his food."

We were saying good night at my door about twenty minutes later. Stuart gently squeezed my hand and told me he'd talk to me soon. But as he was turning away, I stood on tiptoe and kissed his cheek. "Still friends?"

"Always," he assured me solemnly.

Chapter 39

I was getting ready for my dinner with Murphy—and, in the process, managing to demolish whatever microscopic amount of self-confidence I might have been able to bring to the evening. "You have shitty taste," I announced out loud to the woman glaring at me from the full-length mirror. She didn't argue. Funny. I loved that dress when I bought it, which was only two days earlier. How could I have thought it made me look thinner? My hips stretched from here to New Jersey. And the color was all wrong for me, too. Taupe, the saleswoman had called it. It was more like mud brown. It did wonderful things for my hair, she'd said. Maybe. But she didn't bother to mention that it made my skin look slightly chartreuse. Well, there was nothing I could do about the damned dress now. I didn't have anything else to wear. (Honestly.) Besides, it was too late to start changing.

And the dress wasn't the only thing getting me nuts.

Ridiculous as this may sound coming from me, I found it almost impossible to eat when I was with Murphy. And, while down the road this could wind up being a blessing, it was as embarrassing as hell right now. Last week I'd only managed a few nibbles of my burger, but I kept holding it in front of my face and faking it. Then, when Murphy wasn't looking, I put the thing down and plopped my napkin over it, so he couldn't see how small a dent I'd actually made in it. And even if he did, it really wouldn't have been any big deal.

But tonight was different. Tonight he was preparing

the food himself. It would be just terrible if he thought I wasn't enjoying it.

As it turned out, I needn't have worried. Both the dress and my appetite came through admirably.

"You look wonderful," Murphy told me when he was helping me off with my coat. We were standing in his foyer, and he turned around to hang the coat in the closet. Then he glanced back over his shoulder. "I really like that dress," he announced. "The color's sensational on you."

As soon as I was seated on the sofa, he opened the bottle he was chilling in the wine bucket. It was Dom Perignon. "A gift from a true rarity: a grateful client," he said. "I've been saving it for a special occasion."

By my second glass of champagne, I could have eaten New York.

Murphy disappeared into the kitchen a couple of times, leaving me with a platter filled with tiny mushroom turnovers and miniature quiche lorraines. It was only because of my feelings for the man that a half dozen of the hors d'oeuvres awaited his return.

The dinner itself was superb: roast Cornish game hen with cherry sauce, baked rice with almonds and currants, a green bean and red onion salad with a tangy vinaigrette dressing, and for dessert—the pièce de résistance—a cloud-light, but intensely flavored, chocolate mousse. When he'd boasted about his culinary talents, the man was telling it like it was.

Conversation at dinner was easy and fun. Murphy had me doubled over with a priceless story about his first real date at age fourteen. And I reciprocated by relating a very weird encounter I'd had at college with an oversexed and underachieving Yale man.

Things turned more serious after we returned to the living room with our second cups of coffee. It began when I mentioned Louise Constantine's embezzlement referral. "I can see Louise isn't a favorite of yours," he commented.

"You won't get any argument about that," I agreed.

"She really *is* a nice person, Dez. I admit she's reserved—keeps everything bottled up—so it takes a while to get to know her. But there's a lot of decency there."

"Could be," I conceded very grudgingly.

"You're a real sport, you are," he said, with a laugh. "Her personality wasn't always this constipated," he continued, reflecting. "Not that she was ever the life of the party, but Neil's leaving made her withdraw even further into herself."

"Come on. That was ten years ago."

"He had a lasting effect on women." Murphy's face was taking on his Neil Constantine look again, so I tried changing the subject.

"You could qualify as a four-star chef on the basis of your coffee alone. Did anyone ever tell you that?"

He appeared not to have heard me. "You never did meet him, did you? No, of course you didn't. I have to admit the bastard had *style*. He was talented. He had warmth—at least on the surface. And he had a terrifc sense of humor. Plus—and this is the big one—he knew how to listen. You *know* how unique *that* is. Oh, he was good at impersonating a human being. Real good. Women found him just about irresistible."

"His looks didn't hurt any, either," I put in.

"Yeah, he was handsome, all right; I'll give him that."

"But it wasn't just that he was handsome. He looked ... well ... *nice*. I know he wasn't," I added hastily, "but that's how he *looked*. Oh, Selena showed me his picture," I said in answer to Murphy's puzzled expression.

"*Nice* is the last term I'd use to describe Neil Constantine. You know, when he had his mustache, he didn't look so 'nice.' It made him look smarmy—you know, like one of those old-time movie villains. And that's what the man was: a smarmy son of a bitch." He put down his coffee cup and met my eyes. "I wish I could say that I'm sorry he's dead. But that would make me as big a phony as Neil."

It was as though the murdered man had entered

the room, casting a pall over the evening and putting Murphy in the darkest mood I'd seen him in yet.

I was trying feverishly to come up with something that would bring things back to where they were. Then Murphy asked a question that stopped me dead.

"Would you like to know why I *really* hated him?"

I nodded dumbly.

"He killed my niece."

I know I looked every bit as shocked as he intended me to be.

"Not legally," he went on, "but certainly morally." He swallowed hard, and for a couple of seconds I was afraid that was all he planned on telling me. But then he continued.

"My niece Carol Ann was only twelve years old when . . . when we found out she needed a bone marrow transplant. She's the little girl in the picture." He gestured toward the photograph I'd commented on when I was in the apartment before. "Leukemia," he said grimly. "That was in the beginning of July, almost a year after I'd lent Neil the money. My brother Frank, Carol Ann's father, is—and I know this isn't a terrific thing to say about your own brother—the dregs of the earth. He drinks. He can't hold a job. And I wouldn't be surprised if he was physically abusive to Didi, my sister-in-law. Maybe to Carol Ann, too."

"God!"

"He's a beaut, my brother is. Anyway, Didi worked from the day they got married, but thanks to Frank, they were never able to save a dime. So when this transplant thing came up, I was desperate for cash. Donor tests are very expensive, and just about all my money was tied up in the agency. I could have cashed in this CD I had, of course—except that I'd *already* cashed it in so I could lend the money to Neil."

"A bank loan?" I suggested, as though it might still do some good.

"Afraid not. I did *that* a couple of years ago to pump some money into the business. In fact, I have a summer house in the Hamptons, and, a few months after the bank loan, I took out a second mortgage on

the house for the same reason. Oh, I'm a real tycoon,"
Murphy muttered bitterly.

I ached for the man. Somehow, though, I was able
to keep the tone of my voice almost conversational.
"Selena never even mentioned your niece when she
told me about your feud with Neil."

"I doubt very much if she knew. We never discussed
it in front of her. And why would Neil tell her about
it? He may have been a bastard, but he wasn't a *stupid*
bastard. It certainly didn't make him look too good."

"No, it didn't."

"Anyhow, when I explained the situation to Neil
and said I had to have the ten thousand dollars back,
he gave me that bull about the will still being in
probate."

"According to Selena, that was true."

"Who cares? Look, Louise is a wealthy woman. Neil
could have asked her for the money to repay me. She
would never have refused him. And don't tell me it
would have been awkward with Selena in the picture.
We're talking about a kid's life, for Christ's sake!"

"I wasn't going to say—"

"Besides, there was always his sister in Ohio, who
happens to be married to a very rich pharmaceuticals
manufacturer. If his sensibilities precluded his asking
Louise, he could have borrowed the cash from *her*."

"Did you suggest it to him?"

"Only about a thousand times. He kept saying if
the inheritance thing wasn't cleared up by next week
he'd talk to Louise. Every damn week it was next
week."

"What about asking Louise yourself? Did you ever
consider it?"

"Listen, I considered everything. I was even talking
to some prospects about buying the business. But
those things don't happen overnight. And time was
crucial. A couple of close friends *did* manage to scrape
together a few thousand, which wasn't easy. They're
in the same bind I am—decently fixed, but not much
in the way of liquid assets. At any rate, the money
they raised helped, but it was only a start. I needed a

helluva lot more. Besides the medical expenses, which were staggering, there was the cost of relocating Carol Ann and Didi up here. You know, arranging for a decent apartment for them—all that stuff. Did I mention they were from this small town in Minnesota?"

"No, I don't think so."

"Oh. Well, I got them a place right near Sloan-Kettering. There's an excellent man there. The best. And that's what I wanted to be sure Carol Ann had: the best. We were very ... She meant a lot to me. I ..." He stopped, his voice choked with emotion. "Sorry," he said after a minute or two, "it still hurts like hell." Another pause. Then, unexpectedly, Murphy broke into a smile. "Hey, I seem to recall that, sometime in the distant past, you asked about Louise. The answer is yes. When I finally realized that Neil had no intention of even trying to come up with the money, I decided to go to Louise myself, although the relationship certainly didn't warrant it. But suddenly, *very* suddenly, there was no reason to call her—or anyone else—anymore." He said it almost matter-of-factly. But his mouth had this funny twist, and the gray eyes were filled with pain. Then, as an afterthought, he added tersely, "Except Neil; I *did* keep on calling him."

"I can understand why," I told him softly.

He looked at me gratefully. "I couldn't let him get away with it. Although, God knows, it didn't make all that much difference after ... afterwards."

Now, I have been known to cry watching cartoons, so it was all I could do to keep from breaking down. Which, of course, was the last thing Murphy needed. "I'm so sorry. So very sorry," I murmured, taking his hand.

He withdrew it gently a few seconds later. "How about some anisette? And enough with your sad stories," he teased. "Will you please lighten up and try not to depress me anymore."

"Yes to the anisette, and I apologize for being such a downer," I responded with mock gravity.

We spent another hour at Murphy's apartment, sipping our liqueurs and making small talk. But neither of us was quite able to put Carol Ann's death behind us that night.

Murphy insisted on seeing me home. At my door, he asked if I was sure I'd enjoyed the dinner. It was my fourth or fifth go-around at complimenting the chef. But, hey, if he needed reassurance ... "The meal was exquisite," I told him without stretching the truth.

"I really know how to pick a caterer, don't I?"

Sometimes I am not terribly swift. I must have stared at him, mouth open, for three or four seconds before I grasped what he was telling me. "You mean ... ?"

"Right. The whole dinner was prepared ahead of time. All I had to do was pop the stuff in the oven." He grinned impishly. "To be honest with you, Dez, I can't cook worth a damn."

To be honest with *you,* I found Murphy's little ruse totally endearing, but I had no intention of letting *him* know that. So I did the only thing I could think of: I punched him in the stomach.

"There's something else I want to say," he declared, quickly grabbing my wrist. "If, by the vaguest chance, you've been wondering why I haven't made a pass at you, it's because I want to take this slowly. I think we've got something very special here. I hope you do, too." With that, he barely grazed my cheek with his lips, then turned and left.

I've never had a sexier kiss.

Chapter 40

Ellen called at 10:00 Sunday morning. "I want to hear all about it. How did it go?"

I was aching to share my evening—and my delirium—with her. But knowing how abysmal she'd been feeling, I limited myself to: "I had a very good time."

"Is that all? A very good time?"

"What's wrong with that?" To prove the point, I related the incident concerning my fantastic dinner and its bogus chef, which Ellen said she found "positively adorable." Although you couldn't tell from her voice, which was, not surprisingly, uncharacteristically subdued.

"But how do you feel about *him*? I mean, do you still like him as much?"

"Yes, I like him a lot."

"Look, if you're holding back because of what happened with Herb and me, please don't. The best thing you could do for me would be to help get my mind off myself for a while. It would really do my heart good to know things are going right for you. Honestly."

The situation being what it was, only Ellen could have made that statement—and meant it.

"How about if I come over for some brunch and the details? There's nothing like inviting yourself, is there?" she said with a giggle. It really wasn't much of a giggle, but it let me know that the old Ellen was still in there somewhere.

Ellen arrived just before noon, looking like death. She must have lost at least ten pounds in this post-Herb week. And she was a stick to begin with.

I couldn't have felt worse about feeling happy.

I mixed up a batch of mimosas to kick off our brunch and, at Ellen's insistence, started to fill her in on my evening. At first it was with reluctance, but I soon warmed to my subject—and the mimosas—and the telling became easier and easier. Ellen, too, seemed more relaxed. When I got around to repeating the conversation at the door, I heard a squeal of delight that was pure Ellen.

"You know what the best part is, though? Or at least one of the best parts?" she asked.

"What?"

"It wasn't only the money. What I mean is, Murphy didn't hate Constantine just because he didn't repay him. Not that I blame anyone for getting angry when someone welshes on them—especially when it involves big bucks—but to hate your best friend so *much* over something like that . . . well . . . it always seemed a little . . . extreme to me."

"You know, I was troubled by that, too," I admitted, marveling, as I always did, at the things Ellen picked up on. "Until you just mentioned it, though, I'd sort of repressed it."

"But now we know the money wasn't *really* the issue. In fact, when you think about it, in a way, Constantine was a murderer himself. I mean, by not doing anything about paying back the loan, he contributed to that little girl's death. That makes me feel *so* much better about Murphy. Well? When am I going to meet him, anyway?"

"Soon, I hope."

"Of course, we can't make it a double date anymore," she said levelly.

I didn't know how to respond, so I reached over and squeezed her hand. It was ice-cold.

Ellen left at 5:00 and Murphy called at 6:00. "I have tickets to a Rangers game on Wednesday," he told me. "Think you can make it?"

"Rangers?" I repeated blankly.

"Hockey."

"I'm aware of that," I retorted indignantly. "I just

wanted to be sure you said Rangers. This connection isn't too good."

"Well, how about it?"

My interest in hockey is on a par with my skill at bowling, but that didn't stop me. It didn't even slow me down. "Sounds great," I told him.

If I'd been nervous about our last date, it was nothing compared to how I felt now. For the next two days, I was totally wired.

Then everything changed. And I mean *everything*.

It was a little after 5:00 on Tuesday, and I was still at the office, trying to get through the few hours' work I'd started on at 9:00 that morning. But when the phone rang, I was grateful for the interruption.

A muffled voice said something totally unintelligible.

"What?"

Silence.

I tried again. "Who is this? I'm sorry. I couldn't hear you."

"It's ... it's ... me, Aunt Dez," Ellen sobbed.

My heart stopped. "Ellen! What's wrong?"

"It's ... Herb," she managed to get out.

"Are you home?"

"Yes."

"I'll be right there."

I was at the door of Ellen's apartment in twenty minutes.

I have never seen my niece so distraught. The area around her eyes was so puffy that the eyes themselves were reduced to mere slits. And those slits seemed to be producing a virtually endless supply of tears. As soon as she'd brush the wetness away, a fresh procession would trickle down her cheeks.

She was barely able to speak. And the few words she did get out were garbled by the tears.

"Don't try to talk now, Ellen. Just come over to the sofa and lie down." She meekly complied, and I fluffed up a few throw pillows and slipped them under her head. I sat on the edge of the sofa, next to her. "Have you had anything to eat?" (I was raised on the precept that there is no tragedy so great it cannot be mitigated by a little nourishment.)

She shook her head.

"I'll fix you something."

She shook her head again.

"Just a little tea and some toast?" I persisted.

She shrugged. I took that as a yes.

When I came back from the kitchen a few minutes later, Ellen was—amazingly—sound asleep.

I covered her with the afghan her grandmother had crocheted for her mother about thirty years ago, dumped the tea and toast, then took the afternoon paper from my attaché case and settled back in a chair. I'd been reading for maybe an hour when the phone rang. I dashed into the kitchen and made a grab for it, hoping it wouldn't wake Ellen. "Hello, is Evan there, please?" said a high-pitched voice that could only be the property of a prepubescent little girl.

I returned to the living room to find Ellen raising herself to a sitting position. She was flushed, but calm. I coaxed her into the kitchen with me and put up the tea kettle again, along with two slices of fresh toast. It took a lot more coaxing to get her to eat, but she finally gave in. (As you may have noticed, I can be an awful nag sometimes—but, of course, only when I have to be.)

While Ellen was nibbling away at her toast, I reminded myself that this was going to be a very long night and I'd better eat something myself. I scrounged around in the near-empty refrigerator for something without molds on it and finally settled for a peanut butter sandwich on not-too-stale rye bread. Then I poured the remains of an open and fizzless can of Coke into what, in a previous existence, had been a jelly jar and was now serving as one of Ellen's "everyday" glasses. When I joined her at the table, she was just finishing her last bite of toast. "I guess I *was* a little hungry," she admitted.

"Can I get you something else? How about a peanut butter sandwich?"

"No, thanks; I couldn't." She looked down at my plate. "I'm sorry there isn't more for *you* to eat."

"Are you kidding? I've been crazy about peanut butter since I was a kid. As long as it's the good kind like this—without all those lousy chunks."

"I can't stand the chunky kind, either," she said. At which point she burst into tears.

Ellen's sobs were so intense it was frightening. I wasn't much help, either. All I could do was put my arms around her, make soothing sounds, and feel rotten about not being able to do more for someone I loved. Fortunately, this new wave of tears didn't last too long. And after a few minutes—and a fistful of tissues—Ellen said softly, "I'd like to talk about what happened."

So, haltingly and convolutedly, she told me what had occurred that afternoon.

She had, it seems, reached that point of despair when she could no longer just *sit* there. So she left work at 11:30 in the morning to plant herself in front of Herb's office building. He came out a few minutes after noon with another man. He was absolutely livid when he saw her. Telling his friend—or whoever— that he'd catch up with him in a minute, he asked Ellen what she wanted and why she persisted in calling him when it was obvious they were through. "Until that instant," Ellen said, "I was shaking like a leaf. But when he talked to me that way, I became *furious*. I told him that if he had any decency at all, he'd have broken it off like a man, and he said I was behaving like a child, that a *real* woman wouldn't have needed it all spelled out for her. And *then* he said, 'Look, don't blame yourself. It wasn't you; these things happen, that's all. You're a nice kid. I'm sure you'll find somebody else.' And *then* he just said 'Take care of yourself' and walked away."

Ellen had come straight home, flung herself on the bed, and cried for five solid hours. "I didn't know I had that many tears in me," she told me. A moment later, she whispered plaintively, "I'm very glad you're here."

We talked until 4:00 that morning, starting with a blistering indictment of Herb and later working our way through all the other louses we'd loved. It wasn't until we had segued into a condemnation of the male sex in general that I finally coaxed Ellen into going to bed. Then I took the place she'd vacated on the sofa.

It seemed like only minutes had passed before the smell of coffee wakened me. I checked the clock on the end table. I couldn't believe it: 9:00. I followed the aroma into the kitchen, where Ellen was making some toast. She looked a mess. Which was a great improvement over the night before. There was still some puffiness around her eyes, but they were a normal size again, or close to it, and they were dry. And when she said "Good morning. Sleep okay?" her voice was steady.

"Like a corpse," I answered. "Look, I don't have to go in to work today. I'll stay here and we can talk some more or we can go to a movie or whatever you feel like doing."

"I'm okay now, Aunt Dez. Or I will be, once I forgive myself for getting taken in by that ... that ... *person.*"

"It wasn't your fault, Ellen," I said, smiling inwardly at Ellen's idea of an expletive. "Men like Herb are very good at their game. That's why they get away with it. Don't think for a minute that you're the first to fall for his crap. And you're definitely not the last."

"Imagine. Expending all that energy just to get a woman into bed," she marveled.

"It's the challenge," I told her disgustedly. "Mentally, your friend Herb never got out of high school."

"I guess you're right. I just need some time to accept this ... this ... whole thing. You have no idea how much I cared for him."

"I think I do."

"Anyway, you can go to work. Really."

"I don't have to. I'm not that busy," I protested.

"You may as well. I just called my boss; I said that my grandmother's sick and I have to go down to Florida for a few days. I'll catch a flight to my parents' place this afternoon."

"Are you sure that's what you want to do?"

Ellen nodded. "I have to get out of the city right now. I intend to spend the next few days at some remote spot on the beach where I can be as weepy and self-pitying as I feel like."

I left at around 10:30. "Take care," I said, giving her a kiss on the cheek and a prolonged hug.

"You, too. I'll call you when I get back Sunday night."

"I'll call *you* tonight at your mother's."

It was the only time I can remember breaking my word to Ellen.

Chapter 41

That unmistakable creak heralded the elevator's arrival on the fourteenth floor. Just as I was about to get in, the door opened and Selena Warren walked out.

"Selena!"

"Desiree!"

We threw our arms around each other. "What are *you* doing here?" she asked at the same moment that I exclaimed, "I didn't expect to see *you* here at this hour!"

I said I'd been visiting Ellen the night before and it got late, so I just stayed over. And she informed me she'd quit her job and was preparing for a trip to France next week.

It looked like everyone was leaving town.

"I just finished doing the laundry," she told me, which explained the bleach and detergent she was clutching to her chest, "and now I'm going to have some coffee. Come join me."

"I'd like to, but I'm late for work as it is."

"Please."

I'd already called Jackie and told her I'd been delayed. So why not? "I can't stay too long ... but okay, thanks."

I doubt I'll ever make a more fateful decision.

We were sitting at the kitchen table, Selena noticeably paler and more drawn than she'd been only two weeks earlier. "Neil's laywer said his aunt's estate was finally settled and that I'll be getting the money pretty soon. I *was* planning to go to Europe *after* I got it, but Frannie is flying to Paris on business next Tuesday and she convinced me to make the trip with her. I have a little something put aside—enough for the trip, anyway—so . . ."

Taking a break from my Entenmann's pecan Danish ring—obviously a favorite here—I voiced my approval. "I think that's a wonderful idea. You've been through an awful lot these past couple of months."

"I have, haven't I?" Selena replied with a short, bitter laugh. "First the man I love is murdered. And then I find out my husband, who I *truly cared for,* is the one who murdered him."

"It was a terrible shock for you, I know. Are you . . . have you been feeling all right? Physically, I mean. You look like you've lost some weight."

"I never bother to weigh myself. But I wouldn't be surprised if I *did* lose a few pounds. My appetite hasn't been anything to brag about lately. I guess it's finally sunk in that I will never—ever—see Neil Constantine again." Her face seemed to crumple, but she held up admirably. "The last time I saw him, he was in his coffin." Her eyes misted over. "He was wearing his one good suit—it was navy blue—and it went so beautifully with his silver hair and his blue eyes. . . . And I finally got a look at his mustache. It gave him such a distinguished—"

"Mustache?" I broke in.

"His first. He told me he'd always wanted to try it. He started growing it a week or so before I left for Chicago."

Selena said something else and then something else after *that.* But I didn't hear a word. I think she was in the middle of a sentence when I pretended to check my watch and told her brightly that I'd have to be getting to work.

She walked me to the door. And I smiled mechanically, wished her a good trip, and then got the hell out of there.

Chapter 42

All the way down in the elevator, I kept replaying Murphy's words: "When he had his mustache . . ."

I didn't let myself contemplate what that meant just then. Like Selena, I was postponing the trauma of reality.

I hailed a taxi in front of the building, gave the address of my office, and immediately realized I wouldn't be able to deal with anything—or anybody—else that day. I had the driver take me home.

When I walked into the apartment I headed straight for the kitchen to make some coffee. Not because I wanted any. But because it was preferable to thinking. I carried my fourth cup of morning coffee into the living room and curled up on the sofa. That's when I became aware that I hadn't taken off my coat yet.

I remedied the oversight, then picked up the mystery I'd begun that week. After reading the same paragraph for fifteen minutes, I gave up and turned on the TV. No help there, either. That same damned phrase crept into my mind and refused to budge: "When he had his mustache . . ."

There was no alternative but to admit to myself that Murphy *couldn't* have last seen the dead man months ago, as he claimed. Constantine had begun growing a mustache *for the first time* just before he was killed.

I felt physically ill. For a split second, I was so giddy I thought I might faint. But I wasn't that lucky. I remained fully conscious—and unable to avoid the terrible, inescapable fact: Bill Murphy had murdered Neil Constantine.

After a few moments, another thought occurred to

me. Could he have shot Agnes Garrity, too? I rejected the idea almost as quickly as it came into my head. Murphy had no reason to do away with the old woman, and he had been in the building too many times to have made a mistake with the floors. No Warren shot Garrity. I was sure of it. And he was so upset when he realized his error that he dropped the plan to eliminate his rival. Either that or Murphy just beat him to it.

Hey, wait a minute . . . it didn't *have* to be that way. Could be there was a perfectly innocent explanation as to how Murphy got to see the victim's mustache. Maybe he went up to talk to Constantine when Selena was in Chicago but figured it might not be too smart to admit it. Or maybe he ran into him on the street somewhere. It was conceivable, wasn't it? But I knew the answer. And the truth.

I had fallen in love with a killer.

Well, what was I going to do about it? Turn him in? I couldn't even *think* about that. And it wasn't as though I had what you would really call evidence. On the other hand, with this new information, the police could reopen the investigation if they wanted to. It should really be their decision. Besides, knowing what I did, could I possibly continue to see the man?

And then there was Jack Warren. What if he should be convicted of a crime he didn't commit? Never mind about Warren, I told myself. Even if he didn't kill Constantine, he *was* a murderer. Of course, so was Murphy. But the circumstances were entirely different, weren't they? In Murphy's shoes, I'd have wanted to blast the hell out of Neil Constantine, too.

Hold on. That was the whole point: *wanted to.* But would I—*could I*—have actually gone through with it?

I didn't think so. But then, no one had ever been responsible for the death of someone *I* loved. . . .

I must have sat there for hours, turning things over—and over and over—in my mind. Eventually I remembered about my date that night. I called Jackie.

"Where are you?" she demanded. "You said you'd

be a little late, but it's after three. I was beginning to get crazy."

"I'm sorry; something came up. Look, I need you to do me a favor."

"What?" Her tone was not exactly warm.

"Call Bill Murphy for me"—I gave her the number—"and tell him I came down with the flu and I'm going to have to break our date for tonight. Say I just left the office."

"You sound very strange, Dez. What's all this about?"

"I can't go into it now. Just bear with me, okay?"

"Are you all right? You don't really have the flu, do you?"

"No, but I've got some problems I have to work out. I probably won't be coming in to the office for a couple of days. If anyone should call, just say I'm home sick and try to discourage them from calling me here."

"Okay. And Dez, if I can help in any way, well, you know . . ."

"Yes, I know. And thanks, Jackie."

That night I couldn't eat a bite of dinner. I went to bed at 11:00, after staring at the television for four hours without seeing a thing.

I spent a sleepless night, followed by a miserable morning. The phone rang a few minutes before noon, and I picked up when I heard Jackie's voice on the machine.

"Ellen called." (Ellen! God! I'd forgotten all about her!) "She was pretty worried. She told me you were supposed to call last night. I gave her that business about the flu and convinced her you needed your rest and not to disturb you at home. And your friend Murphy checked in first thing this morning to find out if I'd spoken to you since yesterday. Said he didn't want to bother you in case you were sleeping. I said that was very wise."

"I appreciate this, Jackie."

"Don't be a jerk. What are secretaries—and friends—for?"

I went to bed that night still miles away from reaching any sort of decision. I must have drifted off at some time or other—at least for a few minutes—because I had this dream about Murphy being strapped in the electric chair and Mario Cuomo taping my eyelids open so I was forced to watch when they turned on the juice. (I didn't let a little thing like the fact that New York State has no capital punishment inhibit my masochism.)

On Friday I dredged up something else to plague myself with. What would happen when it dawned on Murphy that he had given himself away—if it hadn't occurred to him already! Would he see me as a threat to his freedom? I had feared an attack from the killer. But maybe it was the wrong killer. . . .

I wrestled with that delightful possibility for most of the day. Then, in the evening, my thoughts drifted back to that dinner in Murphy's apartment and the way he'd spoken to me about his niece. It put me in close touch again with the kind of caring, vulnerable man he was. No, I decided. Even if *he* knew that *I* knew, Bill Murphy would never harm me.

But did that mean it was okay for him to get away with murder?

For the third straight agonizing night, I went to bed telling myself I'd have to do *something*. Even if it was to make up my mind to do nothing.

At 3:30, I gave up trying to fall asleep, turned on the light, and opened my mystery. It did the trick.

I woke up a little after 9:30, feeling like I'd been caught in the eye of a hurricane. My body was drenched with perspiration. The blankets were on the floor in a heap. And the top and bottom sheets were so rumpled and twisted together I had to battle my way out of bed.

I was in the bathroom brushing my teeth when the phone rang. I went to the door so I could hear the message.

"Jackie would have my life for this," said the familiar voice, "but I was worried about you." My vital signs threatened to give out, but I made it over to the machine and stood there staring at it as the voice went on. "Please pick up if you can. I'm really concerned. Jackie has you practically playing footsie with the angel Gabriel."

Suddenly, inexplicably, the whole thing was clear. What was all this angst about what I should do? There was, after all, really only one thing that I—being me—*could* do.

I tossed my toothbrush on the end table and, with shaking hands, picked up the phone. "Besides, there's something I have to tell you," he was saying.

I swallowed a mouthful of Crest. "Wait," I said to Tim Fielding. "There's something *I* have to tell *you*. . . ."

Here is a preview of the next suspenseful mystery featuring Desiree Shapiro, a delightful—and unlikely—P.I.: *Murder Can Ruin Your Looks*

No more grizzly murders. No more desperate killers. No more life-threatening encounters. I'd had a taste of the heavy stuff, thank you. And I'd made myself a promise: There was no way I'd take on any case likely to cause me any injury more serious than a paper cut. Not ever again ...

Up until a year and a half ago, being a private investigator was—for me, anyway—a really benign way to earn a living. I always managed to pay the rent and some pretty sizable food bills, thanks to a small but fairly steady share of New York's unfaithful wives, philandering husbands, and phony insurance claims—along with some missing animals here and there.

Okay. Maybe they weren't the kind of cases you could really sink your teeth into. But they weren't the kind of cases that were likely to land you in the morgue, either.

Then my niece Ellen got me involved in this double homicide that almost evolved into a triple—with my own amply proportioned five-foot two-inch frame coming *that close* to occupying a third slab in the city morgue. (I'd prefer that slab to revealing just how ample these proportions of mine are.) Anyway, while I eventually solved the murders, even now I get crazy just thinking about that whole fiasco. Which is why I swore off the kind of cases that could in any way endanger either my physical or mental well-being.

And while I admit that my one and only murder

case turned me into a coward, the truth is, I hadn't been all that brave to begin with.

I suppose I have a nurturing thing when it comes to men. It's the only way I can explain being totally unsusceptible to the good-looking ones and having this penchant, instead, for the little skinny guys. You know, the ones who look truly *needy*. I guess my maternal bent stems, at least in part, from the fact that Ed and I never had any children—Ed being my late husband Ed Shapiro who was also a P.I. Anyway, when it came to the man who walked into my office that Wednesday afternoon, I was prepared to make an exception.

He was over six feet tall and well built, with dark hair, light eyes, and the most beautiful cleft chin. He was, in fact, good-looking enough for me to consider losing thirty—maybe even forty—pounds for. But when he drew closer, I noticed, with just a tinge of relief, that the sacrifice would not be necessary after all. This guy was definitely not a candidate for romance. His eyes—I could see now they were blue— were red-rimmed and dead-looking, and there was a bleak expression on that handsome face. Besides, he was a couple of years younger than I am. (All right. More than a couple.)

"I'm sorry I didn't make an appointment," he said in the sort of hushed tone most people reserve for church or, at the very least, the public library.

"That's okay," I told him, motioning for him to take the seat alongside my desk. "There's no line outside my door today."

"The thing is, I just found out about a half hour ago that you were a private detective here in New York, and I didn't want to waste any time in coming to see you."

"Do I *know* you?"

"You *did*. I'm Peter Winters."

It took a moment for that to register. "Peter Winters ..." Came the dawn. "*Little Petey* Winters?"

My visitor managed something close to a smile. "Guilty."

"My God!" I could hardly believe it.

I jumped up and rushed over to him, and we hugged for a minute. "I wouldn't have known you in a million years," I said.

"I would never have recognized you, either. You're a redhead now." Then, apparently concerned that I might be offended by this reminder of the humble beginnings of my most striking attribute, he added hastily, "Looks good on you."

What a nice, sensitive person Petey'd become, I decided, as I self-consciously patted my gloriously hennaed hair. I hadn't always been so kindly disposed to him, though ...

Little Petey Winters and I had grown up next door to each other in Ohio—with me, I confess, doing the growing up a long time before Petey did. Nevertheless, because his sister Maureen and I, born just three days apart, were practically joined at the hip since kindergarden, I saw a lot of him back then. Actually, a lot more than I wanted to.

I can't even count the number of days and nights I kept Maureen company when she had to baby-sit with her little brother; it was really as if he were my little brother, too. I guess that's why I often resented him like hell just for *being*. (As you can gather, my nurturing nature did not have its roots in my teen years.)

But anyway, Petey abruptly stopped being much of a factor in my life at the beginning of my senior year in high school. Because that's when Maureen formed an even stronger attachment than the one she had to me. His name was Roy Lindstrom. And right after graduation, he and Maureen got married and moved to California.

At first, there were letters and snapshots and, of course, an exchange of birthday and Christmas cards. But gradually it all stopped.

As for me, I went on to college and from there to

New York—and a career, marriage, and eventual widowhood.

But, right now, for a moment or two, I was in Ashtabula, Ohio, again with my very best friend.

I could picture with absolute clarity (although probably not complete accuracy) the long, straight brown hair; the tall, angular frame; and the tiny dimples hovering at the corners of those kewpie doll lips. But what I remembered best about Maureen were her wide, deep-set blue eyes. They were the same color and the same shape as the blue eyes that were filled with so much anguish right now.

"How *is* Maureen?" I asked.

"She's doing okay. She moved back to Ashtabula about six years ago, you know. These days, she's got five kids—three of them still at home—and an ex she can't even find. But Maureen's a strong lady. She opened her own travel agency last fall, and it seems to be going pretty well. She's the one who suggested I get in touch with you."

"I didn't think she even knew my married name or that I was living in New York."

"She said an old friend from Ashtabula, Amy somebody-or-other, had heard where you were and what you were doing and that you were Desiree Shapiro now." He didn't smile when he said the name; didn't even look like he was *suppressing* a smile. So I knew that Petey Winters (I'd have to stop thinking of him as Petey) had a whole lot on his mind. That was verified a second or two later.

"I need your help, Desiree," he said, leaning toward me. "*Really* need it."

"What's wrong?"

"The woman I was engaged to marry may have been murdered."

"*May* have been?"

"Well, no one's sure if she's the one who's dead or the one who's in the hospital damned *near* dead. And I *have* to know." Then slowly, haltingly, he began to tell me this horrifying story . . .

It seems that two days earlier his fiancée and her

twin sister had been shot in their Chelsea apartment. And now one was in the morgue, and the other lay in a coma in St. Catherine's Hospital. "And nobody can tell which is which," Peter said, his voice cracking. "Because whoever did this shot them in the face. Both of them . . ."

"God! I'm so sorry," I murmured. I rummaged around in my suddenly vacant head for some comforting words and came up empty. So I just told the truth. "I wish I knew what to say to you," I admitted weakly.

"I know. It's okay."

"Do you have any idea who might have wanted to harm them?"

"None." It came out in a whisper.

"Let me put you in touch with an investigator who—"

"But I was hoping *you'd* take the case."

"I can't, Peter. I don't take murder cases."

His voice, no doubt bolstered by desperation, was suddenly stronger. "You don't understand. Finding out who committed this—this— finding out who *did* it is the last thing on my mind right now. All I'm interested in is whether Mary Ann is dead or alive."

"Why not wait just a little while? Let's hope the woman in the hospital regains consciousness soon."

"They—the doctors—have no idea when that will be. Or even *if* it will be. Please, Desiree."

I shuddered at the thought of getting embroiled in another murder investigation. But here was Peter who was once almost like family to me and who was now in one of the most terrible situations I could imagine. I just couldn't bring myself to turn him down. (It also didn't hurt that those gorgeous blue eyes were looking at me so pleadingly.)

So, in the end, I agreed to handle the investigation. After first warning myself that I'd have to keep some emotional distance from the proceedings and then stipulating to Peter that my sole purpose would be to establish the identities of the victims. "I won't take it any further than that," I said firmly.

"That's all I'm interested in," my new client assured me.